SHAMROCKS AND SECRETS

SHAMROCKS AND SECRETS

TABLE OF CONTENTS

SHAMROCKS AND SECRETS

ACKNOWLEDGMENTS

Every author takes a moment to thank everyone who was involved in the creation of their book. I will continue that tradition and thank everyone that had a large impact on this story coming together. First and for most, my husband, you have been so understanding during the long road to make this a reality. To my two editors, Ms.Dolly and Elizabeth Simonton. I can't thank you enough for your hand holding and, when needed, hand slapping. To Nicole, you swore to me that if your hair looks good, the rest of you will follow. Midnight C, you were the first person I let read this story, you told me it was really good and you became my biggest cheerleader. To all my Mathisson fans, for without you, this story would still be running around in my head. I can't say a big enough thank you to Mayhem design for blowing me out of the water with the cover of this book. But most of all, I thank you, the person who is reading my words.

DEDICATION

To every girl who has ever looked up just in time to see that guy come into the room, you know the one; hair just right, eyes so deep that they take your breath away, chin chiseled so perfectly it could cut glass. You may never know his name or how he takes his coffee. If you're lucky enough to hear his voice, you mentally record it so you can play it back later. He's the guy you tell your friends about over a glass of Chardonnay. You describe in detail just what you would have done to him given the chance. He appears different to each of us. While we are at it, here's to him as well.

CHAPTER ONE

1n each and every one of our lives, we all come in contact with memorable people at some point. For some, it's a simple smile paired with brief but penetrating eye contact, while for others it's slightly longer and more intense, like with the handsome cashier at the corner grocery. A select few actually change who we are. This is my story and how one man changed everything about my life and those around me.

I guess you're wondering who the hell I am. That's actually the easiest part of my entire story. My name is Christina O'Rourke. My friends and family call me Christi. Well, that's not entirely true, but that'll come later. It all started one night while I was doing what most of us do every day, my job. I can still remember nearly every detail of what happened that night...

I had been working at *Penciled In*, one of the most successful catering companies in Chicago. The owner and my good friend, Charlotte, had entrusted me with this particular event. The guest list was long at over four hundred, and yet very distinguished, as the amount of security onsite proved. The Connor-Donnelly wedding was said to be the event of the year. Charlotte had hired additional servers a month ago and had spent that time training and grooming them to the bride's specifications. For this particular wedding, all of the staff had had to undergo an extensive background check. Like most things in my world, I didn't ask questions. If a client wanted to spend that kind of money to feel important, then who was I to question them. My job was only to make them happy.

I had just finished my preliminary meeting with the entire staff of one-hundred-twenty. Yes, that was correct. The bride's family wanted their guests to be served in a quick and flawless fashion. All of the bar2tenders had to be male and wear all black. All of the servers were to be female and had to wear black pencil skirts with peacock blue halter tops to match the bride's colors. I was at least able to wear a black blazer over mine.

The bride's family, the Connors, were from New York and I was told they were from 'old money'. The groom's family on the other hand, came from Ireland and were rumored to be just as well off. I wasn't certain how you came to a new country and suddenly have money, but, again, it wasn't my place to question.

I noticed my sister, Shannon, was talking with a very attractive man that had arrived with the bridal party. I motioned for her to get back to work and the handsome man kissed her cheek, and then squeezed her hand. I would have to ask her about him later. My sister didn't have the best track record with men.

Shannon and I were twins and also of Irish descent. Shannon had met her ex, Kevin Delaney, our senior year in college. He had been nice in the beginning, taking her to nice restaurants and buying her pretty things. All of that changed the day she gave birth to his daughter, Abigail. Abigail was four now and seriously the most beautiful little girl on the planet. Her sperm donor on the other hand, was a scumbag. Our other sister, Coleen, was two years older than us.

Colleen wasn't any luckier in love. Her long-time boyfriend, Jimmy—well, he got her mixed up in some pretty heavy shit, and then he got her killed.

Shannon and I lived together in a tiny three bedroom house. It took the two of us to take care of Abigail, she sure as hell couldn't count on Kevin to help her out. Shannon had taken him to court and proven paternity, yet he still refused to pay his child support. Like I said, he was a scumbag.

Dinner had been served and the cake had been cut. Now it was time to stand around and watch people get drunk and happy.

Looking back, I should have questioned the people in that room. I should have listened to just a few conversations. Instead, I watched my staff and made certain people were having a good time.

It was just after ten o'clock that night when one of my bartenders alerted me to a situation. Apparently, a couple was in a heated argument outside of the restrooms. This was one of the many things I was good at, breaking up fights and diffusing situations.

I smiled at the many people that were still present on my way to deal with the problem. Once I got there, I nearly turned around and left. Standing with his back to me was none other than Kevin Delaney. He was currently in a heated conversation with a very pretty girl. As I stood there and watched briefly, the girl slapped him across the face. For a tenth of a second, I thought about getting her a drink for that. I smiled to myself as I crossed the room toward the couple.

"Excuse me," I said, putting forth my most professional tone, complete with toothy grin and calm stance.

Kevin turned his entire body in my direction. The look on his face was one of pure rage. I decided to direct my attention to the girl as she appeared to have complete control at the moment. The look on her face was rage at first, or so I thought. A closer look showed a large amount of white powder caked on the outer septum of her nose.

My dad had always told me to expect the unexpected when it came to people who were under the influence. He told me of a guy who had once actually broken out of the handcuffs because he was high on LSD. Yes, my dad was a cop, a detective, actually.

"Yes, hello, nice dress by the way, I absolutely love that shade of blue."

Make the situation about her, check.

"Oh, um..."

Distracted, check.

"Listen, I can't agree with you more that this piece of shit deserves to be hit a hell of a lot harder than what you just did. However..."

"Fucking butt out, Christi!" Kevin spat from my left.

I turned my attention to him. "Really, fuck-nut, you want me to get her a set of boxing gloves or save you a trip to the ER?"

"Fuck you, bitch."

"No, fuck you, you son of a bitch!" the blonde interrupted, yelling at Kevin. *Gotta get control, Christi...*

"Hey, thank you..." I motioned for her to tell me her name.

"Mandy, Mandy Owens."

I held my hand out to shake hers. "Hello, Mandy, pleasure to meet you, Christi O'Rourke." I made a move to wedge my body between theirs. "As I was saying before we were so rudely interrupted by pencil dick here," I motioned behind me. Mandy began to giggle; ladies and gentlemen, situation defused. "I think you can do so much better, I also think you might want to go back into the restroom and remove some of your face powder you must have missed when you freshened up your makeup," I motioned to her nose.

Without a second thought, she turned on her heel and walked right back into the restroom. Now I had to deal with Kevin...then take a bleach bath.

I turned around, ready to lay into him, when I noticed a group of men behind him making their way down the hall in our direction. The five men walked with authority in a 'V' formation, like mallard ducks heading south for the winter. Without saying a single word, people were moving out of their way, clearing a path for them to pass through with ease.

Kevin hadn't realized that my eyes had left his and were fixed on the man in the lead position. He was tall, well over six feet. His black tux looked like it was made just for him and I wasn't surprised by this, as most of the men in attendance tonight had that same appearance. This man, however, was different; the fit was due to more than just a great tailor. He had a certain air about him. His face was absolute perfection, like a model straight off the runway. I couldn't decide if his hair was brown or dark red, but that was not what had me nearly speechless. It was his eyes. They were a shade of green that I couldn't remember ever seeing.

"Goddamn it, Christi..."

Great, dick face just had to interrupt my eye fucking...

"I can't fucking believe you're still fucking up my life. That girl you just pissed off was my pussy for the night!"

Before I could respond, a very husky voice interrupted. "Is there a problem here, Douce?"

What surprised me more than that voice was how quickly Kevin managed to turn around to face him. His entire body quaking as he stared at the tall handsome man.

"Oh, hey, Boss. No-no problem here."

Suddenly, Kevin was all smiles, and then he placed his arm around my shoulders. "That's not how I see it, Douce."

Douce?

"Oh...this is a friend of mine's sister. We were just catching up." Kevin replied, trying to pull me into his side, like we had been friends since birth.

I noticed the men behind him were listening intently to everything he said. Disgusted, I managed to remove Kevin's arm and moved away from him a few steps, glaring at him. This didn't go unnoticed by Kevin's boss. Boss?

Kevin hadn't paid Shannon any child support in all these years. If this was his boss, then maybe I could find out where he was working. I had no problem with helping Shannon file a garnishment on his paycheck.

"I'm sorry to interrupt, but did I hear correctly that Kevin works for you, Sir?"

I looked directly into his staggering green eyes. His chiseled jaw was a little distracting, but getting Abigail some much needed financial help was very grounding.

Green eyes looked between me and Kevin, almost in confusion, with a slight hint of annoyance. I then turned to look at Kevin; he was white as a ghost. Something just wasn't right.

"Douce...perhaps you should talk to Legs about your position."

I turned back to Green eyes in time to catch his eyes scanning me from head to toe. I watched as his tongue came out and covered his top lip, sucking it behind his teeth. With a chuckle and an arch of his eyebrow, his eyes met mine.

"Boss..." one of the guys behind Green eyes spoke at his side. Green eyes turned to look at the man, who in turn leaned in close and began to whisper quickly to him.

"Douce, I'll see you first thing tomorrow," he said to Kevin without making eye contact. "Ms. O'Rourke, this was the best party I've attended this year. I'm told you're responsible."

I was shocked because I had no idea how he even knew my name. I decide to quit acting like a mute and answer the man like the professional woman that I am.

"I have a great staff, it was a team effort," I smiled and folded my hands in front of me, always remaining professional.

"Yes, well, you managed to save poor Mandy from Douce."

Everything I had ever been taught told me that I had to maintain a courteous and professional manner. I took pride in the fact that I had always done that when representing *Penciled In*. So the words that fell from my mouth next should have remained unsaid...

"Oh, well, Kevin told me he had plans for Mandy tonight. However, he still has his hand to help himself out later."

Green eyes began to chuckle and then all five men behind him joined in. A shiver ran down my spin at the situation. Green eyes was clearly an influential man, his men seemed to follow his lead at every turn. His presence even had Kevin about to piss his pants.

"Legs, I like how you work." With that he walked past me, taking his entourage with him. I watched as again people moved to get out of his way. Men giving him knowing glances and head nods.

I was so shocked at the scene that had just played out that I had forgotten the question that had popped in my head...who the fuck was Legs?

"Fuck!" Kevin spouted as he dragged his hand through his hair. His frustration evident in more than just his words. If it wasn't for all the guest surrounding us, I would be very nervous being this near to him.

I was so confused right now. I had no idea what the hell had just happened. The only person standing here with any possible answers was known for fucking people over.

"Kevin, what the fuck just happened?"

Kevin looked pissed. He was mumbling under his breath and I couldn't understand a word he was saying.

"I could slit your fucking throat for what you just did!" Kevin hissed, his face less than an inch from my own. I opened my mouth to say something back when Brandon, one of my bartenders, interceded.

"Ms. O'Rourke, you okay?"

Was I? I was confused as hell. Before I could even answer, Kevin was backpedaling. Talking a mile a minute, his fake assed smile back on his face.

"Hey, Man, I was just telling Christi here goodnight."

Brandon was a big guy, almost as big as Green eyes. He was one of the extra staff Charlotte had hired for this event. If I didn't know better, I would have sworn Kevin knew him, and more than that, he was scared shitless of him.

"Is that true, Ms. O'Rourke?"

I took advantage of Brandon standing here. Kevin was clearly about to piss himself. I was going to get some answers.

"Kevin, who the hell was that and who the fuck is Legs?"

Kevin gave Brandon a wide-eyed look and then turned and ran out the door as if he was on fire, leaving me still confused and my questions hanging unanswered.

Brandon very gently placed his hand on my arm and began leading me back into the ballroom. I hadn't realized I had been out in the hall so long and most of the guests had already left. I noticed the staff had already begun to break down tables. Shannon was sitting at the end of the bar and the smile on her face was radiant. I hadn't seen a real smile on her face that wasn't because of Abigail in years. Sitting next to her was the dark haired man from earlier. She was looking at him as if he was the only person in the room. Just like green eyes, his suit was tailored and he held himself with confidence. His smile was almost as big as hers.

"Christi, let me buy you a drink and we can have ourselves a little chat."

At this point, I was too tired to argue.

Brandon handed me a cold beer and then leaned his entire body toward me. "All right, Brandon, start talking. What the fuck just happened?"

"That, my fair Christi, was Patrick Malloy. He's a close friend of the bride and groom's families."

I took a long pull of my beer. Okay, so he was a guest; that was obvious. What was with the personal bodyguards though?

"Brandon, spill," I said, my voice clearly conveying my agitation.

"Patrick Malloy is someone you want on your side. He has a lot of influence in what goes on in this town. He isn't someone you want as an enemy."

Another part of my job was being able to read people, and I could tell Brandon knew a shit-ton more than he was letting on. He was choosing to give me the cliff notes on green eyes, aka Patrick Malloy. I also knew when to cut my losses. If this Patrick guy was so influential in this town, then someone else would certainly know him.

"All right, then who the fuck is Legs?"

Brandon moved in closer and spoke in hushed tones. "When Patrick likes someone, he gives them a name that he'll remember. You, my fair lady, must have made quite an impression. *You* are Legs."

I sat at the bar and continued to sip my beer. The room had been cleared and all of the staff had been paid and escorted out. Shannon had finally said goodnight and was being escorted home by the dark haired man. His name was actually Dillion and he was an accountant. He offered to take me home as well, but I politely declined. I would tell Shannon in the morning that Kevin was working for Patrick Malloy.

It was late when I finally got everything wrapped up and went to the restroom to change my clothes. I hated being in my uniform one second longer than I absolutely had to. With my Nikes laced up, I made my way to my car in the parking lot. George, the night security guard, walked with me and made certain my car started. I waved goodbye and turned left onto the street.

My mind must have still been on the evening, because I never noticed the black sedan that followed me home.

CHAPTER TWO

When I got home last night, or rather very early this morning, all I could concentrate on was getting into a scalding hot bath. However, the last thing I wanted to do was to wake up Abigail. I silently made my way to her room and slowly and quietly opened her door. Her bedroom was the epitome of princess perfection. She had pink painted walls, her name spelled out in white wooden letters stood out against the color and there were fluffy pink curtains covering the windows. Her canopy bed was my favorite feature in the room, with its dainty ruffles and massive amounts of stuffed animals. I envied her. How pathetic was it to envy a four year old and her princess bedroom? It was more than that, though. Abigail had her mom, me, and our dad to take care of her. Growing up, it was just my dad and he didn't have a clue how to decorate little girls' rooms.

When I was six, our mom had disappeared. I could remember asking my dad when she was coming back and he would always say she was off on a vacation. I remember that we packed up the car one day and Dad drove us to Chicago. Now, all these years later, I still didn't know where she was and Dad wouldn't talk about her so we avoided the subject of her entirely.

Abigail was sleeping soundly and I knew she wouldn't wake if I ran the water. So that was just what I did. As I lay in the tub surrounded by bubbles and silence, I replayed the events of the night in my head. I had been told in the past that I had a nice set of legs. I never agreed, but then again, a lot of women don't like their bodies. Somehow it felt almost offensive to have Patrick Malloy make reference to them. It didn't really feel like a compliment, more of him naming a place he wanted to be—between my legs. I decided that it didn't matter. I'd lived in Chicago all this time and this was the first time I had ever encountered him. What did matter was getting in touch with him again. I needed to let him know what a piece of trash he had in his employ. I had to find out what kind of business he ran and then let the courts know. Abigail was growing everyday and her needs were becoming more and more expensive. It was time Kevin was forced to pay. The hot water and fragrant bubbles had done their magic. I felt relaxed when I finally crawled into my bed and fell into a dreamless sleep.

The downside of living with a four year old was that they tended to have schedules. Abigail was no exception. When she was awake, she expected everyone in the house to be as well. She didn't care that you had only gotten three hours of sleep.

Abigail woke me by bouncing energetically on my bed. "AUNTIE CHRIS, TIME TO GET UP!" she shouted as she continued to jump.

"Oh God, who gave you sugar so early?" I asked to no one in particular

"Auntie Christi, Mommy's making pancakes. Hurry up, I'm hungry!"

She finally quit jumping as she mercilessly removed the covers from my bed. It was a damn good thing she was cute. I groaned as I heaved my tired body over the edge of the bed. My feet were sore and the chill of the hardwood floor felt so good.

As I made my way into the kitchen, I smelled the one thing that would make my life better, coffee.

I watched as Shannon was flipping pancakes and humming, swaying her hips to the song that must have been playing inside her head. This was a bad sign. Shannon was notorious for falling in love fast and thinking later. This wouldn't be the first time I would have to rein her in. I took my seat at the bar and Abigail quickly followed.

"Okay, who are you and what have you done with my sister?"

Shannon turned around as she placed a plate full of pancakes on the counter. The smile on her face was huge and I could only guess what, or rather who, had put it there.

"Can't I just be in a good mood?" She questioned with a smirk on her face.

"Just please tell me you slept in your own bed last night?" My face serious.

"Mommy, can I have pink juice?" Abigail interjected as she headed toward the refrigerator.

I wasn't going to let Abigail's question derail my need for answers. Shannon had been hurt time and time again. I refused to let that happen this time. I would kill Dillion if he tried to hurt my sister.

"No, Baby, you can have milk."

"Can I have pink milk?" her big blue eyes sparking at her Mother

"Good try, but no, you can have white milk." Shannon said with a chuckle. Shannon placed the cup of milk in front of Abigail. Her attention again focused on me.

"Yes, Christi, I slept in my own bed...alone."

I knew I had to be careful with Abigail in the room. I wasn't always able to keep my emotions in check when it came to my family.

"I like him, Christi. I like him a lot. I want to get to know him better and see where this goes. He listens to me, he actually looks me in the eyes, and is interested in what I have to say."

I completely understood what she was saying. All too often men were too busy staring at my chest, rather than paying attention to the words I spoke. I still wanted her to be careful, though.

"Well, since you went to all the trouble of trying to bribe me with carbs, what do you want from me?"

Shannon hated to cook. Even though she was really good at it, she only did it when she wanted something.

"Wow...nothing gets by you, Watson."

"Pfft, please, I am so Sherlock." I countered.

"Whatever, I know it's your day off, but I have a date and I need a sitter."

"I will, on one condition." I stipulated, completely serious

Shannon rolled her eyes and turned around to get more coffee.

"Ok, I'll bite, what's your condition?" she asked.

" Don't shave your legs before your date." I responded matter of factly.

"Um...okay...but why?" her tone clearly curious

"Because I heard somewhere that if you have stubbly legs, you're less inclined to...have relations." I whispered, looking quickly to Abigail.

Abigail was beyond excited to be spending the night having a sleepover with Auntie Christi. I promised her we would order pizza, watch all her favorite movies, and stay up late. She didn't really understand why she couldn't go with her mommy on her date. I told her they would be doing boring things and that we would have so much more fun.

I told Shannon it might be better if I had Abigail in the bedroom when Dillion came to pick her up. I didn't want her to be confused if things didn't work out. Shannon agreed and I distracted my niece with an impromptu dance-off. We stood in her bedroom with my iPod and danced around the room. When I was certain Shannon had left, I took Abigail out into the living room and was about to order pizza when my dad called wanting to know what we had planned for dinner. He insisted he take us out for pizza when I told him of our plans.

Dad took us to a little mom and pop place called Gino's. They made the best Chicago-style deep dish pizza on the planet. Once we devoured our food, Abigail asked if she could go play the video games. Since we both had a clear view of the machines, dad gave her money and told her to go get quarters from the cashier. With Abigail safely occupied, I decided to pump my dad for information.

"So, Dad, you seem to know everyone in this town, what's the story on Dillion Parker?"

My dad never took his eyes off Abigail as he spoke.

"Chris, you can trust Dillion with Shannon. He's a good guy, he'll treat her right."

This surprised and yet angered me at the same time. Dad knew all of the pieces of shit that Shannon had dated, yet he knew of a decent guy and he never brought him around.

"If you knew he would be good for her, why haven't you introduced them before?"

My dad actually chuckled at this one. "Fathers don't tend to get involved in their daughter's love lives."

He had a point I guess. I decided to go for broke.

"I had a run in with Kevin last night at the wedding. Shannon didn't see him. I found out where he's working and I got his boss's name."

"Did you tell your sister?"

"No, she was too damn happy this morning. I didn't have the heart to mess that up." I admitted.

"I can't blame you there, Sweetheart. So, who's the fucker working for?"

I took a drink of my Coke. I wanted to know as much as I could about Patrick Malloy. My dad had a lot of contacts and if anyone had information on him, I knew my dad would have it.

"A man by the name of Patrick Malloy, ever heard of him?"

My dad took several minutes before he spoke. He wasn't a man of many words, but when he did speak, he meant every word he said.

"Did you speak with him about Kevin?"

"Not really, he noticed Kevin and I were fussing and he asked if there was a problem, then he called Kevin, Douce." The last word coming out as if a question.

My dad pulled out his phone, checking it quickly and then pocketing it.

"Tell me something," my dad shifted his body closer to mine, "did you tell Patrick how you and Kevin knew each other?"

"Actually, Kevin told him that I was the sister of an old friend."

I watched as Abigail jumped up and down at whatever was happening on the video screen. We both chuckled as she yelled out in excitement.

"Did the subject of Abigail come up?"

I noticed my dad start looking around; he was starting to creep me out.

"No, he got really nervous and then tried to play it off like we were just talking. Patrick told him he would see him later then left with his men."

"Did Douce stick around?"

"No, as soon as Patrick left, he shot out of there. I talked to Brandon, the bartender who seemed to know Patrick, and I asked him what the deal was."

"Brandon was working your party?"

"Yes, Kevin got really nervous when Brandon came over."

"I'll bet he did more than get nervous."

Now I was really curious. Who the hell was this guy?

My dad was again silent. I let him be; knowing if I pushed, he would just clam up and I would never get any more answers.

"Christi, what I'm about to tell you doesn't leave this table, you got me?" I nodded my head and leaned in closer to my dad. "Not even your sister, do you understand?" Again I nodded.

"I've known the Malloy family for a very long time. I've been good friends with Thomas Malloy since we were boys."

I listened patiently as dad continued his story. His far off gaze told me he was telling it just as he lived it.

"When you were a little girl and your Mother and I started having problems, she threatened to take you girls and run. I was just a street cop in a small town and didn't have two nickels to rub together. Thomas had called me out of the blue and I told him what was going on. He hired a top-notch attorney that dug up information on your Mother. She signed the divorce papers and disappeared into the night. Thomas got me the job here and told me he would call on me in the future for a favor. He told me that family was the most important thing in this world and I agreed with him. Patrick took over the family business from his dad, Thomas, about six years ago."

He looked at me again, a serious look on his face.

"I'm not surprised that Douce didn't want Malloy to know about Abigail. I can guarantee you that that was why he left."

Abigail began to laugh at a little boy who was playing beside her, apparently he lost his game and was throwing a fit. She had such an infectious laugh that you just couldn't help but join her.

"Did Patrick say anything else to you?"

I thought for a minute before I answered him. "He called me Legs."

My dad chuckled and then turned to me and looked me directly in the eyes. "Keep that one filed away, you may have to use it someday."

Abigail came back to the table after she had used up all of her money, and I noticed it was getting late, so my dad went and settled the bill, while I waited with Abigail. We said goodnight to the owners and headed out to the parking lot. I had just finished getting Abigail fastened into her booster seat when I heard laughter coming from across the parking lot. I looked over and noticed that none other than Patrick Malloy was getting out of a black Mercedes. He had a voluptuous blonde at his side and she was giggling at every word he spoke. He noticed my dad before me and said something to the blonde and the guys that surrounded him. He made his way across the lot in my dad's direction.

"Sir, how are you?" As he stood in front of my dad, the two men embraced in a manly, back-slapping hug.

"I can't complain, young man. How's your father?"

"Da is good. I'll tell him you inquired. It's been too long since you've been to the house, my Mum would enjoy a visit."

It was at this point that Patrick made eye contact with me. "Ms. O'Rourke, a pleasure to see you again," he winked as he spoke.

"Mr. Malloy," I smiled as I acknowledged him.

The blonde had made her way over and was shooting daggers in my direction. She had on a skin-tight pleather mini dress with thigh-high fuck-me boots. I had my doubts that anything on her was real.

My dad said goodbye to Mr. Malloy and we got into the car. I noticed as we passed them, that Patrick winked at me, while the blonde flipped me the bird. I guess she wanted me to know her IQ.

CHAPTER THREE

Shannon and Dillion had become inseparable in the past three weeks. He had been to our house several nights a week for dinner and to play with Abigail. He seemed completely smitten with the both of them. Shannon swore to me that they hadn't slept together and I honestly believed her.

Dillion showered her with gifts, flowers, and dinners out. He would bring Abigail dolls and hair bows. He was really trying. He had even gone so far as to ask our father's permission to date Shannon. Yes, he would do nicely.

Last weekend, Dillion took both of them to meet his family. Abigail came home with nearly a whole new wardrobe and a Barbie Corvette. I had never seen Shannon happier or smiling so much. I'd definitely never heard Abigail giggle more. This made me happy.

Dad informed Shannon that he was stealing her and Abigail away this weekend for dinner and a movie and I was asked by Charlotte to go clubbing with her. This weekend was a rare occurrence that we had no clients booked. I jumped at the chance to have an actual non-work related adult conversation.

Charlotte agreed that we would stick to low-key bars. I didn't want to have to wade through drunken people or shout over loud music. Charlotte rolled her eyes, but agreed. She knew of a great jazz bar not far from *Penciled in.*

After a long hot shower, I applied my makeup a little heavier than normal, and then spritzed on some fragrance. I dressed in a simple but elegant little black dress. It wasn't anything fancy, but you could never go wrong with the right dress. A nice pair of heels and I was out the door to meet Charlotte.

We let the valet park the car and made our way inside to find a table in the corner of the room. The bar was all black with dark blue lighting illuminating the ceiling throughout the club. Each table was covered in a white tablecloth and had a small lamp in the center. Charlotte signaled for the waitress and then proceeded to order a martini for each of us. The music was nice and not very loud, and I was really enjoying myself. We had been there about an hour when two guys approached our table. They were very polite and asked if they could join us. The taller, more handsome one was leaning into me and inhaling deeply, before the other guy elbowed him, backing him off me.

Well, that wasn't creepy at all.

Charlotte explained to them that we were just trying to relax and thanked them anyway. Fortunately, they took the hint and moved along. I had just ordered my second martini when I noticed none other than Kevin walk by our table. He noticed me immediately. Throwing his hands in the air, he turned completely to our table.

"Fuck, can't I go anywhere and not run into you?"

His arrogance was diluting my buzz. I had been so busy with work, that I hadn't had an opportunity to find out where Kevin worked.

"Oh, God!No, you're the one who's fucking up my night! I haven't had nearly enough to drink yet to deal with your low-life ass."

Kevin was there with a different girl this time. She was pretty, with long black hair. I couldn't tell what color her eyes were as they were dilated. The thought crossed my mind that he had to get all of his dates stoned before they would go out with him. I turned to his date and noticed she was looking behind me.

"I'm sorry, I didn't catch your name," I addressed Kevin's date. She didn't answer me; she just kept looking behind me. "Listen, I just wanted to give you a piece of free advice, run as quickly as you can from this low-life right here. You see, Kevin will promise you the world, but the second he gets what he wants, he's out the fucking door. And whatever you do, don't have a baby with him, he doesn't take care of the one he has."

The girl still had not made eye contact with me; whatever was over my left shoulder had her complete attention. "Is that the truth, Douce?"

I turned in the direction of the voice. Standing there in all of his glory and his ever present entourage, was Patrick Malloy. His grey shirt had the top two buttons undone and his blazer matched his pants. His hair was styled perfectly, not a hair out of place. His eyes, however, were black and his face was absent of any emotion. The room seemed to grow very quiet as he waited for Kevin to answer his question. When he got no response, he then turned his attention to me.

"Legs, care to elaborate?"

I didn't know if it was the alcohol or because I was already pissed that Kevin was still sharing my oxygen, but the fact that he couldn't say my name really pissed me the fuck off.

"Okay, first of all, my name is not Legs, it's Christi. That shit just pisses me off. I have a fucking name, *Patrick*, and I'd appreciate it if you'd fucking use it when you address me."

The look on his face changed as I proceeded to stick my finger in his face, well more like his chest as he was considerable taller than myself. I watched as a tiny smirk began to form at the corner of his mouth.

I didn't let him speak as I continued my word vomit.

"This waste of fucking skin here is the father of my beautiful niece, Abigail, and the fucker knows it, too. He hasn't seen her in years and he refuses to pay one god-damn dime of court-ordered child support. So yes, Mr. Malloy, you have a low-life motherfucking dead-beat father working for you."

His expression changed from the cocky smirk to one of anger. I should have been afraid of this quick change, but in reality, I was getting turned on.

"Smiles' baby?" He questioned Kevin, his tone even, yet suspicious.

Again with the code names, this was too much. Can't the man call people by their given names?

"Who the fuck is Smiles? I'm talking about my sister, Shannon." I shouted, exasperated. Ignoring me, he voiced his next question directly at Kevin. "Giggles is your daughter, Douce?"

Kevin didn't answer, and frankly I was confused and getting even more pissed off. I then turned to Charlotte, who was watching this entire scene play out like a tennis match.

"Who the hell is Giggles?" I asked her, since no one else would answer me. She looked at me wide eyed and started to answer me when Patrick questioned Kevin.

"Does Books know, Douce?"

Kevin lowered his head, finding his shoes very interesting all of the sudden. I looked around and noticed nearly everyone in the bar was watching us.

"No, Boss, he doesn't know, and yes, Giggles is mine. Smiles and I had a thing a long time ago."

I felt as if I had been transported to another country and they were all speaking in a language I didn't understand.

"How far is he in arrears, Ms. O'Rourke?" Patrick's voice and facial expression changed back to his prior cockiness.

"He owes roughly ten thousand dollars in unpaid support."

One of the men in his entourage leaned into his ear. Patrick's face never changed as he listened to what he was being told. I looked at Kevin and noticed that his entire face was now white as a ghost. His date had completely disappeared. Two men suddenly appeared and grasped Kevin on each side.

Patrick was now looking at Kevin, whose face had gone completely ashen. No words were said as the two men escorted Kevin out of the bar and into the night.

It was like that scene in a movie; the one where once the fight was over, the music came back on and people carried on with what they were doing. Our waitress suddenly appeared with a fresh round of drinks and Patrick began speaking with the men in his entourage. Once the waitress sat our drinks down, Patrick handed her two crisp one hundred dollar bills.

"Make certain Ms. Christi and Ms. Charlotte are kept happy while they're here."

I watched as the waitress flashed him a smile and pushed her chest out just a little more. I rolled my eyes at the shameless way she was flirting with him.

He then turned back to us. "Ladies, always a pleasure, enjoy the rest of your evening."

He spoke to a few more people in the room and after each one, he would turn his attention back to our table. As he made his way to the front door, he turned one final time and nodded his head as he stepped into the darkness.

Monday came all too quickly. Shannon and I were sitting in my office going over the calendar for the week. We had a wedding and a sweet sixteen party this weekend. It was agreed upon that I would work the birthday party and Shannon would do the wedding. A knock at the door stopped our list making, as a courier had a package for Shannon. Honestly, with as much attention as Dillion had been giving her lately, it was probably tickets to Aruba or something. Nothing could have prepared me for the truth.

"Oh, my God."

I turned my attention from the Gucci shoe-inspired cake that the young birthday girl wanted to the papers that now sat in Shannon's hands.

"Chris...look."

I took the paperwork from her and began to read the letter that sat on the top. It was from the president of People's First Bank here in Chicago. It was addressed to Shannon O'Rourke and Abigail Grace O'Rourke. The letter basically stated that a college fund had been opened in the name of the minor child and currently held a balance of twenty thousand dollars. Furthermore, it would increase by twenty thousand dollars every year until the child reached twenty-one years of age. Another slip of paper clipped to the letter was a cashier's check in the amount of fifteen thousand dollars. A second letter stated that the check was for back child support and that from this day forward, a check for five thousand dollars would arrive on the first of every month for the benefit of said minor child. This would continue until the child was twenty-one, or until the child was legally adopted by any man Shannon decided to marry.

My mind went immediately back to the conversation at the bar between Patrick and Kevin. All of these years and Kevin had never made an effort. One conversation with his boss, suddenly Kevin was made of money.

I didn't have time to ponder the matter any further, since Charlotte made her presence known when she walked into my office. She entered, followed by two women. The first was an older, yet very beautiful woman. She was so graceful,and reminded me of the Hollywood stars from the forties and fifties. Her beautiful red hair flowed onto her shoulders in soft yet perfect waves. Her complexion was peaches and cream and sickeningly flawless. Her beige-colored pantsuit looked as if it was designer made and cost more than what I made in a month. It was her eyes that stood out to me, vivid green.

The petite woman who stood beside her was just as beautiful. Her hair, however, was much darker and longer. Her skin was just as flawless, but her eyes were a beautiful blue. Shannon clearly knew theses women as she leaped from her desk and embraced them in a warm greeting.

"Chris, I'd like to introduce you to Mrs. Nora Malloy and Ms. Paige Malloy."

The two women smiled brightly as they continued into the office. Charlotte motioned for them to have a seat in the chairs that faced my desk and then asked if they would care for a drink. Nora spoke first and requested a cup of hot tea in the most enchanting Irish accent I had ever heard. Charlotte excused herself and left to go make a pot of tea.

"Christi," Nora spoke, her green eyes shining, the look on her face was one of pure joy, "I was a guest at the Connor-Donnelly wedding and I was impressed to say the very least." As she spoke, she turned her direction to Paige who nodded her head in agreement. "I was told by Mrs. Connor that you'd been very helpful in making her daughter's day very special."

"It wasn't just me, Mrs. Malloy, I have an amazing staff."

"Please, call me Nora."

Charlotte appeared with a tray of tea. Once all of our cups had been prepared, we continued with the meeting.

"Christi, I'm going to get right to the point here. Paige is getting married in eight months. As big as the Donnelly wedding was, this one is going to be huge. Practically everyone that attended that wedding will attend Paige's. That guest list, however, wouldn't compare to this one considering the additional size of the grooms family. The Montgomerys were a well-to-do family from the South and will more than double the Connor-Donnelly guest list. Christi, we're looking at over eight hundred people."

When you'd done this as long as I had, you learned a few things besides how to break up a fight. You learned that money talked and bullshit walked. It didn't matter if you were planning a party for eight or eight hundred, the process was the same. Nora may have been wearing a designer suit and had a pretty accent, but did she have the cash to buy the wedding she was describing?

"Nora, I can give Paige just about anything when it comes to her reception, but the bottom line is that it'll cost a great deal of money."

Nora didn't even flinch when I told her the Connor wedding cost nearly a thousand dollars per person. That roughly meant her reception alone was over four hundred thousand dollars. The additional people would increase that cost significantly.

Paige began to list the kinds of food she wanted to have served. She wanted to have a speakeasy-style wedding theme. She showed me photos of her bridesmaid's dresses that were silk and had lace appliqués adorning them. She wanted all of the drinks served in martini glasses with the exception of the beer. She wanted all of the wait staff to be male and wearing white waiter's jackets with black bow ties, cummerbunds, and black pants. There would be a band playing and at least ten bars set up throughout the room. Everything she had chosen was even more high-end than the last wedding. The last item that I needed to address was that of security. For the Donnelly wedding, we had had to charge security as a separate fee.

"Oh no, Lass. My son, Patrick, will take care of security."

It hadn't occurred to me before that Nora Malloy was Patrick's mother. So with a plan in motion and a tight hug from Nora and Paige, the meeting was over and a wedding reception scheduled. I sat in my chair going over everything that had happened in the past few weeks. With a careful decision made, I grabbed my cell phone and scrolled down my contact list. I pressed send and waited three rings before getting an answer.

"Brandon, if someone wanted to get in touch with Patrick Malloy, how would they find him?"

CHAPTER FOUR

You know that scene in horror films where the creepy music begins to play and you shout at the television for the girl on the screen not to go into the house? Well, that was how I felt as I sat inside my car, parked outside under the neon sign that flashed, *Whiskers Gentleman's Club*.

Gentlemen my ass...

Brandon assured me that Patrick had an office inside the club and that he could normally be found there every evening. I needed to thank him. I needed him to understand that I knew what he had done, even though he didn't have to do it. I could have just called him, or have sent one of those fancy edible fruit basket things. I could have taken Shannon's advice and sent him the equivalent of guy flowers, a six-pack of his favorite beer. However, with the amount of money he had made Kevin pay, none of those things would do. I needed to look him straight in the eye and say thank you. So, with a deep breath and my hand wrapped tightly around the can of pepper spray I had in my pocket, I exited my car and made my way to the doors.

There was nothing special about the building that housed Whiskers; it was in the middle of a rundown industrial area. The building stood alone, surrounded on three sides by parking lots. The sidewalk out front had seen better days as it was littered with cracks. The tattoo shop across the street was missing the last 'O' so that it now read 'Tatto.' Several bars lined the street on either side, and at the end was a pawn shop and an adult bookstore.

I took a deep breath as I placed my hand firmly on the metal handle of the door. I could do this, ten minutes tops and I would be back in my car and headed home. I could feel the vibration of the thumping base as I pulled the door of the club open. Once inside, I came to a wall that blocked the view of what was going on from any innocent passersby. To the left was a bar, behind which stood two of the biggest guys I had ever seen. They looked me up and down with huge smirks on their faces. I pulled the belt of my coat tighter around my waist and nearly vomited in my mouth. The way the human wall of a man was sucking his front teeth and cleaning his finger nails with his pocket knife was disgusting and caused my stomach to turn.

"Can I help you, Sweet Thing?"

I hadn't noticed the short, stocky guy that stood in the entryway. He had on white dress pants that were pleated in the front and secured with a patent leather belt.

Hello, the seventies are calling, they want their pants back.

The black shirt beneath his white suit jacket was open most of the way and clearly showed the three thick gold chains that hung from his neck, nestled amongst his bushy chest hair. Try as he might, he was no John Travolta. I turned my attention to him and shot him a quick smile.

"Yes, Sir, I'm here to see Patrick Malloy."

All three men snickered and glanced at each other. Human wall looked around the corner at what I can only assume was a girl dancing. Gold chain guy was still undressing me with his eyes. The last guy was older than the other two, his head completely bald, a striking black soul patch stood out from his tiny lower lip. He wore sunglasses that obscured my view of his eyes, although I'm certain he too was dreaming up ways to get me naked as the girls on the other side of that wall. I never understood people who wore sunglass even at night. Did they feel they had something to hide?

"Boss doesn't do the interviews, Baby. That's my job," gold chain guy responded.

"Do I look like I need a job?" My voice clipped, gone was my politeness. I needed to see Patrick and then get the hell out of here.

"Everybody needs a job, Sweetheart." He quickly retorted, his tone eluded that he thought he was funny. His grin devilish and the hair on the back of my neck began to stand up.

"Yes, well, I didn't ask for a job, I asked to see Patrick Malloy." My voice may be firm, but inside I was about to bolt and run. Thanking Patrick be damned.

"Can I tell him who's asking?"

'Christi, Christi O'Rourke"

The human wall and Mr Clean again chuckled and one of them began playing with his cell phone, shaking his head

"Listen, Babe, I know every piece of pussy in this town and Boss don't know no Christi O'Rourke. Now either you want to apply for a job or you turn around and head right back out the way you came."

Before I could get too frustrated, my father's words came back to me.

"What name did he give you? File that one away; you may need it sometime."

"Then tell him Legs wants a quick word."

Suddenly, it was as if I held the key to the city. The two guys behind the bar immediately stood up straight and wouldn't make eye contact with me anymore. Gold chain guy suddenly found his manners and actually smiled at me, a warm, apologetic smile.

"My apologies, I didn't recognize you, Miss."

He picked up the phone that was sitting on the bar beside him and spoke in hushed tones. Finally, he glanced up at me and spoke, "Yes, Sir, Boss, right away."

"Legs...er, Ms.O'Rourke, if you'd please follow me."

I wasn't about to let gold chains touch me and so I stayed a half step behind him. Once we passed the bar, the room opened up and the music got much louder. The room was painted black, I think. The lighting around the room gave everything a red hue. There were three stages, with poles in the middle of each. All three stages had different naked girls dancing to a song I didn't recognize. To the right I noticed a staircase that led to a wooden door at the top. The sign on the door read private. Gold chain guy asked me if I would care for a drink, but I smiled and declined.

The door at the top of the stairs opened and a young girl came out. She was fully dressed in jeans and a t-shirt and couldn't have been a day over sixteen. Her mascara was running as if she had been crying. She stormed past me and ran out the door. Gold chain guy instructed me that Patrick was in the office at the top of the stairs. I carefully climbed the stairs and stood outside the door. Here goes nothing, I said to myself as I twisted the handle and opened the door.

Ever entered a room and have the conversation suddenly stop? Yes, that was where I was now. Once I opened the office door, everyone stopped talking and looked in my direction. Truly, this was more than likely a good thing; conversations that were held behind closed doors in strip clubs usually weren't garden party subjects.

Patrick sat behind the massive desk that stood majestically in the center of the room. The desk looked to be an antique and yet well cared for. His high-backed leather chair towered over his head. The desk was clean and only housed an expensive looking desk set. The green desk lamp illuminated the glossy surface. Patrick however, looked like the captain of a ship. He dominated that desk, as well as the room.

The room wasn't anything like the décor downstairs; the walls were all paneled with rich dark wood. Not like the paneling from the seventies, no, this was like the kind you would find in old English homes.

The painting that hung behind Patrick's head looked to be a portrait of a very hand-some Irishman. The plaid sash that crossed his chest reminded me of a picture that my grandmother had had in her house when I was a little girl.

To the left stood three men. The first I recognized immediately as Ryan Donnelly. Ryan was a massive man with very broad shoulders, and I was certain his biceps were as big as my thigh. All of my dealings with him in the past had been pleasant.

Next to him was another man just as big. However, his skin was much darker; he wasn't making eye contact with me. His hands crossed in front of him.

The last man was just as tall, not nearly as built, and his hair was a nice shade of dark blond. He, also, wasn't making eye contact with me.

"Ms. O'Rourke to what do I owe the honor?" Patrick's deep voice sounded and brought my attention back to him.

"Please, take a seat," he motioned and then stood for me to sit in one of the chairs that faced his desk. "Does your father know you're here?"

Patrick Malloy held himself as a man who expected to be intimidating. He oozed power, from the constant group of men who surrounded him, to his black Armani suit he was currently wearing. He wanted people to fear him, but why?

I prided myself on being a strong, intelligent woman. Which was probably why I hadn't had a date in over a year. I wasn't going to willingly let Patrick see that he made me just a little nervous.

So, instead of addressing him, I turned my attention and made my way over to Mr. Donnelly with my hand out for a handshake. "Mr. Donnelly, such a pleasant surprise to see you. How is your beautiful bride?"

I watched the surprised look on his face as I continued to hold my hand out. He quickly looked at Patrick and out of the corner of my eye, I noticed Patrick do a quick nod. It was then that he took my hand in his and very softly shook it.

"Ms. O'Rourke, always a pleasure to see you. My Allyson is excellent, thank you for asking."

I smiled brightly at him, "I've asked you to call me Christi, meeting you here doesn't change that." Again he looked at Patrick, his face contorted with confusion. I didn't understand what was going on between these two men, so I decided to be polite and give Ryan an easy out.

"Please tell her I said hello." He nodded with understanding and I turned back to-ward Patrick.

All of the men in the room waited until I had taken my seat before they sat down. I thought this odd since we were in a strip club.

"Mr. Malloy, you're a busy man and I only want to take a minute to personally tell you thank you. Thank you for helping my sister and my niece."

A devilish grin spread across his face as he looked directly into my eyes. "I'm not certain I know what you're referring to, Ms. O'Rourke."

"Please, Mr. Malloy, call me Christi. After everything you have done, it seems only right."

He smiled his devilish smile and moved his left hand up to rest under his chin. His green eyes sparkled in the light from the lamp on his desk.

"Only if you call me Patrick" His voice was doing strange things to my insides. I only smiled at his request.

"You and I both know you had everything to do with Kevin, err rather Douce, owning up to his responsibilities. I simply wanted to say thank you, it'll go a long way toward paying for her education."

There I said it, now to get the hell out of here.

"Giggles is a smart little girl, she deserves the best."

I was so sick of these names he had given to the people I loved, "Her name is Abigail." It came out very snippy, though I didn't mean for it to.

"Sorry, Christi, *Abigail* is a smart little girl," he emphasized her name as he corrected himself. "Smiles did a fine job of raising her by herself, and it shows."

"Why do you call my sister Smiles?"

He didn't bat an eye as he looked directly into mine. "Because giggles start as smiles. Your sister is always smiling every time I see her, and your niece has a laugh that makes my Ma giggle."

Fair enough. However, I refrained from asking why he called me Legs.

"Yes, well, again, I know you're a busy man and so I won't keep you..."

"You didn't answer my question, Christi; does your father know you're here?"

For a brief moment, I thought about telling him to mind his own business. I was an adult after all. However, I decided that since he had just gotten Kevin to pay up that I would remain nice.

"No, Patrick, I haven't spoken to my dad today. He has no idea I was coming to thank you," I answered and began to rise from my chair.

"This isn't a safe neighborhood, Christi. A beautiful woman such as yourself could attract some...unwanted attention."

"Yes, you're right, thank you for your concern. I'll see myself out."

"Not so fast, Christi," Patrick rose from his seat. I turned my attention back to him and sat back down in my chair.

"Although it was very courageous for you to come here and thank me for helping your sister, I'm afraid I cannot accept only that." His eyes never left mine as he continued. "After all, I did get Douce to pay your sister a large sum of money, did I not? I'd say that mere words would not be quite sufficient."

I was at a loss for what to say at this point. This had not gone as I had planned. This was only supposed to take a few minutes and I would be on my way home. He was right; I was attracting unwanted attention.

"Then please, enlighten me on how I can properly thank you." Again with the clipped tone, I was in way over my head.

"Easy, Christi, have dinner with me."

His suggestion was not what I had expected, although I really had no clue about what he would deem acceptable. However, just as I was about to tell him where he could stick his request for dinner, Patrick began to unbutton his suit jacket and leaned back in his chair. He then casually lifted his long legs and placed them on his desk. It was at this point that I noticed the shiny handgun that sat in the waistband of his pants. I quickly looked away, only to notice that the other three men in the room were also packing. Suddenly, it was as if all the puzzle pieces came together, like a chain made of thousands of tiny magnets. Everything I had witnessed that related to Patrick Malloy pointed to just one thing—the Mafia.

I had watched enough movies focused on organized crime that I felt I knew enough to steer clear. I also knew they tended to make people do what they wanted. I decided the best approach was to convince Patrick that I didn't fit into the standard mob arm candy role.

"Thank you for the offer, Mr. Malloy. However, a man in your position undoubtedly requires a certain type of woman to fulfill his needs. I'm sorry, but I'm not that type of woman."

"Patrick. I *asked* you to call me Patrick"

His voice eerily low and I swallowed hard. I could feel the fear crawl up my spine. This had been a very big mistake.

"Jesus Christ, Christi! I'm asking you to dinner, not to give me a fucking lap dance."

It was sheer self preservation that motivated me to say what I did next.

"You may not be requesting a lap dance, *Mr. Malloy*, but you would require something from me that I'm not prepared to give."

He looked hard into my eyes, a battle line had been drawn. On one side was Patrick, a man who was, I am certain, accustomed to getting everything he wanted. Myself on the other, only wanting to leave this room in the same condition I entered it in. Patrick leaned his body back into his massive chair, a sly smile forming on his face.

"So, if I promise to conduct myself as a perfect gentleman and not demand a blow job at the end, would you reconsider?"

Patrick was a handsome man, used to having women fall at his feet. How sad it must be to never know if they wanted him for his money or the power they must feel when they are with him. I would gladly trade them positions, they could have his undivided attention.

"I'd have your word that this would only be dinner, no other expectations?"

I didn't give a shit how good he looked or how full his bank account was, he stood for something that I wanted no part of. One dinner and we were even.

"Yes." His answer rained with assurance and strangely I believed him. "Then, yes, I'd reconsider." My voice soft and still a little unsure.

"Good, done!" He slammed his hand on the desk as he spoke the words. *Fuck me!*

He pushed his chair away from the desk and slowly came around toward me. "Let me begin my role as a gentleman by doing proper introductions."

He motioned for me to join him by the three men who were again standing.

"Gents, this is the lovely Christi O'Rourke. Muscles, aka Ryan, you already know." Ryan smiled and nodded his head in my direction.

"This is Tonto, one of my inner circle."

Tonto was just as big as Ryan, or rather Muscles. I extended my hand out to shake his. I noticed that again, Patrick nodded his approval.

"Pleasure to meet you, Sir," I smiled at Tonto.

"And this is someone you would've been meeting in the very near future. My soon-to-be brother in law, Caleb Montgomery."

"I had the pleasure of meeting your beautiful bride recently, Mr. Montgomery. Congratulations."

Caleb didn't wait for Patrick, he grasped my outstretched hand and instead of shaking it, he raised it to his lips and kissed the back of it as he bowed slightly. "Thank you kindly, Ms. Christi, the pleasure is all mine."

"Christi, let me escort you to your car. I'm sure your father would worry if I let you go by yourself." Patrick interrupted as Caleb's lips touched my knuckles. He dropped my hand slowly, glaring in Patrick's direction.

Tonto and Caleb left the room first, while Patrick held the door for me. I followed the other two down the stairs, Patrick close to my left side. Once I got to the last step, I chanced a glance toward the bar. Sitting on a barstool eyeing Patrick was another overdone, scantily clad blonde. Clearly those were his type, so why was he interested in me? This only reassured me that he would be seriously disappointed with me after our dinner. Once he realized that my panties would be staying firmly on my body and not the floor of his car.

I turned my attention back to walking out the door when the blonde suddenly crossed my path.

"Hey, Baby, I've been waiting for you," she cooed, reaching out and running her blood red nails up Patrick's arm. I continued to walk. I could have cared less who he was sleeping with.

I felt his hand wrap around my arm as he kept me from moving forward. I turned back and gave him a questioning glare.

"Harley, I've told you to stay out of this club." He spoke to the blonde, but his eyes never left mine. "I know, but I have something for you."

I really didn't have the desire to listen to her any longer. I wanted to go home, see Abigail, and then take a very long, very hot bath.

Patrick ignored her as he urged me toward the door. Once outside, I noticed that Tonto, Muscles and Caleb were standing guard around my car. I clicked the remote, unlocking the doors. Patrick was at my driver's door before I could blink. He opened the door and stood waiting for me to get into the car.

"Christi, I'll pick you up Friday at six o'clock."

His eyes now soft, whether from the low lights of the club or change in venue. His voice calm, warm, and dare I say...sexy.

I watched as Patrick and his men stood in the road as I drove off. Again, I failed to see the black sedan that followed me home.

As I pulled into my driveway, I had to laugh at myself. My plans to simply thank him had gone up in flames. I now suspected Patrick Malloy was a serious member of the mafia and I had a date with him, I should have stuck with the fruit basket.

My dad was waiting for me when I opened my front door. This wasn't an unusual thing to happen, he was always stopping by. My gut told me he had a reason for being here, though.

"Patrick Malloy called me, Christi."

"Oh?"

"He told me everything, so you can drop the act."

"Okay, so I went to see Patrick Malloy."

"No, you went to a rough and dangerous neighborhood, Christi. What the hell were you thinking?"

"I needed to talk to him and it isn't like he has an office on Michigan Avenue."

My dad was silent as he pondered his thoughts. I left him alone, not wanting to do battle with two men tonight. "Christi, Patrick's a good guy and I want you to give him a chance. I trust him."

"Well, good, because he invited me to dinner."

"I know; he asked my permission first. Just promise me you'll give him a chance?" My dad made his way toward the door. He opened it and went to leave. Suddenly, he turned around and said, "Christi, he doesn't have an office on Michigan Avenue, but he does own a condo in the same building that Oprah lives in."

It was an hour later that I had settled into the pillows of the couch with a deep wine glass. As I closed my eyes and listened to the creaking of the house, I began to play the events from earlier in my head. Patrick had not acted as I thought. Clearly he and my father were friends who loved to gossip about me. As I took a large gulp of my wine, I nearly choked. If Patrick was a member of organized crime and he and my father were as close as I suspected. Was my dad a dirty cop?

CHAPTER FIVE

$\mathbf{T}$his wasn't a date; this was simply two people eating at the same time. Everyone ate dinner, we were just doing it together. Shannon nearly blew a gasket when I told her. She couldn't believe it took me so long to figure out that Patrick was in the Mafia. She said it took her ten seconds to figure out that Dillion was.

"How can you be okay with this, Shannon?"

"Easy, its just a job. It isn't any different from being a lawyer or whatever." She threw her hands in circles in the air to emphasize her point.

"Are you kidding me? They commit major crimes and kill people." I shouted back at her.

"Oh, and I suppose you're are honest in everything you do? People lie, cheat and steal every day, Chris. Get off your self imposed high horse. He is just a guy with a different job, don't judge him for things you know nothing about."

Since this wasn't a date and only dinner, I wasn't going to dress up. Yeah, that lasted long enough for my father to see me and demand that I change out of the jeans I had selected. I hadn't gathered up enough courage to confront him about being a dirty cop. So here I sat drinking the last sip of my wine, wearing a sexy little black wrap dress and heels.

If one positive thing could be said about Patrick, he was punctual. My dad raced to the front door like a kid on Halloween. Patrick looked so different tonight, his suit still tailored to his build, his features impeccable. However, his face didn't seem so fierce and his body didn't seem so rigid. This version of Patrick I could grow to like.

"Good evening, Christi, you look very lovely this evening," Patrick said with the biggest smile on his face as he handed me a huge bouquet of lilies.

My dad was so excited that he quickly snatched the flowers from my hand and began ushering us out the door. I knew with Patrick being in the position he was in, luxuries were a given. What I didn't expect was the stretch limo that was parked in front of my house.

I also didn't expect him to have the entire restaurant reserved for just the two of us; well, the two of us and the four huge guys who sat across the room.

Clair's was a local supper club and had been in business since the early 1900's. The building it was housed in was rumored to have been a speakeasy at one time, with caves that ran underneath. The walls were made of red brick and the walls that separated the different rooms had rows of arches. The tables were all square and draped with white tablecloths. Tiny votive candles illuminated our table.

Patrick, acting as the proper gentleman he pretended to be, pulled my chair out and then took his own seat. This time, I noticed the gun he'd had earlier in the week was gone.

I loved the feel of the old buildings here in the city. I had always wondered if the bricks could talk how exciting the stories would be.

Clair's was old-style dining, where they took great pride in being over the top, from offering you hot towels to wash your hands, to placing your napkin on your lap for you. They were the only restaurant in town that employed a sommelier.

"I'm impressed, Patrick, you must know someone to get them to close this restaurant on a Friday night."

Patrick's eyes met mine as his trademark smirk crossed his face. "I'd love nothing more than to say I pulled a few strings, but I want to be honest with you. *Clair's* has been my family's business since my great-grandfather built this building and named it after his first wife."

"Honestly, I'm impressed a little more now. I've always had a fascination with older buildings."

"Well, anytime you want to take the grand tour, I'll be happy to set that up for you, get you down into the caverns."

"Those aren't just rumors?"

"No, Christi, this was a speakeasy during prohibition."

"Then I'll be taking you up on that offer of a tour."

Patrick ordered a Delmonico and I went with the lamb chops. Our salad was made table side and was by far the most amazing salad I had ever had.

"So, are there any other places your family owns that might impress me?"

Patrick leaned back in his chair and wiped his face with his napkin. "Actually, yes, I just recently acquired the building you work in, as well as the banquet hall next door."

"You bought that building? I thought Charlotte owned it."

"No, it was actually owned by a rival family, I bought it with one of my ghost companies. They weren't being very professional with Charlotte and I don't tolerate those kinds of actions."

I wasn't about to ask him what had happened, it clearly was not my business. I did find it odd that he didn't like bad business; he was in the Mafia after all.

"Tell me, Christi, do you enjoy working for Ms. Charlotte?"

"What , no nicknames for her?"

He chuckled and then took a drink of his wine. "No, I'm certain Ms. Charlotte would have me dragged by my shorthairs if I gave her a nickname."

I began to laugh along with him. He was correct about her being tough. I had learned a great deal from her when it came to handling people.

"My grandfather, whom I'm named after, taught me his rules for business. I've lived them since I took over for my da. He and my da have taught me more lessons by watching them than any college class I ever attended."

"You went to college?"

He again began to laugh, "Does that surprise you? I went to Yale, actually."

"I'm sorry, that was quite rude of me. I did just stereotype you, didn't I?"

He looked at me very seriously as he leaned into me and whispered, "Yes, you did, Legs, but you can make it up to me by having a drink with me."

I let the nickname pass for now. After all, I did just insult him. It wouldn't be that big of a deal to have another glass of wine with him. However, I should have known that he would want to go to a different place to have the agreed drink.

Our waiter appeared again and Patrick slipped him what I believed to be a large amount of money. He helped me with my chair and once again we were in the limo.

Patrick began to type on his cell phone and never once told the driver where we were going. It was almost as if this had all been pre-planned.

The drive was only a few blocks, and we honestly could have walked. However, being in heels and a dress, I was glad we didn't.

The building we pulled up to I recognized immediately as being *Pieces*, the new club in the downtown area. I avoided downtown, certain areas simply were not safe.

Tonight though, the thought of my safety wasn't a concern. I knew Patrick could and would protect me.

The club was housed in an old warehouse that had been on the mayor's list of 'make our city beautiful' restorations. The city offered huge tax breaks to anyone who would take over the buildings, make repairs, and open businesses. I had read that the O'Leary Foundation had come in and fixed up several buildings and I wondered if this was one of them. The entrance to the building was impressive. There were two massive oak doors with "*Pieces*" written in dark green and outlined in gold.

I had been so busy taking in the sight of the building that I had failed to notice Allyson and Ryan Donnelly standing just outside of the limo. I smiled and Allyson pulled me into a tight hug.

"Oh, my goodness, it's such a pleasure to see you again, Mrs. Donnelly."

"Oh, Christi, it's Allyson to you."

"Very well, Allyson"

It was then that I noticed Patrick's entourage had joined us. Black suits now surrounded Allyson and myself.

"Christi, I have someone I need to speak with, can I leave you to visit with Allyson for a few minutes?"

Before I could assure him I would be fine, Allyson did the honors.

"Oh, don't worry about us, we'll just catch up, just find us a table," Allyson waved her hand dismissively at Patrick.

Patrick shocked me when he reached down and took my hand in his, leading me into the building.

Once inside, I noticed that the place looked like an old Irish pub straight out of Ireland. The bar was long and glossy, made of a beautiful oak-stained wood. The brass footboard glistened in the lights that illuminated from the ceiling. The bar was packed and I didn't think we would find a table. I blushed as man after man looked toward Allyson and myself, their eyes raking down our forms.

I watched in amazement when their eyes then landed on Patrick and my hand in his. It was as if the bar caught on fire as barstools began to empty. Men were tripping over themselves, trying to grab their beers and make their way to the back of the room.

Patrick led me over to the center of the bar and pulled out a chair for me. He snapped his fingers and a very handsome man appeared behind the bar.

Patrick instructed him to give me anything I wanted, and then he leaned down and kissed my forehead.

"I'll try not to be too long." And with that he joined a tableful of men in black suits behind us. I looked around and noticed a man in a black suit on each side of Allyson and myself.

"He's never been subtle a day in his life," Allyson chuckled while taking a sip of her martini.

Then it hit me, this was all a set-up. He had brought me here so that Allyson could talk to me. He knew I had dealt with her for several months, and considered her to be a friend.

"All right, girl, what's this about?"

I was able to see Patrick's table clearly reflected in the mirrors that hung behind the bar. He wasn't looking at me, but I could see him talking to the men at the table.

"He told me you showed up at *Whiskers* alone the other night. I have to hand it to you, Christi, you've got balls."

I took a drink of my martini and then crossed my legs in her direction.

"I wouldn't necessarily say that. In hindsight, it was really stupid and I could've been hurt."

"He'd never let that happen, you know?" I shook my head.

"He won't always be around to protect me."

"Thats not true, Christi."

"Really?" My tone was condescending.

"Patrick always has an eye on you."

I looked into the mirror again and saw that Patrick was still talking with the men at the table.

"No, he doesn't, he's having a conversation over there, see, look in the mirror for yourself."

Allyson smiled and then shook her head, "The bartender, Christi. He hasn't been more than a few feet from us since Patrick gave him his instructions."

I hadn't noticed it until now, but she was right.

"I'll bet you also don't see the car that follows you around all day?"

"What car?" I questioned.

"My point exactly."

Allyson and I sat in silence for a few minutes. As I continued to sip my drink, I took more notice of the room. When I first arrived, there were mostly men that you would find in any corner bar getting a drink after work. Now in addition to them, there were ladies dressed to the nines, huddled around tables sipping colorful drinks. There were more suits than I had ever seen. A scene from *Goodfellas* came to mind where the lead character came into the room and instantly a new table was placed near the stage for his date and himself.

"You do know who and what Patrick does, don't you?"

"It didn't take me long to figure it out, although my sister disagreed."

Shannon and I had barely spoken two words since that conversation. She felt I was wrong for wanting nothing to do with Patrick. Maybe Dillion wasn't as good of a guy as she deserved after all.

"He's a very powerful man, Chris."

I took another drink and nodded my head, "I thought so."

Allyson then turned to me and placed her hand on my knee. I looked first to her hand, and then back to her eyes. "He may be the most powerful man in this city, but right now, you have more power than he does."

I blinked at her and then tipped my head to the side. "How do you figure?"

"He's willing to do pretty much anything to have you by his side."

And just as quickly as she got my attention, she lost it.

"I can't give a man like him what he needs," I stated as I turned my body back to the bar.

"Just what do you think a man like Patrick would need?"

I began to run my finger around the rim of my glass. "Allyson, I've seen *Casino* and *The Godfather,* and I've watched enough episodes of the *Sopranos* to know that the women who are beside the powerful men are expected to ignore certain things."

"Please enlighten me, what kinds of things?" Allyson questioned, defensiveness in her voice. "Because I'm pretty sure that I'm married to one of his inner circle and not much happens that I don't know about."

I turned my body back toward hers, "Okay, for instance, the wives are expected to turn their heads so that the men can have the *goomah*, I can't do that. I can't just sit back and let him get his dick sucked under the dinner table just because he carries a gun. I'm just not built like that."

"Let me interrupt you on one thing; *goomah* is Italian, Patrick is full-blooded Irish, so it would be *mot*. Furthermore, his Ma would kill him if he tried that. Italians and the Irish are different in more ways than just nationality. The whole girl on the side thing is frowned upon; he would lose respect from his men."

"Why me though? Why not one of the trashy bleached blondes that are hanging off of him nearly every time I see him? They'd be better suited for him than me, especially that one with the huge boobs."

"Who, Harley?" Allyson made a look of disgust.

"Yes, he did call her Harley. Why not her?"

Allyson turned back to the bar and took another drink from her glass, before she motioned to the bartender for another.

"Miss O'Rourke, can I get you another?"

"No thank you, I'm fine for now."

"First," Allyson began when the bartender walked away. "Harley isn't Irish, she's actually Italian. However, it's more than that; she didn't come by that name by accident."

"What, does she enjoy that brand of motorcycle?"

"No, she got that name because she can quite quickly suck-start a Harley."

I began to choke on my drink and I noticed that several men in the room turned their attention to me, just as the bartender came over and made sure I was all right.

I quickly recovered and asked for a glass of water. Once I regained my composure, I thanked the bartender who informed me his name was Devin.

"So, you're saying it's important for Patrick to be with an Irish woman?"

"It's non-negotiable, actually. He can choose whom, but they have to be of full Irish descent. Patrick must produce full-blooded Irish heirs."

"So why not just make a trip back to Ireland, scope out a girl, and then take her to the altar?"

"That would be ideal, right? As far back as anyone can recall, though, the Malloy's have made arrangements for marriages between other influential Irish families. However, when Thomas made the arrangement with the McCreary's for Patrick, it was before Mr. and Mrs. McCreary had eight boys."

I had to laugh, as that would make it difficult for an heir to happen.

"Anyway, it just so happened that Thomas touched base with an old friend, your father, and he made him an offer."

My father's words came back, *'He said he might need a favor someday.'* "Please don't tell me..."

"Oh, no, Christi your father told Thomas that Patrick would have to earn your hand if he really wanted it. You just made it easier for him to approach you by going to *Whiskers*."

I looked again at Patrick in the mirror. This time he looked directly at me and winked.

"Listen, Christi, putting aside what he does for just a moment, at the end of the day he's a really good guy."

I already knew he was a good guy, the reason I was sitting at this bar was because he was a good guy.

"Christi, do you ever wonder why his men avoid eye contact with you? Or why Harley tries so hard to stay by his side?" I just shook my head. "It's because he commands so much respect and carries so much power." Allyson leaned into me again as she lowered her voice, "Now that you know all that, tell me you don't enjoy this new power you have over him, hmm?"

I didn't want to have this so-called power over him. I had only wanted to say thank you, not start a war.

"Yes, but Allyson, arranged marriages, guns, drugs..."

"Hold on, Christi, the arranged marriage isn't like it was back in the day. Ryan and I were an arranged marriage. We were introduced once we were sixteen and we had the choice of whether or not to marry. Same with Paige and Caleb, it's to strengthen the families."

"Wait...Paige is...?"

"Yep."

"Oh, my, Caleb talks so highly of her."

"That's because he's head over heels in love with her. Caleb and Amex are soul mates, its perfect."

"Amex?" I looked at her confused.

"Oh yes, you haven't been schooled in Patrick's nicknames. Well, you already know that you're Legs."

"Yes, I'm well aware, and I can't say that I take that as a compliment, more like a bad porn name."

"I knew I loved you for a reason," Allyson laughed as she patted my leg. "Paige is Amex because she can burn through a credit limit like no one's business. Ryan is Muscles because, well, he has a lot of them, and I'm..."

"Wait, let me guess." Allyson was a beautiful woman, her dark brown hair and hazel eyes would stop traffic, she was also very well-endowed. "My guess is Stacks, due to..."

"My boobs? Nope, its Ammo. I can take apart and put back together any gun you place in front of me in less than fifteen seconds." She spoke with pride and I suspected she had a gun somewhere on her person.

I felt so horrible for saying that to her now. "Allyson, I'm so sorry..."

"Nope, you don't get to apologize with words, the Malloy's are a family of actions and I want to show you something."

Allyson slid her drink away from her and grabbed her clutch. She stood fluidly from her stool. Wrapping her arm around me, she leaned over and whispered, "Are you aware that sitting at that table are some pretty heavy hitters in Patrick's world?" I shook my head. "Any man in this room would rather eat his own tongue than interrupt that conversation, yet if you were to walk over there right now, they would all Miss O'Rourke you to death. And Patrick, he would stop what he's doing to make any request you had happen right then and there. Like it or not, by kissing your forehead, he told the entire room how important you are to him. Want to see if I'm right?"

I rolled my eyes at her, "I need the ladies room."

Since talking with Allyson, I was now more aware of the things happening around me. I watched as people who were standing in our way suddenly moved without being asked. When we reached the ladies room, there was a line of about six women waiting. Once we entered the hall, all six moved to allow us to move to the front of the line. Allyson opened the door and I followed her. Standing beside the sink, however, was the girl who had been with Kevin that night in the jazz bar. She didn't notice Allyson or I enter the room as she leaned over the counter and snorted some white powder into her nose.

I watched in horror as she passed the rolled-up bill to the girl standing beside her, Harley. Knowing what they were doing brought the reasons behind Colleen's death to the forefront of my mind. I turned on my heels as fast as I could and headed back into the bar. I could not and would not tolerate anything to do with illegal drug use. I practically sprinted back to the barstool that I had been sitting on and turned the corner to tell Patrick I needed to leave.

Allyson's words about the members at the table were long forgotten as my desire to get as far away from those girls as possible won out. My steps never slowed as I came to an abrupt stop at the table. I had no idea what was being said, and I didn't care.

"I'm sorry for interrupting, gentlemen," I turned to Patrick. "Patrick, I have had a lovely time and thank you so much for dinner, but I have to go."

I didn't wait for him to respond as I turned and ran for the door. I had no idea how Patrick got to the door of the bar so quickly, but he managed to open it for me. The limo driver was standing beside the car with the door open and waiting. I quickly slid inside and closed my eyes, resting my head against the back of the seat.

Patrick's phone rang and I heard him answer it, but didn't process what he was saying.

I opened my eyes and was able to let out the breath I had been holding. I noticed Patrick was in the middle of making another call. I heard the muffled noise as they picked up, but I couldn't hear their side of the conversation on the other end.

"A cheadaítear Michelle imo mbarra."

I was sure he was trying to hide the conversation from me by speaking in Gaelic, but I had spend enough summers with my grandmother to be fluent. Besides you couldn't live in the section of Chicago that I did and not pick it up. The girl from the Jazz bar was named Michelle, he was upset that she was allowed into the bar...his bar apparently.

"Bhí sí ag déanamh buille arís le Harley."

Now he was upset because the trashy blonde, Harley, was doing it with her. "Aimsigh agus a dhéanamh air seo a ghlanadh suas. "

I should have known Kevin was still under his employ as he gave instructions to whom ever he was talking about to have him clean up the situation. Would he have Michelle killed? I shivered as I thought about it.

Tá mé ag cur léi go dtí mo theach"

His last sentence made me want to jump from this moving car since he told them he was taking me to his house.

He closed his phone and remained silent as he looked out the window. He reached over and gently took my hand in his.

"You do know I'm fluent in Gaelic, right?"

He chuckled as he turned his face back to me. "Yes."

"Then why didn't you just speak English on the phone?" I asked as if it was the dumbest thing I had ever heard.

"Because, the person I was speaking to doesn't speak English"

Well,...foot meet mouth.

When the driver finally stopped in the underground garage, Patrick didn't let my hand go while he helped me out of the car. Once in the elevator, he slid a gold card into a slot at the top of the number panel. The ride was quick and the door opened to what I assumed was his condo. The floors were marble and the walls were painted a neutral shade of cream. The chandelier that hung from the ceiling was crystal and absolutely beautiful. The room we were currently standing in appeared to be a foyer. I saw that directly in front of us was a long hall that led to a wall of windows. I didn't wait for an invitation as I walked toward them to look out onto the city.

My eye caught the ferris wheel at Navy Pier and it held my attention. This had been an interesting night. It definitely wasn't what I had planned it to be, although that seemed to be the norm when it came to Patrick. I watched as the lights on the wheel went round and round, like the events of the last few days. I no longer felt that I could trust my gut when it came to the people around me.

"Come sit and talk with me."

I turned and saw Patrick had two glasses of wine sitting on the coffee table. He was keeping his word at being a gentleman and was waiting for me to sit.

I slowly walked around the table and took my seat beside him.

"I'm so sorry about the bathroom, Christi; she wasn't supposed to be there."

"It's not your fault, Patrick. She doesn't realize that she's throwing her life away."

"No, she knows it; she just doesn't care right now. I've tried to get her to get help, but she isn't ready. Listen, I know Allyson had a talk with you tonight..."

"That was a set up, wasn't it?"

"My Ma thought it would sound better coming from a woman, one that you already trusted."

"I understand why you did it," I sighed.

"Then you're not upset with me?"

I chuckled as I turned to him. "No, I'm not mad at you," I looked directly at him as I spoke, "But I can't be what you need me to be, Patrick" I leaned forward and took the wine glass off the table, taking a large drink before continuing. "I refuse to be an accessory for you to wear when you feel like it. I refuse to turn a blind eye to any extracurricular activities you feel the need to have."

Patrick leaned forward, resting his forearms on his thighs. "Who said that's what I want or need?"

"Please, a man in your position has a role to portray."

"So you're saying that every successful businessman is a man-whore?"

"You know what I mean."

"Clearly I don't, Christi. If I wanted a trampy, uneducated sex toy, I would have Harley in here. What I want is a highly intelligent, beautiful lady."

"Why do you keep her around then?"

"Well, I assume you know why I call her Harley?"

"Yes, Allyson told me several nicknames you have for people," I giggled as I remembered the conversation.

"Well, even though she has her mouth open most of the time, she always has her ears open, too. Men seem to want to tell a woman who is currently on her knees all kinds of interesting things. She just feels the need to tell them to me."

"So, you and she have never...?"

"Me? Fuck Harley? Not in this lifetime." His tone was laced with disgust.

"Good to know."

The conversation I'd had with Allyson raced through my head. Patrick had been more than generous to my family. Could I really have a relationship with him?

"Come on, Christi, what do you say? Give us a chance. You never know what might happen."

Yeah, it was that last part that had me worried.

chapter six

Early the next morning, I phoned my father and asked that he meet me for breakfast at the diner near my house. After last night, I was definitely more aware of my surroundings and I noticed the black sedan was nowhere in sight.

I parked my car and made my way inside the diner. When we were little girls, dad would bring us here all the time and buy us pancakes with strawberries and whipped cream. Although I had changed to coffee and an omelet, the diner was still the same.

My father was already seated with a cup of coffee raised to his lips when I sat down across from him.

"Morning, Daddy."

"Good morning, Christi." His face broke into a wide smile.

Doris, the same waitress that had served me those pancakes all those years ago, stood to my left, pouring my first of many cups of coffee.

"Good morning, Christi. Cheese omelet is already on the grill and should be out shortly," Doris spoke in her usual friendly tone.

"Thank you, Doris. How's your family?"

"Everyone's good, Ian is in his second year of med school and Mary just got engaged."

The bell dinged three times indicating food was ready, so Doris excused herself to retrieve it. I took a much needed sip of my coffee and let the caffeine fill my system.

"So, how did it go?" My father asked.

I didn't look at him as I responded, "I'm sure you already know."

"I know he wants to pursue a relationship with you and I've given my blessing."

"Jesus, Dad, this isn't the 1800's, I don't need your blessing to have a boyfriend."

My father only looked at me over the top of his coffee cup. I knew that he was of the old school mentality, where you did ask the family for permission. I also knew that *if* I decided to date Patrick, my father would assume a wedding was on the horizon.

"He gave me a lot to think about," I replied, looking into the caramel-colored liquid that rested in my cup like it had the answers I needed.

My dad placed his cup down and folded his hands on the table top. "What's there to think about? You go to dinner with him, he gives you a ring, we call the priest, and this time next year I have more grand babies."

I rolled my eyes at him as he chuckled, although I knew he was completely serious.

"I can't be what he needs, Dad."

My dad cocked his head to the side and gave me a bewildered look. "Can't be what he needs?"

"Yes, Dad, he's a man of power and he's used to having things his way. Which I'm sure includes any woman he wants, whenever he wants them." I took a deep breath and turned my gaze briefly to look out the window. I now noticed a guy in a black suit standing on the corner. I turned my attention back to my father, "I can't turn a blind eye to him having other women, Dad. I don't care how much money he has, how many people he knows, or how many good things he does for people. I deserve to be loved and respected, and he can't truly do that if he's bed-hopping."

"Does he, as you call it, bed hop?"

"His office is in a strip joint, Dad, what do you think?"

"I think you're assuming and that isn't fair."

He did have a point, I *was* assuming.

"Why are you suddenly his biggest fan? You do recall what he does for a living? Have you forgotten you're still a cop? Or has that changed too?"

I knew as soon as the words left my mouth that I had crossed a line.

"Christina Anne, I'm well aware of my duty and I don't need you to remind me what it is. My advice to you is to quit pointing fingers at Patrick and remember there are always three pointing back at you when you do. I choose to let certain activities slide and look the other way when needed. Because at the end of the day, Patrick and Thomas Malloy have done a great deal of good for this city."

His words stung and I knew he was right. People that claimed to be honest cheated the system every day. Whether it was a banker or a teacher or even a doctor, people sometimes did illegal things.

"Sorry, Dad, you're right."

"Is that the only reason you won't give him a chance?"

I thought for a second and took another sip of my coffee.

"I just can't see how you're okay with being involved in this. Beside the fact he'd possibly want other girls on the side, what about the other things associated with organized crime? What about the prostitution, guns, and the drugs, Dad? I know you can't be okay with illegal drugs."

I watched as my father took another drink of his coffee. "Well, since you mentioned it, the Malloy's aren't involved in drug trafficking. That's an area they leave to the Porchelli's."

I felt shivers go down my spine at the mention of that name. The Porchelli's were a well-known Italian crime family in New York and Miami. They were known to be very violent and stopped at nothing to get what they wanted. I had read news articles where certain members had even killed children of people who got in their way.

"Did you even ask Patrick what his involvement in all these 'illicit' activities was?"

"Why would I ask him that, Dad? Last night was supposed to simply be two people having dinner, not Pre-Cana."

Before my father could respond, a dark figure appeared at the end of the table.

"Mr. O'Rourke, Miss O'Rourke, I apologize for the interruption. Mr. Malloy wishes to extend you a good morning and instructed that I deliver this." His glove-covered hand slid an elongated black velvet box onto the middle of the table. The green ribbon that surround it reminded me of Patrick's eyes. "Mr. Malloy also asks that you allow him to take care of the bill, which I've already done."

My dad thanked the very large man and even shook his hand before sitting back down in his seat.

"Well, I guess that answers my question of whether you two are dating now," my father chuckled as he took another drink of his coffee

"I didn't agree to date him, Dad." He quickly set down his coffee cup and looked at me questioningly. "He told me that he didn't need to have a girl on the side. I told him he'd have to prove himself, and that he could say anything he liked, it still didn't make it the truth."

My father only lowered his head and shook it back and forth.

"Well, then I hope you're ready to be courted, because you gave him a challenge. I have a feeling that's something he'll enjoy more than you."

By the end of the day, I would see how true my father's words were.

I didn't bother looking inside the velvet box; it didn't take a rocket scientist to tell me it was a bracelet, and probably an expensive one. I tossed the box into my purse and headed to work. I had to stop for gas and once I had pulled in, I noticed the black sedan was parking behind me at the pump. I was barely out of my car when the same large man got out, grabbed the nozzle, and began filling my gas tank. He reached into his pocket and handed me a large envelope.

"Ms. O'Rourke please open this one. You wouldn't want to get me into trouble, would you?"

His smile was genuine as he finished filling my tank. Once thing was for certain, Patrick surrounded himself with loyal and efficient people.

I took the envelope and tore it open. Inside I found a gold credit card shaped card inside. A small note was wrapped around it.

Christi,
Next time you want to pay me a visit, come to my condo, not my old office.
I want to keep you safe.
Patrick

I hadn't been in my office thirty seconds when a knock sounded on my door. A large bouquet of flowers made their way in followed by Charlotte. She sat them on the corner of my desk and gave me a simple lopsided grin.

"Someone made an impression," she spoke in a singsong voice.

"UGH!" I shouted as I flung myself into my chair back. I could just hear my father laughing at my pain.

"I take it this isn't the first thing you've received this morning?" She questioned as she poured herself a cup of coffee before walking slowly over to my desk and taking a seat.

"No, but I hope it's the last."

"Why would you want that? You have a man paying some serious attention to you and you want him to stop?"

Charlotte questioned with a shocking tone. I guess for some women this would be considered romantic, but for me, it felt like more of a challenge. Patrick was trying to wear me down.

"Yes, because he's just...ugh!"

Charlotte leaned over my desk and spoke very softly.

"Talk to me, Christi." She looked at me with sadness and concern.

"He wants to pursue a relationship with me. He asked me to give us a chance."

"Do you not want that?"

"I...I want...I don't think I can be what he needs."

"What does he need? A girlfriend? Someone to share dinner with, go to movies?"

"Charlotte, be serious. This is Patrick Malloy we're talking about, he doesn't stand in line for movies or take walks in the park on Sunday afternoon. He carries a gun, has men who carry guns surrounding him constantly, and has his office in a strip club. He's a mafia boss for God's sake! He needs some hardcore, gun-carrying, tramp-dressing, sex addict that's content to look the other way. I'll never be that." I said exasperated.

Why was it that I was the only one who saw this? Patrick needed someone like the trashy, pleather wearing bitch I saw him with. He chose to have those kinds of women around him, so it was obvious to me that they were what he really preferred.

Charlotte looked at her shoes and then back to me. "He also owns most of the buildings in this part of Chicago, contributes millions of dollars a year to various charities in the city, and attends mass at Saint Josephine's every Sunday with his family, which, correct me if I'm wrong, is way more than you. The last time you attended mass, young lady, was... when?"

Goddamn it!

I was scheduled to have a meeting with Nora and Paige this afternoon to begin planning Paige's engagement party. I had a few errands to run before the meeting, but honestly, I was worried that one of Patrick's men would follow me and pay for the tampons I needed to buy.

Before I could get out the front door, Charlotte came running after me. "Christi, change of plans, you're now meeting the ladies at *Amoré* for lunch."

I didn't have a single second to question her as a husky voice spoke from behind me.

"Ms. O'Rourke, your car awaits."

I turned my body toward the voice to see the same driver from last night opening the door of a black sedan. Deciding against an argument, I crossed the sidewalk and headed for the car. It wasn't this driver's fault for making me angry and I didn't plan to take it out on him. This kind man was only doing his job. I made myself comfortable as he closed the door behind me.

"Sir?" I questioned once he was seated behind the wheel.

"Yes, Ms. O'Rourke?"

"Since I have a feeling that I'll be seeing quite a lot of you, may I have your name, please?"

Looking at me through the rearview mirror, he nodded. "It's Angus, Angus McCoy, Ms. O'Rourke." He spoke with a thick Irish accent and his grey eyes never meeting mine. His face reminded me of Liam Neeson.

"Very well, Angus, and in the future, it's Christi."

"I'm sorry, Ms. O'Rourke, Boss says I'm to refer to you as Ms. O'Rourke."

"Well, Angus, he isn't here now, is he?"

"Sorry, Ms. O'Rourke, I have orders to follow."

I couldn't argue with Angus, he was loyal to Patrick even if he wasn't around. I would remember that in the future. Little did I know it would come in very handy.

Angus drove me the twenty minutes to *Amoré*, a restaurant that was just north of Michigan Avenue. The large green awning hung over the entrance and covered the valet area. Angus pulled in and a man in a red suit opened my door for me.

"Good afternoon, Ms. O'Rourke lovely to see you," the man in the suit addressed me. Clearly he worked for Patrick since he knew my name.

"Thank you."

The door to the restaurant was being held by a man in a black suit and I had no doubt he, too was one of Patricks hired hands. I made my way through the door, thanking the man who held it open for me. He tipped his head, but didn't make eye contact.

A busty blonde in a tight, black business suit was waiting for me once I entered the foyer. She looked familiar, but I didn't have time to ponder on it long before she turned on her heel, curtly snapping at me. "Ms. O'Rourke, if you'd please follow me. Mrs. Malloy is waiting in the garden room."

The blonde gave me a quick look up and down over her shoulder with a tight lip and a furrowed brow; she was clearly sizing me up.

"Oh, Christi, how lovely to see you again, Lass." Nora rose from her chair and greeted me with a kiss to the cheek. Paige was seated to her left and Allyson to her right. I saw only one empty chair and I waited for the blonde to finish pulling it back for me.

"Thank you, I can manage." I told the blonde as I took my chair from her.

"As you wish," she snapped and then quickly turned on her heels and left the room.

"Oh, dear, sorry about Simone, I'm not sure why Patrick hasn't fired her yet. She usually isn't this rude, though," Nora stated as I took my seat.

"That's because she knows Patrick has his sights set on our Christi, Ma," Paige stated. "Caleb told me he kissed your forehead the other night at the bar. Word travels fast for such a big town." Paige added

"Like that would change anything when it comes to Patrick, you know as well as I do he doesn't cross those lines." Allyson spoke her voice serious.

"Wait...Patrick owns this place, too?"

All three ladies looked directly at me, and then began to giggle.

"Yes, Christi, Patrick owns a lot of restaurants, bars, and hotels here in Chicago," Paige informed me.

"Christi, please say you'll forgive my scheming from last night," Nora voiced, changing the subject completely.

I smiled at her. I knew she only meant well and I highly doubted she had ever been told no a day in her life.

"There's nothing to forgive, I assure you."

"So, my son tells me you've given him some homework, so to speak."

"I'm sorry?" I questioned, completely taken off guard.

"Don't worry; I think its good for him to work for something. Your father was right in giving you the choice and not just handing your hand over to him. You're exactly what he needs, Christi. You have a good head on those pretty shoulders of yours, and good for you for not just falling down at his feet. He needs to work hard at something once in a while."

I was astonished at Nora's words. She thought I was playing some game with Patrick, for what I wasn't certain.

"Nora, I feel the need to clarify some things with you. I didn't agree to a relationship with your son not because I'm playing a game of sorts with him, but I honestly feel there's someone else more suited to his needs out there than me. I truly want nothing from him."

"Told you," Allyson interjected.

"Oh, I agree, Allyson, she's perfect." Nora took a sip from her tea cup and then addressed me again.

"You're exactly what Patrick needs. He's always gotten everything handed to him, ever since he was in short pants. For the first time in his life I believe, he has to work at getting what he wants. Now, my question to you is...are you ready for tropical storm Patrick?"

"I'm sorry, but I don't follow you, what storm?"

All three ladies began looking at each other and laughing. Paige spoke first.

"How many gifts have you gotten today?"

"Three."

"Only three? He really isn't taking this seriously, is he?"

Paige had barely spoken the words, when the waiter brought a plate of food and set it down in front of me.

"I'm sorry, I didn't order this," I said to him.

"No, Ma'am, Mr. Malloy gave instructions to serve this to you with his compliments."

I looked at the plate that now sat in front of me. It was a huge, thick-cut steak with the bone resting on one side. It looked incredible and smelled heavenly. I wanted nothing more than to dive into that steak.

"Sir, could you remove this and then bring me a Caesar salad, please?"

He looked at me bewildered and then took the plate away. "My pleasure, Madam."

"You do realize you just sent back the house steak that's dry aged three months and costs over two hundred dollars?" Nora questioned me.

"I didn't want steak for lunch, I wanted a salad. He can't make me eat something I don't want."

"Oh, my sweet lass, you're more perfect than I thought. I would however, like to have tea with you this week. I have some things I would like to discuss with you."

I wanted to simply tell Nora that she might as well tell me what she needed to here and now, something told me that not only was this family strong, but there were no secrets to be found inside the inner circle.

My suspicions were correct when I did finally make it to the pharmacy; my purchases had already been paid for, including Shannon's birth control . I made the two-block walk back to the office to find the black sedan was parked across the street. This time I felt bold and waved to the driver.

Once inside, I tossed the bag into a chair and proceeded to finish my work. It had been nearly two hours since I'd had any deliveries and I began to think he had finally given up. I was certain Nora or one of the girls had phoned him and told him I had sent back his food, and even worse, that I had paid for my own lunch and gave the waiter a tip.

I still hadn't opened the first gift he had given me this morning and honestly, I didn't feel as if I should. I was going to return them to him. It was only fair that if I didn't plan to have a relationship with him that they should go to someone who would.

Charlotte came bouncing in and sat on the corner of my desk. "You have very large balls, my love."

"What?"

"Returning a gift from Patrick Malloy; that, my dear, is ballsy."

I closed my eyes and tossed my head back into the headrest. I was so tired of this.

"Charlotte, I'm returning everything. It isn't right to keep any of it."

Charlotte then handed me a robin's egg blue box; the box that needed no introduction. "What the hell...when did that show up?"

"Does it matter? It's from Tiffany's! Why not take it for a test drive?"

I just rolled my eyes, shaking my head. This was just too much. Next he would be sending me a diamond-studded pistol with a matching leather combination holster and garter belt.

The box sat on my desk, taunting me, teasing me. I wanted so badly to pull those white ribbons off and tear into that blue box, but I couldn't. I would return both boxes and enough money to cover all the purchases he'd made today. He clearly didn't get me. I wasn't someone who could be bribed with bobbles and shiny objects. I needed to see real tangible proof that he wanted to be with me. Patrick Malloy was obviously not the guy for me.

Tossing the blue box into my purse, I headed to the one place I knew he would be. Ignoring the black sedan that was still parked across the street, I jumped into my car and then drove to the club. I had what I would say to him all planned out. I would be polite, yet firm. As I turned the corner and parked my car in the parking lot, I made certain my pepper spray was still in my purse.

Once inside, I noticed the same two men standing behind the bar. They noticed me instantly, and the taller of the two came around to stand in front of me.

"Ms. O'Rourke, why are you here?"

"I need to see Patrick," I went to walk by, but he quickly stepped in my way.

"Boss isn't here, Ms. O'Rourke, he said you knew."

"Knew what?"

"He works out of his condo now. He moved his whole office over there."

The gold card...the note...shit, shit, shit!

"Thank you." I turned and began to walk out.

"Oh no, Ms. O'Rourke, let me walk you out. This neighborhood isn't safe for a lady such as yourself."

I made it back home to find Shannon and Abigail having a tea party. I loved how simple things were in our house.

"Auntie Christi!" Abigail called out.

I smiled as I crossed the room and joined them. Shannon had a mischievous smile on her face.

"Abby, honey, why don't you go get a cup for Auntie Christi"

"Yeah!" she shouted as she hurried off to her bedroom.

"Can I see what he gave you?"

I rolled my eyes and handed her my purse. Shannon found the two boxes and took them out.

"Christi, you haven't even opened them yet!"

I then turned to look at her and reached for my purse.

"I'm giving them back so what's the point?"

"Quit being a stuck-up bitch, Christi."

One thing about my sister was she always spoke her mind. Not always at the most opportune time, mind you.

"Just open the fucking boxes."

She placed the two boxes in my lap and waited. I would have waited all night except that I knew my sister would wait right along with me. She was more stubborn than I could ever be. I took the long black box first and slowly removed the green ribbon. Resting inside was the most beautiful tennis bracelet I had ever seen.

"It's just like mine," Shannon spoke as she showed me the same bracelet that wrapped around her right wrist. "It's a tradition in the Malloy family to give one to the woman you're dating. Dillion gave me mine after our second date. I'm surprised you haven't noticed the Malloy ladies wearing theirs. Although I'm jealous, as yours has a little bigger diamonds than mine."

Shannon was right; the diamonds were slightly bigger. Finally, I opened the Tiffany's box.

"Do you know what this is?" I questioned holding the box up.

"I have my suspicions, but no, I'm not certain."

Resting inside the box was a shamrock pendant. The leaves were emeralds and the stem was made of platinum, the chain was also made of platinum. I gasped as I touched the green stones.

"Oh, my God. Christi, that's breathtaking."

"Do you know why he gave me this?"

"No clue, you should ask him."

Shannon was right; I did want to know why he felt the need to give me these particular pieces of jewelry. The bracelet was so beautiful and a huge part of me wanted to keep it, but that wouldn't be right. It was still early and I decided that if I was going to give them back, I should just do it.

The drive to his condo went quicker than I had hoped. All the courage I'd had when I'd gone to the club was long since gone. I shouldn't have opened the damn boxes.

I slid my card into the slot as I had seen Patrick do and the elevator sprang to life. I remembered that there wasn't an additional door once the elevator opened and I hoped I wasn't interrupting anything.

The door opened to reveal a very handsome Patrick Malloy standing there waiting. I couldn't help but smile at him as he greeted me.

"Hello, beautiful," he smiled and then quickly kissed my cheek. "Have you had dinner yet?"

"No, not yet. Um, I actually just came to return these." I said as I held the two boxes out to him.

"Come, sit with me, Christi, have dinner and let's talk."

He didn't give me an opportunity to argue as he led me to the kitchen. There were already two place settings on the bar with glasses of wine at each. Patrick pulled out my chair and motioned for me to sit.

"I hoped you'd be by tonight, I'm glad you're here," he smiled as he took a sip of wine. "So, you said you wanted to return my gifts?"

I had just taken a sip of my wine, so he surprised me by diving right in.

"Yes," I choked. "But it's not that I don't like them, I really love them, actually."

"Then keep them," he said matter-of-factly.

"Patrick, you know I can't do that," my tone was defiant.

"Shannon told me the significance of the bracelet. We aren't dating, so it isn't fair for me to keep that."

"Did she tell you about the shamrock?"

"No, she didn't know."

He smiled as he took another drink from his wine glass.

"Well, there are many old stories about the history of the shamrock. I could name at least fifteen different businesses that use it on their logo. However, the history behind why the Malloy men give them is a lot less corporate and a lot more of tradition.

When my great-grandfather left Ireland and came to America, he left behind my great-grandmother. He came here because he wanted a better life for his future family. He had three dollars and a ticket for his passage on him when he left. When he was telling her goodbye, he gave her a shamrock that he had picked from the hill where they were standing. He told her that someday he would come back for her and he would take that shamrock from her and give her one that was made with emeralds that matched her eyes. He swore to her that he was going to come back to her as the man she deserved."

"After he left, the women of her village told her he would forget all about her and he would find a woman in America. She waited for him for two years, and when he did come back, he presented her with a pendant cut from the same emerald that one is and asked for her hand in marriage. She had kept the real shamrock and placed it in her shoe. She had it in her hand when they buried her in our family plot."

I had tears in my eyes when Patrick finished telling me his story.

"Christi, I've not begun to show you the type of man I can be, a man you truly deserve, I'm asking you to be patient and let me show you I can do it. I know you say we aren't dating and I respect your feelings on that. However, that's not how I feel. I'm devoted to you; I just need to prove that to you."

Patrick placed his hand over mine and gently squeezed.

"I know I've gone about pursuing you all wrong. You made my Ma's day at lunch today by the way."

I had to laugh at him. As powerful as he was, his mother still called the shots.

"So I promise to show you I'm the right guy for you, and I swear I'll cut back on the gifts," he chuckled as he spoke, his eyes pleading with mine.

"You moved your office."

"Believe it or not, there's a history behind that as well."

I cocked my head and turned my entire body toward him. He smiled and then took both of my hands into his.

"When my Da took over the business and was told he was going to marry my ma, he paid for her to come to America and see where she would be living. She had brought her sister along and they spent the day shopping. My Ma was having a hard time getting my Da to answer the phone, so she hopped in a taxi and gave the driver the address she knew for his office. When she found out it was in a strip club, she told him in no uncertain terms that she was going to return to Ireland and for him to never call her again."

Patrick's face looked excited and his eyes were sparkling as he continued his story.

"So, picture my Da, the most feared man in Chicago at the time, chasing this woman out of his club as she's cussing him out in Gaelic. He's begging her to calm down, and all the while, his men are watching this go down. He swore to her that he'd move all of his dealings out of the club if she'd agree to stay and marry him."

He was laughing hysterically as he finished his story.

"So, I have to ask, did he move? I mean your office is in a strip club."

"Oh, he moved it all right. He even bought all new furniture so she'd come visit him."

It was at this point I began to laugh. I could totally see Nora going 'postal' on his father.

"Took me less time to move my office, though, I just locked the door." His words were spoken from his heart and I was losing the fight to stay away from him.

"Damn, and I was looking forward to cussing you out in Gaelic." We both were laughing at this point.

"Christi, I'd gladly let you beat the living shit out of me with all my men watching if you'd agree to be mine when you were finished."

ChAPTER SEVEN

The next day, Patrick kept his word and only sent text messages, no flowers or jewelry. I had agreed to wear the Shamrock pendant, since I wanted to give him a chance to prove himself. He agreed to keep the bracelet in his safe.

I contacted Nora and went over the final decisions for Paige's engagement party. She informed me that they had increased the guest list due to some last minute additions. I then contacted the caterers and increased the food amounts.

I had promised Shannon that I would watch Abby for her so she could go to dinner with Dillion. I loved my time with Abby, she was such an easygoing kid and it was more fun than work to keep her. We played a few games, painted toenails, and even had a tea party before she crashed in my lap during the movie, Beauty and the Beast. I chuckled, I could relate to poor Belle having a beast to contend with. I made myself a cup of tea and settled in on the couch and began watching mindless television. It was just after nine o'clock when a news anchor broke into the program I had been watching.

"We interrupt this program to bring you this special report. Here now is CNBC anchor Todd Stevens with breaking news."

"Good evening, ladies and gentleman, this just in from our New York correspondent outside Sing-Sing Correctional Facility. Just this afternoon, a federal judge ordered the immediate release of Anthony Porchelli, son of Velenci Porchelli, head of the alleged Italian crime family. Anthony Porchelli had been sentenced to fifteen years for alleged tax evasion. However, new evidence released today overturned that conviction. Mr. Porchelli is a suspect in many crimes throughout the New York and Miami areas and is still under investigation, but tonight, he's a free man. For further updates, stay tuned to CNBC..."

"I'm getting married!" Shannon shouted as she charged through the door, interrupting anything else Todd had to say.

"Christi, he wants me to marry him!"

Dillion and Shannon walked in and Shannon tackled me as she ran through the living room. She was so excited, I didn't think her feet ever even touched the ground.

"He bought us a house and he wants me to quit my job. He wants to have babies right away and he even began the paperwork to adopt Abby."

She was bouncing with excitement as she told me how he had asked for her hand. Dillion just stood there grinning from ear to ear, obviously enjoying Shannon's enthusiasm.

"Oh, Christi, it was so romantic. He had the entire restaurant rented out and he had the table all decorated with pink roses, he knows how much I love pink roses..."

She was giggling so much that I began to laugh with her.

"He didn't even let me order dinner before he dropped down on one knee and asked me."

"Oh, my God, I have to call Daddy." She ran off, clearly in her own little world

"Well done, Dillion," I said in congratulations.

"She is my world Chris. I can't imagine my life without her and Abby."

For the first time in my life, I was green with jealousy. Dillion truly loved my sister and was willing to do anything, be anything for her. There were no obstacles for them. Dillion was an accountant, he dealt with numbers not guns and prostitutes. He would be home every night for her, take vacations and throw birthday parties. Even if Patrick and I made it to the same place, it would be different.

I was very excited for Shannon, she deserved to be happy and I was glad that Dillion wanted to adopt Abby. She deserved to have a daddy that cared for her as much as he did.

My father was just as excited as I was, and many bottles of champagne were opened that night. Poor Abby slept straight through the hugging and kissing. As Dillion and my dad were getting ready to leave, I took Dillion aside and spoke softly in his ear, "You'd better be good to both of them. I don't give two shits who you work for, hurt my family and I will fuck up your world."

Dillion looked me straight in the face as he spoke loudly and clearly, "On my honor."

Dillion did indeed want to marry in a hurry. Being Catholic, they still needed to attend classes. Dillion and Thomas Malloy had spoken with Father Murphy and the classes were sped up a bit. Shannon quit working and concentrated full-time on planning their wedding.

Paige's engagement party had arrived. I would be working it; however, Nora wanted me to be a guest as well. I agreed to dress up, yet still be in charge of my staff. The room was incredible, Paige had wanted to introduce the whole same speakeasy theme as her wedding. She had a large jazz band that would play during the party and she also wanted to have a singer like the ones from the movie *Chicago*.

Patrick was quickly worming his way into my world. He gave me enough space to still be me, but when the opportunity arose, he treated me like a queen.

I hadn't heard from Patrick all day which was a little unsettling. He had grown on me and I would have to admit that I missed him terribly. We had made plans to have dinner at his condo the Sunday after Paige's engagement party. It seemed the more I knew about Patrick, the more I liked him. I didn't exactly like his job, but I hoped that one day I could ignore it completely.

I was very impressed with how everything came together. I made my rounds and everything was going well. I still hadn't seen Patrick and I was getting a little nervous. I did one final check to see that the bars were stocked when I noticed something odd about the black suits.

At each of the exits were posted two men dressed in suits, one on each side of the doorway. I recognized many of them as being Patrick's men; however, the men that stood opposite them I didn't recognize. Furthermore, each of the men I didn't recognize had a strange looking lapel pin. Patrick's men never wore visible jewelry.

I noticed Dillion and Shannon sitting at a high-topped table and so I decided to ask Dillion what was going on.

"Hey, guys, having a good time?" I stood between them with my hands on each of their backs.

"Wow, Christi, I can't imagine this many people attending my entire wedding," Shannon joked.

"Sweetheart, there'll be just as many there, I promise you," Dillion replied kissing her hand.

"Hey, Dillion, what's the deal with the guys wearing the lapel pins at the door?"

"Well, they're here because of three particular guests tonight." I turned my gaze directly at him. "See that man standing beside Thomas Malloy?"

I found Thomas standing near the main bar. The first time I was formally introduced to Thomas, I nearly swallowed my own tongue. Patrick was without question an insanely handsome man, but with Thomas's striking blue eyes, it was clear where Patrick's looks came from. He was the perfect blend of both parents. Thomas, however, was a huge flirt and I found myself fanning my face during dinner. Thomas had a fresh drink in one hand and four men behind him. The man that stood directly beside him was about two inches shorter than Thomas and looked thirty years older.

"Yes?" I replied.

"That's Velenci Porchelli." An instant shiver ran up my spine. I knew that name and what it represented. I was instantly frightened.

"Oh, fuck me." I gasped

"Seems he's trying to mend fences with Thomas and trying to have better relations with the Malloy family. Velenci's son just got out of prison so, he's trying to find some work that would keep his nose clean, so to speak."

The news report came to the front of my mind and I began to pray that he wasn't sending his son to live here in Chicago.

"He also wanted to offer his daughter, Sophia, to the family..." Next to Nora was one of the most beautiful women I had ever seen. She was tall, nearly as tall as Allyson, with olive-colored skin and long, dark hair that seemed flawless. Her one-shouldered, teal dress only accentuated her perfect features. I knew this was Sophia without being told. "...and offer her hand to Patrick as a sign of good faith, but..."

Dillion didn't get to finish his statement as a deep, thick-accented voice interrupted him.

"Please excuse my intrusion; however, I had to come over and introduce myself to two of the most beautiful women in the room."

I turned to my right and came face to face with the man who's mug shot had flashed across my television. His hair was combed straight up and looked to be coated in too much hair gel. He reminded me of those kids from that reality show from New Jersey.

His hand was extended to me and without thinking, I placed mine in his. He leaned over without breaking eye contact and kissed the back of my hand. The uneasy feeling he left behind made me want to cut off that hand.

"May I have this dance, Miss...?"

"O'Rourke, and you, Sir, are...?"

"Oh, how terribly rude of me, I'm Tony, and may I say what a pleasure it is to meet such a beautiful lady."

His eyes left mine briefly as he looked at the shamrock pendant that hung from my neck. I noticed a sudden smirk appear on his cold face as if he was calculating his next move. Just hearing his name made me tremble. This man had just been released from prison and I knew he was known for not simply killing his victims; he would play with them first. I could feel my entire body vibrate.

"Is everything all right, Miss O'Rourke?"

I turned my attention to the very tall man that stood over Anthony. I remembered him as being one of Patrick's personal bodyguards, I believed Tonto was his name.

"Oh, um, y...yes. If you gentlemen will excuse me, I have to get back to work."

I quickly made my way to the kitchen. I wanted as far away from the Porchelli men as I could get. I stepped into the large walk-in refrigerator and began to take several deep breaths, pressing my back against the cold steel. Once I had my breathing under control, I made my way back out into the ballroom. I looked around, but I could no longer see either of the Porchelli men. What I did see, though, was worse.

Patrick stood beside the bar, with his arm around Sophia Porchelli. He was smiling down at her and she had her hand on his forearm. He turned, placed his drink on the bar and then took hers as well. She stumbled slightly as he took her by the arm and left the room. Dillion's words came back to me then.

"...*Offered her hand to Patrick, as a sign of good faith...*"

Of course he would accept the offer of marriage. Patrick would have no choice. I kept a low profile for the remainder of the party, completely avoiding the Malloys, Patrick in particular, and as soon as the last person left, I slipped out the back.

It was quiet when I arrived home. Shannon would be staying at Dillion's house and Abby was at my father's. I was glad to have the house to myself, since I barely made it to my bedroom before the tears came.

It was my own fault. I had given him such a hard time about being enough for him. Sophia was exactly what he needed, she knew how to act and she knew what was expected of her. Ever so slowly, I unclasped the chain from around my neck and placed it back in the Tiffany's box.

I would return it tomorrow with dignity. As I crawled into bed, I ignored the sound of my cell phone ringing. I knew it would be Patrick and I just didn't have it in me to deal with him right now. As I closed my eyes, I could picture my father telling me that I should be careful what I asked for; you just might get it. It wasn't supposed to hurt this bad to tell him goodbye.

CHAPTER EIGHT

Sleep did not find me. I tossed and turned and tried to remind myself that this was exactly what I had wanted. As I got ready for work the next morning, I stayed a little longer in the shower, hoping the hot water would wash away the hurt I felt.

I had too much to do to sit and wallow. It wasn't like we had committed ourselves to each other. I mean, my God, we hadn't even shared a kiss.

I chose to wear jeans. I wasn't in the mood to be pretty and I certainly didn't feel it. I stopped by the diner on my way and grabbed a large cup of coffee. It wasn't like I needed the caffeine to keep me awake. I thanked Doris and made my way to my office.

Once inside, I checked my email and deleted all the junk. My voicemail had a few messages, I would return them later. It was then that I noticed I had no idea where my cell phone was. I clearly remembered having it on me last night at the party. I checked my purse twice, and still couldn't locate it. I was just about to sign on to the internet and do a search, when Nora walked into my office.

"Good morning, Christi, I just wanted to personally stop by and thank you for making last night a huge success."

The words had barely left her mouth when a man dressed in black entered my office, carrying a large bouquet of red roses. He sat the vase down and tipped his head at Nora. She looked none too happy to see him. He returned three more times with more roses. It looked like a florist shop in here.

Neither Nora nor I said one word as he continued to parade in and out of my office, the size and quality of the bouquets getting larger and larger. Finally, he came back in with a large white envelope and what looked to be a cell phone.

He handed me the envelope and the phone and then tipped his head at me. I noticed as he left that he had the same strange lapel pin on his suit jacket the Porchelli guards had worn.

I opened the envelope and skipped down to see that my worst fear had been realized. Tony Porchelli had sent these flowers and he'd had my cell phone.

Dear Christi,
Accept these flowers as my official invitation to dine with me this evening in my hotel room.
Yours,
Anthony Porchelli

Something in me snapped and I was so angry, I was seeing red. I tossed the card across the room with a roar, and then grabbed the first vase full of roses I came to. I picked them up and marched outside to the dumpster and hurled them into the trash. Nora watched me, shock written all over her face. Once the last vase had been tossed and I could hear the breaking of the glass in the dumpster, I marched back into my office, took the Tiffany box from my purse, and crossed the room to where Nora stood, still shocked at my outburst. I placed the box into her hand.

"Please, give this back to him. I know you came to tell me about Sophia and I hold no ill feelings toward Patrick. I know he has no other choice."

With that, I stormed out of the office and ran to my car. I needed to talk to the one person who would let me talk without interruption.

Colleen Victoria O'Rourke
Always in our hearts

I traced the carved letters on my sister's headstone. Colleen had been my oldest sister. She was the only one who would just listen to me today. She wouldn't judge me or tell me how this whole thing was my fault.

"Oh, God, Colleen, what am I going to do?"

I sat with her headstone directly in front of me, gently leaning my forehead against the cold marble.

"How is it that we allow these men to ruin our lives?" I spoke quietly as the tears began to roll down my cheeks. "I wish you were here, Colleen, I wish you could just tell me a story like you did after mom left and make everything better."

The memory of the three of us dressed in our nightgowns, piled under our covers so dad wouldn't hear us, came to me. The tears and sobs came, too, and I welcomed them. I missed my sister, even with all her problems, I missed my big sister.

I shivered as I felt the wind blow my hair around my face. I could hear it as it tossed dead leaves and grass clippings.

"Shhh, Baby, I've got you."

The warm voice surrounded me like a soft blanket. I knew that voice, but why was he here?

I raised my head as he enveloped me in his arms, drawing me into his lap. I welcomed his touch as I melted into his chest. He just held me as I continued to sob into his shirt. I knew I shouldn't be here, this was so wrong. He was promised to another woman, but dammit, I wanted him to be here, if only for a little while.

Once my tears had finally stopped, I raised my head to look into his face. I knew this was goodbye and the best way to do this was quickly and mercifully, like ripping off a bandage.

He looked into my eyes and for a brief second, I had hope that he had come to rescue me from my sadness. He slowly and yet deliberately wiped the tears from my face.

"I took care of Tony, he won't bother you again," his voice was barely above a whisper, yet deep and masculine.

"How did you know about Tony?" I questioned as I placed my head back on his shoulder.

"For one, I saw him approach you last night. Two, my Ma told me about your quarterback tryout with his roses," he chuckled as he spoke the latter.

My head shot up and I looked at him with surprise. "You saw him last night?"

"Who do you think sent Tonto over to intercede?"

It was now or never, and I began to remove myself from his lap.

"Yes, well, I heard about your upcoming nuptials. She's beautiful by the way."

I couldn't look at him as I spoke, I didn't want him to see how much this affected me.

"Christi, she's a coke-head, and she was so stoned and drunk that she'd started to remove her clothes at the bar. She feels that since she's Venny's daughter, she's above everyone else. She refused to listen to anyone except me. I got her out of the party before she could do any real damage. I took her to her hotel and made sure she got into bed. I had one of her father's guards standing outside the room the whole night."

"I'm sorry; I hope she changes before..." I couldn't even say the words. I didn't want him to have to marry her.

"Christi, please, look at me."

His eyes were pleading and it nearly broke my heart. The words were written all over his face, he didn't want to marry her, either. I watched as the wind blew pieces of his hair around and I so badly wanted to run my fingers through it.

"I'm not marrying Sophia."

I gave him a puzzled look as I tried to understand. He had to marry her, it would be his duty.

"Forget the fact that she's a dope-head and she couldn't hold an intelligent conversation if it came with instructions. Forget the fact that she doesn't have a drop of Irish blood in her, and forget the fact that she has more plastic than Mattel. She isn't you. Venny has spent so many hours trying to persuade my da to blend the families that it's ridiculous. He tried with Amex and now again with me. My da won't budge. More importantly, I won't budge. Venny rules by fear, but it's not enough. Most of his men would turn their backs and run if things got really tough. My men, on the other hand, would take a bullet for me and I for them. He wants to combine the families because he's broke, that's why he moves so many drugs. Well, as much as they can keep out of Sophia's nose."

"Tony knew who you were the second he saw your shamrock. I reminded him of that when I called your phone after I handled his sister and he answered. He only wanted to piss me off by sending you flowers. He knew he'd spooked you last night, and it gave him a rush. I reminded him who he'd have to deal with if he continued to have contact with you."

I felt as if the weight of the world had been lifted off my shoulders. Patrick wasn't marrying Sophia. I could wear his bracelet after all.

"Did your dad ever tell you why we stay away from drug trafficking?" I shook my head as he wrapped me again in his arms.

"My Ma had two older brothers, Declan and Connor. They were already working with my Da before she arrived in the states. Anyway, they were out one night at a bar not far from where *Whiskers is* now when a man came running into the bar and began shooting people. They were shot in the back of the head; they never saw the man who killed them. When the dust finally settled, my Da learned that the man was high on LSD and was having hallucinations. He thought the bar was full of aliens. My Da had to tell my Ma her brothers were dead. He vowed he would never be a part of drugs ever again."

He began to rub my arms and I again let myself lean into him. "Your dad says your sister died from an overdose."

I nodded my head. I hadn't talked about Colleen's death in a long while. "She was in her last semester of college when she met this man, Jimmy. He got her started on drugs and *he* supplied her with the drugs that she died from. *He* didn't actually put a gun to her head, but he killed her just the same. My dad had to identify her body. It was horrible. She was found by a maid in one of those seedy motels. Jimmy had left her there to die, alone and naked in strange place."

I turned my body so that I was again facing Colleen's gravestone. Patrick just kept his arms protectively around me.

"Tell me your favorite memory of your sister."

That was easy, it was the one I always thought of when I came here to visit her.

"When my mother left, Shannon and I would have bad dreams and Colleen would have us come into her bed and she would read us a story, only she would animate it. She would change her voice for the different characters and she would change the story to something different. She would have us so wrapped up in the story that we would forget all about missing mom for a while."

We sat there for the longest time just looking at the headstone. He would touch my fingers with his or kiss the back of my head.

"My Ma said you gave the pendant back. Does that mean you don't want to wait for me?" I closed my eyes and took a deep breath.

"No, I was only trying to do the right thing when I was told you would be marrying Sophia. I knew you didn't have a choice and I didn't want to create drama."

"So, you're still considering an us?"

"Actually, I was going to ask for the bracelet during our date tomorrow night."

I felt him move around behind me and I thought he was getting up to leave, until I saw the necklace dangling in front of me.

"Can we put this back on then, please?"

I turned my head slightly and saw the smile that covered his face. It was quite contagious and I had one just as big.

The chain felt cold as he laid it around my neck. I couldn't help but touch it as it rested on my chest.

"I see no reason to wait until tomorrow for you to wear my bracelet, do you?"

I shook my head no as I felt him lift my right hand from my lap.

I watched as he removed the box from his inside jacket pocket and then he opened the hinge. The bracelet was as cold as the necklace had been and I loved how the diamonds glistened in the sunlight.

"I need you to make me a promise."

I looked from the bracelet to his green eyes. "Anything," I whispered.

"In the future, when you hear someone talking about me, no matter who it is, ask me before you do anything." I smiled as I again nodded my head.

"Good, now hold on to your hat, Christi. I've waited very patiently to kiss those pretty lips of yours."

He didn't give me a chance to respond as his lips connected with mine, leaving me breathless.

When I returned to my office, I found Nora sitting patiently in my chair. She was typing away on her cell phone and smiled as I walked into the room.

"I see my son was able to talk to you."

She motioned to the pendant that hung from my neck.

"Yes, he explained several things to me. I clearly jumped to conclusions, something I have chastised Shannon for on a number of occasions." I chuckled.

"Yes, well sometimes things present themselves in a particular way and it is hard to see the truth. I am happy to see that you were able to find that in the end."

I offered her a cup of tea as I had begun to make one for myself. "That sounds lovely, Lass. I wanted to speak with you as it were."

I handed her the cup and settled into my chair. I watched as she patiently stirred the hot liquid, watching the spoon as it mixed the sweet goodness.

"Did your father ever tell you of the arrangement he and my Thomas made about you?"

I nodded as I sipped my own cup.

"He said that Thomas helped him with his divorce from my mother, but that was all he said." She looked at me with such a gentle look, a motherly look.

"Oh, Christi. The men in our lives try so hard to protect us, thinking we are these fragile china dolls that will break at the slightest touch. If you are to become a member of this family, you should know the entire story."

I was frozen in my chair as I listened intently to her words.

"It is true that Thomas contacted your father at a time when he needed our help. Of course my Thomas rarely did anything back then that didn't benefit himself. He was so angry when Matthew denied him your hand."

It was so strange to hear my fathers first name out loud. He was either dad, grandpa or Mr. O'Rourke.

"But I told Thomas, that it was better that way. Have Patrick prove that he is a man in more ways than just age. If he can't control his heart, how can he control the family business."

I could clearly picture Nora telling an angry Thomas that he wouldn't be getting his way.

"When the time came, we took Patrick to the mall over on Moore Street. He was to bump into you and introduce himself. However as he stood there watching you, he told Thomas that you were too innocent for his world. Patrick was never protected from what his father did. There was no point, he was to be the leader of the family. I told Patrick very firmly that he would attend university and get a good education. I explained to him that any man can point a gun at another and make him do what he wants, but to be successful, you needed knowledge. Patrick Senior and Thomas, tried to teach him everything they knew when he graduated. Patrick took to the role of head of the family like a duck to water. However, I could see it in his eyes that his heart was empty."

I faintly remember the day that Nora spoke of. My father hated shopping, but on that particular Saturday, he insisted on taking just me to the mall. I met several of my friends that day and even found out that Mikey O'Toole had a crush on me. Mikey and I dated for several years, he was my first kiss as well as the one who took my virginity. He joined the military and married Rebecca Stone from the neighborhood.

"Now, Christi, I know that my son was no saint while he was away at university. Thomas made certain he had eyes on him the whole time. But I do know for certain that he never dated a lass with red hair like yours. He has always leaned toward the floozie types. When he took over the family, I cornered him at dinner and asked him why he didn't date a good Irish girl. He smiled and told me that he wasn't ready to fight for her yet."

My mouth was gaping and my eyes wide.

"Yes, Christi he was talking about you. He was smart enough to know that he had to establish himself before he pursued you. He took the advice of his elders and made certain he could provide for you."

Just like the moment I figured out that Patrick was in the Mafia, finding out that he knew me all this time. He took the risk that I would marry someone else. He deliberately dated girls who were the complete opposite of me, not because he preferred them, but to avoid duplicating me. Looking back, I understand why he had a different blonde with him every time I saw him.

"Thats why you chose *Penciled In.*" My statement was to no one in particular, just a verbal result of what was whirling around in my head.

"No, Love, Charlotte has a reputation that we respect. However, she did do us a favor by placing you in charge that night. I have always known that you would be his equal. That night he came by the house and spoke with Thomas until the wee hours of the morning. He wanted advice on how Thomas persuaded me to marry him."

I laughed at her words. Patrick was such a confident man and for him to go to his father for matters of the heart.

"Christi, Patrick may be the head of this family, but his Da gave him the best advice he could. As the woman he chooses to have by his side, you will always be the neck, turning the head in the right direction."

CHAPTER NINE

With Shannon leaving and the wedding season quickly approaching, Charlotte placed an ad for her position in the local newspaper. She wanted me to do the interviews because I would be working directly with them.

It had been a month since my visit to Coleen's grave and I honestly smiled as I thought about Patrick. He wasn't the person I had thought he would be. It was almost as if he had a split personality. With me he was gentle and caring, but when we were out to dinner and we ran into anyone else, he had this mask that he put into place. At times, it was somewhat unnerving, as if I didn't know who I was with. Then in an instant, he was back to being the loving man who held my hand and kissed my forehead.

Unfortunately, that was all we had done, kiss and hold hands. He had this crazy notion that he still had to prove himself.

So for now, I settled for what he was willing to give me.

Charlotte had set up two interviews for today; the first was a no-show and the second was waiting in her office. Imagine my surprise when I walked into the room to find Harley sitting in a chair.

Harley looked completely different. Gone were the trashy halters, pleather skirts, and knee-high boots. In their place were a silk blouse, pencil skirt, and demure kitten heels. Her makeup was minimal and her cleavage hidden. She actually looked more beautiful.

"Harley?"

My shock could clearly be heard in my voice, I never expected to see her sitting in that chair.

"Hello, Ms. O'Rourke, and if you please, my name is Francesca Ciccone, Frankie for short."

Her voice was relaxed without a hint of sarcasm.

"Oh, I'm sorry. Please excuse me; that was rude. Frankie, it's a pleasure to see you again."

She simply smiled at me and then turned to look at a stunned Charlotte.

"I take it we know each other," Charlotte chuckled and then opened a file.

Charlotte went into detail about the type of person we were looking for and the requirements we had. Basically, we needed an assistant for both Charlotte and myself. She would be responsible for scheduling all the staff, and making certain our schedules were accurate. She would also take care of renting out the ballroom next door.

"So, I'd basically have to make sure you guys weren't double-booked and that people are where they're told to be."

Charlotte and I laughed and then agreed with her. I looked back at Frankie; she had her hands in her lap, fidgeting with her beaded bracelet.

"I know you know about me, but I want you to know that I don't want to be that person anymore." Her voice was lower this time and I could hear the sadness she was trying to hide.

"I won't lie to you and say that I'm the best person for this job. I'm just asking for a chance to have a job that I can be proud of.

"Ms. O'Rourke, I know that you especially don't have a very high opinion of me. It's no secret that I wanted Patrick. He never noticed me though, and I knew the second he gave you the bracelet that all hope for me was gone. I hope that if I get a good job and a nice place to live, maybe then I can turn the head of a good man like Patrick."

I had no doubt that she was being honest. I wanted to give her a chance and I hoped that Charlotte felt the same. There was only one concern I had and it needed to be addressed.

"Frankie, I think it's wonderful that you want to change your life and I'll help however you need me to, but I do have a concern and I think you already know what I mean."

She nodded her head and looked down, fidgeting in her chair. "You're worried that I'm a coke head like Michelle."

"Yes, Frankie, and there's no room for that activity in this business."

She reached into her purse and retrieved a stack of papers. Handing them to me, she continued to speak. "When Patrick found out I was in there with Michelle, he chewed me a new one, and then he made me talk to a counselor. He makes me take monthly drug tests. I've been clean for a while now."

I took the papers from her; they were lab reports that showed she had no drugs in her system. The latest was dated two days ago.

"Does Patrick know you're here?" Charlotte questioned. She had let me lead this interview up to this point.

"No, he just told me to find a real lady and learn from her. I only know two ladies and I'm scared to death of Mrs. Malloy. Since Ms. O'Rourke is my only other choice, I'm going to try to be like her. Patrick said he agreed that Ms. O'Rourke was a real lady and that I could learn a lot from her. That's what I want, to be a real lady."

How do you respond to that? I looked to Charlotte for help, but she was just as speechless as I was.

"Well, Ms. Ciccone, I think you'd bring a new spin to things around here. Don't you agree, Christi?"

"Oh, please, just Frankie. It's hard enough to get used to not being called Harley."

Charlotte looked lovingly at her. She rose from her chair and made her way around, leaning her body against the desk.

"Lady lesson number one: a proper title is the first sign you're being seen as a lady. Now, Ms. Ciccone, I'll expect you here in the office by nine o'clock every morning. Are we clear?"

The shock on her face nearly brought tears to my eyes. In an instant she was on her feet and hugging Charlotte like a life ring being tossed to a drowning man.

"You wont regret this, I swear Ms. Charlotte."

Charlotte smiled back and could only laugh at her excitement, "I'm holding you to that."

Frankie had been working in the office for a little over a week. She wasn't perfect, but she really tried hard. Patrick only smiled and kissed my forehead when I told him we had hired her.

This week was scheduled to be crazy as it was Shannon's engagement party and one of Paige's bridal showers. Patrick insisted that he wanted to throw the engagement party, and since he didn't have anyone to argue with him, he gave me a credit card and told me to make it special.

Paige's bridal shower was being hosted by Caleb's family. It was hard to contain my laughter when Nora would refer to them as "the hillbillies." Caleb's family was from the deep South. His mother was off-the-boat Irish, but his father was as southern as sweet tea. Nora told me that Eileen Montgomery was one to put on airs. She had left Ireland when her father insisted she marry his right-hand man. She didn't agree, so she jumped on a ship and here she came. Sherman Montgomery had been a moonshine runner at the time. He found her working in a rundown diner and fell in love with her accent.

Sherman had taken over for his dad like Patrick had taken over for Thomas. The Montgomery family wasn't as big as the Malloy family, but Patrick wanted to branch out further. Paige and Caleb made a good match, so the family would be joined. It didn't matter if Paige didn't marry full Irish, she wasn't eligible to take over the family business.

According to Nora, Eileen had colorful ways to describe what her husband did. For example, when he was running moonshine, he was in "exporting," When he moved up to take over his father's role, he was now the "CEO and general manager".

Frankie was at the office by six o'clock in the morning for Shannon's engagement party. I had spoken to her and told her that she would be in charge of this event because as my sister's maid of honor, I had to be available to her at all times. You would think that I had just handed Frankie a million dollars the way her face lit up. By the time I stopped by to make sure the flowers were delivered, she had the tables set up and was stocking the bar by herself.

That night as I danced with Patrick, I took a long look around the room and let my mind wander for just a second, I thought about what this would be like for Patrick and me. I couldn't imagine who would be on the guest list knowing that Patrick had more business associates than family.

"What has you so lost in thought, Pretty girl?" Patrick's masculine voice whispered into my ear, his lips making brief contact with the shell.

"I was just daydreaming," I sighed in return.

"Care to share, or can I take a guess?"

I snuggled in tighter as I laid my cheek on his chest. I felt so safe wrapped in his arms; I couldn't remember a time when I felt safer. Every time we were together, he held me just like this.

"Honestly, I was wondering what this would be like for us." I held my breath as he continued to lead me around the floor to the slow song. We hadn't been together that long and I really shouldn't have been thinking this way. It was strange to think that not that long ago, I was trying to push him away. Now I wanted to pull him closer.

Patrick only hummed as he replied, "Not sure if this room would be big enough, Ma would invite everyone she ever knew."

I could only hope that someday we would find out if the room was big enough. I buried my face in further and wrapped my arms around his waist. It was so easy to forget that he carried a gun, until my hand managed to find it hidden in the holster in his pants. The first time it happened, I gasped and jumped away out of pure shock. As it happened more and more, I would just move my hand a few inches away. He would just kiss me and make me forget.

"I promise, it'll be better hidden at our wedding."

His words were what caused me to gasp this time. As I looked at him, he only smiled and looked down into my eyes.

"Shit, you think I worked this hard to just quit half way?"

"I really wasn't certain. I mean, it wasn't that long ago that I was trying to get you together with Harley."

"Oh, Christi, I want this more than you know."

I watched as Shannon and Dillion visited with their guests. Shannon was so happy and Dillion was so attentive to her. I noticed that he would touch her very subtly; it was as if he was reassuring himself she was real.

Patrick had excused himself to make a phone call and when he returned, I noticed that he did the same thing with me. It wasn't much, a brush of his fingers or placing his hand on my back. He was doing this for his benefit, but what he did reassured me as well.

Out of the corner of my eye, I noticed Brad making his way over to where Patrick and Dillion were speaking. I couldn't hear what was being said, but I could tell it wasn't good.

Dillion looked at Patrick and shook his head, and then they hugged. Dillion returned to Shannon's side and whispered something into her ear. Patrick made a phone call and then came over to where I was standing.

"I'm sorry, Christi, I have to go take care of some business."

"Business?" I questioned. "Sorry, its none of my..."

"I have to go and remind someone that loyalty and responsibility doesn't stop when you go home."

I wasn't about to ask him what he meant by that. By his tone of voice, someone might just die tonight, so I deduced the less I knew, the better.

"I would ask you to stay with me tonight, but I know you'll say no."

"You'll never know unless you ask."

"All right, will you let Angus take you to my condo and will you stay with me tonight?"

I smiled devilishly and then pretending to think. "Yes, Mr. Malloy, I'll go to your condo and wait for you."

The party had nearly cleared out when my sister approached me. "I can't thank you enough for tonight, it was so amazing."

She was glowing with excitement. It was worth all the planning to have her smile like this.

"Oh, Sweetie, I'm so happy for you. You deserve to be this happy." I hugged her tightly, a tear escaping that I quickly wiped away.

I noticed out of the corner of my eye that Dillion was speaking with Brad. Again, I really didn't want to know what was happening.

Shannon picked up on my observation. "You'd think Douce would've learned the first time."

"Huh?"

"When Patrick first confronted him about Abby, he told him to take care of his responsibilities. As soon as he heard that Dillion had asked me to marry him, he decided that Dillion could take over supporting her."

I looked at her with confusion.

"Since the truth has come out about Abby, it seems she isn't his only child out there. Douce has four others, the paternity results came out today."

So that was where Patrick was headed.

Once the room was completely empty and I had said goodnight to Dillion and Shannon, I found Angus and instructed him to take me to Patrick's.

Once inside the building, I made my way up to his floor. It felt strange to be there without him. I knew Patrick wouldn't mind if I made myself at home, so I opened a bottle of wine and got comfortable on his couch.

I had just poured my second glass of wine when he came home. He crossed the room and kissed my forehead, trailing down to my neck.

"I could get used to having you here when I get home."

I looked into his eyes as I took another sip of wine. I wasn't going to respond to that one.

Without another word, Patrick took my glass, placed it on the table, and then extended his hand to me. Once off the couch, he led me down the hall to his bedroom.

The only lights in the room came from the glow of the city below. Patrick stopped just shy of his bed and wrapped me in his arms. His lips found mine as he kissed me with purpose. His hands found the zipper of my dress and ever so slowly he began to unzip it as he continued to kiss me.

My hands made their way to the inside of his suit jacket and removed it from his shoulders before I made quick work of his dress shirt. Patrick slowly steered me onto the mattress, never once breaking our kiss. The feel of his weight on me was enough to make me moan, that and the fact that his mouth had found my neck. Patrick reached around my back and unhooked my bra, removing it so quickly I didn't even realize it had been removed.

"Mo dsha, Christi, ta' tu' nois aille' na shamuhlu me' (My God, Christi, you're so beautiful)," his voice was so thick with want.

"A t'u liom go mbraaitheann dheanann sli," (You make me that way.) I replied breathlessly.

"I never thought hearing Gaelic could actually make me hard." He pushed his pelvis into my heated core to show me how hard he really was.

"Patrick…condom…"

He continued as if he didn't hear me. I began to push his chest to make him stop.

"What?" His voice full of want, breathless and yearning.

"I said, condom." I spoke a little firmer this time.

"Why? You're on the pill, right?"

I looked at him with disbelief. "Yes, but that doesn't change the fact that I have no idea if you're clean or not."

The look on his face was one of astonishment, and then anger.

"Are you telling me you think I'm cheating on you?"

"No, but I am pretty certain you aren't a virgin."

"No, but neither are you."

We had recently had the past partners discussion. He wouldn't admit to a particular number, only that it was more than one and less than thirty.

I told him about my only two encounters. My first had been Mikey O'Toole, and it had been over so quickly that I wasn't even certain it really happened. The second came a few years ago with a guy I thought I would marry, thus the reason for the pill.

"Yes, but your number is higher than mine, and besides, you should be asking me if I'm clean as well."

"I don't have to ask you!" His voice was now raised and his face was red with anger. "Damn it, Christi, I didn't sleep with any of the girls at the club! Why would you think that?"

Now I was angry; just because he didn't sleep with strippers, he felt safe?

"Oh, so you always slept with virgins?"

He didn't respond.

I began to move to the edge of the bed.

"Christi, I don't see what the big deal is. If you're worried about getting pregnant..."

"No, Patrick, I'm not worried about getting pregnant, I'm worried about getting some life-threatening or disgusting STD. You seem to think because you've only been with non-strippers that you're exempt. Do you honestly think that girls who willingly fall into bed with a mob boss haven't been with other men?"

I began to get dressed; he was crazy if he thought I was going any further.

"No, Christi, I don't think I'm exempt, but I have no symptoms..."

"Did you not pay attention in health class? Most men get no symptoms...Ugh!"

I was done; he obviously didn't care about the severity of this situation.

"Christi, wait...I...I..."

"You what, Patrick? What can you possibly have to say that would change this?"

He only looked at me, but said nothing.

I spun on my heel and left a naked Patrick sitting on his bed.

"I love you!" he shouted as I opened the door, but I continued out of the condo. Michigan Avenue was actually busy for the late hour. I literally stepped out of the door and into a cab.

There was only one place where I would feel safe right now; only one person who I could just sit with and not be questioned all night. I quickly told the cab driver the address and twenty minutes later, I was standing outside a door I knew well.

I pushed the illuminated button and listened as the bell chimed inside the house. Moments later, the porch light snapped on, followed by the quick opening of the door.

"D...daddy..." I managed to get out before the sobs began.

"Come here," my dad spoke as he pulled me into the house.

I made my way into his living room and then collapsed into the cushions of the couch.

"He's called three times already; I thought for sure you would've gone to your sister's."I shook my head quickly, pulling my knees up under me, wrapping my arms around a throw pillow and sobbing into it.

"She's too happy, and she would've wanted to talk about it."

My father made no comment. He crossed the room and filled two glasses with an amber liquid.

"Here, this'll take the edge off."

I drank what was in the glass, and then handed it back to him. We sat together quietly for several minutes before he began.

"Christi, I have a question that I have to ask." Turning to me, he took my hands in his, "Did he physically hurt you?"

"No, Dad, he didn't hit me."

I turned my entire body and crawled into his waiting arms. Even as a grown woman, I never felt safer than in my daddy's arms.

"Christi, I need to call him and let him know you're safe. Regardless of what he did or didn't do, he needs to know you're here and safe with me."

I simply nodded and curled further into my dad's side.

I could feel my dad dialing his phone. I chose to close my eyes and not think about what had happened.

"She's safe."

Silence.

"She said you didn't hit her and that's the only reason I'm calling you. Leave her alone tonight, all right?"

And with that, he ended the call.

CHAPTER TEN

The sun was shining as I made my way to work. It was just too bad my mood was so cloudy. I didn't sleep very well last night. My dad never said a word after he got off the phone with Patrick.

It was just what I needed, no one hounding me for what had happened, it wasn't anyone's business but mine. I wondered again if I had been right in the beginning, Patrick needed someone to turn a blind eye, I wasn't that girl. I would *never* be that girl.

Charlotte was waiting for me when I got into the office, a large cup of coffee in her hand.

"I would ask how your night went, but by the look on your face and the enormous bouquet of flowers on your desk, I would say someone screwed up."

I took the cup from her hand, rounded my desk and placed the mug down. Grabbing the vase with both hands, I walked out of the office door and to the entry door. I placed the flowers on the sidewalk and then went back into my office.

Charlotte said nothing as I sat in my chair and drank my coffee quietly.

It was nearly eleven when Nora walked into my office.

"If you have come here to defend him you can turn right back around."

Nora stood in the doorway blinking and looking confused. Suddenly the look on her face changed and she reached into her purse, retrieved her phone, and made a call.

"Care to explain why my Christi is ready to strangle you with her bare hands?"

I watched as Nora listened for a few seconds and rolled her eyes.

"Patrick really, this is 2014 not 1954. She has no idea of the types of women that have been warming your bed."

Nora crossed the room and took a seat in the chairs that faced me.

"All I know is you need to fix this and need I remind you that dime store flowers won't even begin to do the job, this is Christi not one of your bobble headed women. Get it together Patrick Shane Malloy, before it's too late."

She was again silent as I suspected she was listening to Patrick's side of the story.

"Well, I'm glad she refused them, I would have hurled them at your head!"

Nora looked directly into my eyes as she spoke.

"I won't tell you if the necklace is still on her neck or not, figure out how to fix it." She didn't wait for his response, as she ended the call and then turned to Charlotte.

"Charlotte, I am going to be borrowing Christi for a few days."

I looked at Nora in shock. What was she thinking, I had her daughter's bridal shower coming up.

"Of course, Nora, but we do have Paige's shower approaching."

Nora turned her attention back to me.

"All you need is a phone and a computer, you can work on that from anywhere, am I correct."

"Y-yes?"

"Good, then it's settled."

Nora reached into her purse and dug out a scarf and a large pair of sunglasses, handing them to me.

"You will need these, Lass."

Two hours later, we pulled off the highway onto a road that was highlighted with a pristine white fence, covered on each side by wild flowers and well manicured bushes. At the end of the long winding dirt road emerged a tall white house. It looked to be an old farm house. To the side, was even a big red barn and behind the house was a very large body of water. Nora was good at getting away from Patrick's men; the car that was parked outside my building never moved as we passed, I am certain they thought it was someone else.

"This house has been in my family's possession for a long time now." Nora answered my unspoken question.

"Patrick won't think about this place since he hasn't been here since he was a boy. He will call me and try to see where you are, but he needs to see what it would be like if you were gone."

I exited the car and took a deep breath. The air was so clean here and you could hear nothing except the wind in the trees.

I got to work in one of the rooms down stairs, Nora was right all I needed was the internet and a phone. I made great progress without having ten different interruptions. That night, Nora returned with Allyson and Paige. They brought several movies and more food than ten people could consume. We sat around the television laughing and telling old, stupid boyfriend stories.

The next day I woke up more rested than I had in a very long time. Allyson left early so that she could get back to Ryan, but Paige decided to hang around and relax.

"Christi, I don't want to know what Patrick did. Knowing him, it was probably insensitive and just plain boarish, but deep down he really cares about you." Paige said as she played with the throw pillow that rested on her lap.

"How do you do it, Paige?"

"Do what, Christi, forgive him?"

"No, not Patrick, Caleb. How did you fall in love with a man that had been chosen for you?"

Paige smiled and had this soft glow about her after I said his name. There was no mistaking it, they were very much in love.

"The first time I met Caleb, we had traveled to Mississippi and my Ma said I didn't have to like him if I didn't want to."

"So you knew of the arranged marriage?"

"I know it sounds so medieval, and I suppose that if you didn't grow up knowing that's how things were, it would bother you. Honestly, it was kind of exciting for me. I knew that when I met Caleb and if we clicked, then we could bypass all of the 'what if' and just discuss our future together."

The smile on her face never wavered as she continued to tell me her story.

"So, clearly you both 'clicked'." I chuckled as I air quoted.

"Oh, you have no idea the ways we clicked that trip."

"Oh, my God Paige, you so did not."

"Yes, we did. He was my first and I never wanted to leave."

I laughed as I recalled my first.

"From the first moment I laid eyes on him, I knew this was right, that we were perfect in every way. Much like you and my brother are perfect for each other."

"I wish I had your confidence, I'm just not so certain."

Paige scooted closer to me and took my hand in hers.

"Christi, Patrick is human and he is a man, so you have to take that into consideration. He is going to do really stupid things because of that."

I rolled my eyes at her.

"But you also have to remember that he is willing to do anything that you ask of him."

"No, that's not true, Paige. If it was I wouldn't be here, I would be beside him, having round three or four. He acted as if I was asking him to cut off his dick or something."

I got up from the couch and made my way to the large window that overlooked the lake.

"I feel as if I am only a number to him, a proverbial notch on his belt."

As the word left my lips, a lone tear traveled down my cheek. What he had done hurt, and it hurt badly.

"But he said he loved you, doesn't that count for something?"

I hung my head at the memory of Patrick shouting those three words at me as I shut the door. The cold glass felt good on my forehead as more tears began to fall.

"He said it in hopes of stopping me from leaving."

"Christi..."

"He said it in hopes I would be like one of his blonde bobble heads, that don't question anything." My voice reflecting my agitation.

"Christi, I have to stop you right there. First Patrick doesn't even like blondes."

"Really, because with the exception of the first time I laid eyes on him, he's always had a blonde crawling all over him." My words more clipped than they should have been.

"But was he touching them?"

Her words hit me like a baseball bat. I thought back to the parking lot, the first blonde I saw him with, had he touched her? No, no he hadn't. Then with Harley, she was again the one touching him.

"I can tell the answer by the look on your face."

Neither one of us said a word as I let it all sink in. I watched as the leaves in the trees moved with the wind. How the light danced off the peaks of the water. A squirrel sprinted across the lawn, stopping only to shove what I assume to be a fallen nut into his engorged cheeks. Oh to have the simple life of a squirrel.

"I know my brother, Christi. He has never said those words to any female that wasn't related to him. He wouldn't do that to you for anything *less* than to tell you his true feelings."

After a few hours of sitting on the deck and drinking coffee, I got dressed and went for a walk around the lake.

It was close to sunset when I finally came back around to the house. I wasn't ready to go inside, thought, so I walked down the wooden dock and sat down at the end. I leaned over and watched the tiny fish swim around under my feet.

I felt the vibration of the dock move and I knew who it was without looking. I glanced up to watch the sun riding along the horizon. The fading light reflecting in the water.

"Christi?" his voice was barely above a whisper.

"You don't have to turn around or say anything, but can you just listen to what I have to say?"

I didn't turn around or even acknowledge his request.

"You're right, about so many things."

I could tell by his tone that he was having a inner battle with himself.

"I am so sorry. I...you..."

I continued to let him have his time to get his thoughts together.

"I disrespected you in the worst way. You have every right to know every detail about my life."

I could feel him getting closer, I felt the dock bounce as he sat down behind me.

"If I could take it all back, I would. I would do as you asked me and not have questioned you. I would take everything back, well, except for telling you that I love you."

I could feel the tears begin to form, causing my vision to blur.

"Granted, I have terrible timing, but it is true nonetheless."

A tear ran down both cheeks, I let them.

"I got tested. I had my doctor run every test he could think of and rush the results. I have them here, if you want to see them—I am clean."

I looked down as his left hand that was wrapped securely around white rolled paper, appeared in from of me.

"Thank you for that. For getting tested, I mean."

"You shouldn't have had to ask me, I should have known better and been more prepared."

I watched as the fading light danced across his face. Sitting here at the end of the dock wasn't a powerful man, or a man to be feared, this was my Patrick. A man who clearly would do anything for me.

"You are the most important thing in my life and I will fight till my death for you."

His words were barely above a whisper, and yet I heard them loud and clear.

I watched as Patrick eyes left my face and traveled to my neck where his shamrock rested. I felt his warm fingers running between the metal and my skin.

"I prayed that you would still be wearing this when I saw you."

His eyes then met mine again.

"Do you understand why I was upset?"

He nodded his head and began to play with my bracelet.

"I felt like I was just another number, like I didn't matter as long as you got off."

His hand left my wrist and then traveled to my face, where he brushed the back of his knuckles across the apple of my cheek.

"You've never been a number to me, Christi, I will prove that to you, I swear."

I was done being angry with him, it was time to move forward. I leaned forward and slowly closed my eyes, Patrick quickly followed as our lips met. This kiss was sweet and tender and exactly suited for this moment.

"For the record, I love you, too." I looked into his eyes, truly meaning the words I spoke.

Once the sun had finally sat, Patrick took my hand and led me back to the house where he built a fire and began to tell me his sordid sexual past.

"When I was almost eighteen, my uncle told me he wanted to give me an early birthday gift."

"Wait, blood uncle or well-uncle?"

When I was growing up, I knew we had two types of family, blood family and well-family. Well-family, were people we had known so long that most likely, our great-grandparents bathed in the same well as their great grandparents. We still considered them family.

"A well-uncle, anyway, he took me to this bar and proceeded to give me my choice of women that he had hidden in the back. I didn't really want any of them because they looked haggard and torn. They smiled and giggled, each trying hard to get my attention. However, I wasn't impressed with any of them. Lucky for me, a fight broke out and my uncle ran out the back with me. He said in the car that he would make it up to me, but he was killed before he could make good on that promise."

Patrick had a piece of my hair wrapped around his fingers as he continued to tell his story. I'm not certain who got more out of it, him or me.

"So, I saw this beautiful girl one day. I wanted to go over to her and ask her out, but before I could get to her, she was talking and laughing with this other guy. I saw her a few more times and each time I thought about going over to her, I changed my mind and turned the other way. I was at this party right before I went away to college and I had just seen this girl with another guy and I was pissed. So, I found another girl who was the exact opposite and took her upstairs. I never knew the poor girls name and I left as soon as I finished. I went away to Yale and I tried to get that girl out of my head. I had a few girls in college but I made it known that I didn't want a relationship."

I got up from the couch and got a new bottle of wine, I poured us both a glass as Patrick continued.

"When I came home and took over the business, I was so focused on proving myself that I took little time for women. That's not to say that I didn't have a hand job or two. But for a long while, I didn't bed any woman. I know my family has very high expectations of me and I will do everything in my power to make sure I keep the family proud."

He turned his entire body to face mine, as he took both my hands in his.

"Christi, when I marry you—and I don't mean if—I want to have nothing between us. I want to have this little glimmer of hope that each time I make love to my beautiful wife, that we may have just created a little Irish miracle."

I had to smile at him. I had never seen him quite so handsome.

"Family is everything to me. That's why I have been so hard on Douce since I found out about Giggles. I believe that if you are man enough to have sex with a woman, then you are man enough to carry the responsibilities of anything that comes from it."

I couldn't help myself as I ran my index finger along his chiseled chin.

"Christi, I'm sorry I disrespected you. I've just gotten so used to having what I want when, I want that I forget you are my equal and have a huge say in what I do. Thank you for being so wonderful and giving me another chance, even though I don't deserve it or you."

I smiled as I responded, "Oh, Mr. Malloy, I have no doubt you will make this up to me."

"Oh, you have no idea all the ways I plan to do just that."

I kissed his lips softly as I whispered, "I love you"

"I love you, so much, my Christi."

CHAPTER ELEVEN

Nora and I had been trying to tie up all the loose ends for Paige's bridal shower. With this being thrown by the groom's family, Nora had been trying to stay out of the planning. However, when it was suggested that a Low Country Boil be done, Nora put her foot down and after a number of heated phone calls, a ladies tea was finally scheduled.

Paige was so excited at the thought of an English tea party, that she begged Caleb to fly in a specialist on the subject. Patrick called me and asked me to have a talk with her. I contacted Allyson, who as we all knew had no issue with telling you it how it was, she gave me advice on how to handle Paige.

I found a local hotel that actually served afternoon tea and hired the lady that hosted it to come and show us what to do.

"All right, Christi, are you ready for this?" Charlotte questioned as I was finishing adjusting the place settings.

"That's a good question, it makes me a little nervous to think that this is just a bridal shower and there are so many people coming."

This would be the first bridal shower where the guest list was over two hundred. It was also the first one where men would be in the next room in case something happened.

I had been thinking about that quite a bit lately. Patrick never went anywhere without his bodyguards, and now I had men that followed me everywhere I went as well. If I were to marry Patrick and have children with him, would those children become targets? Would they have men that followed them everywhere they went? I couldn't imagine trying to attend a soccer game with two or three bodyguards hovering around. I didn't get a second longer to think about it since Caleb's family had arrived.

Mrs. Montgomery was everything Nora had said she was and then some. I politely introduced myself to her as the party coordinator. She eyed me up and down condescendingly before turning her nose up as if I was beneath her.

Nora noticed this and came over to greet me. "Eileen, how nice to see you again, I see you've met our Christi."

"Oh, yes, Nora. Good to see you as well. Yes, she told me who she was, it's the least she could do after what this is costing me."

Excuse me, bitch? You insisted on throwing this thing!

"Yes, well, Eileen, if the money is an issue, I'm certain Christi could just ask Patrick for his checkbook."

I turned to Nora with a raised eyebrow. What the hell was she talking about?

"Patrick? What would this glorified waitress know of Patrick?"

I watched as Nora's face changed to one of pure joy, and a maybe a little mischief.

"Eileen, may I introduce you to Patrick's Christi. I know you've heard he gave her the necklace. This...is our Christi."

You could have shoved a Mack truck in the gaping hole that was Eileen's mouth. I hadn't realized that my accepting the shamrock had been such news. I thought it was just a close family thing. Clearly I was wrong.

"Oh, well, you must be very excited then, Nora, she's very pretty."

Not one time after Nora set her straight about whom I was did Eileen look at me. I was used to this from Patrick's men, but this was new for it to come from a woman.

"I'm happy for my son. Christi is good for him, and she makes him a better man."

Wow...didn't see that one coming.

Once all of the guests had arrived, the tea was served. I made my way to the back of the room. I wanted to make certain the wait staff had everything they needed. I was in full work mode when Nora approached me.

"Christi, you need to take your seat."

"Nora…what are...?"

"You're a member of this family and you need to have a seat with the family."

"Nora, thank you, but I'm also working."

Something you learned fairly quickly, you never argued with the Malloy women.

"Did you not hire Frankie to assist you?"

It sounded like a question, but it certainly was not.

"Then go freshen your face and join us."

Sitting and not helping was a true test of my nerves. I wanted so badly to go to the kitchen and make sure everything was going well. It wasn't that I didn't trust Frankie; I just had issues relinquishing control.

We had barely begun our second pot of tea when I noticed Eileen's face was scrunched up in a disdainful manner. The boss in me wanted to make certain everything was all right.

"Don't even think about it," Nora instructed from my left.

"Sorry, it's just hard to let go."

"Christi, even if she wasn't paying for this, she'd still be unhappy. That's just how she is." It was more than that and I knew it. Nora had no problem reading my expression. "Let's get through the gifts and we'll talk."

The tea itself was really a lot of fun. The tea lady, Mrs. Belvedere, was very informative when she told the history of the different teas that were being served. It was interesting to learn that different teas were served at different times of the day and that this was a tradition that had occurred for many years in England. I hoped one day that I would get to travel abroad and experience an authentic tea.

Sitting next to Allyson was certainly an entertaining event. She and Paige would make up different stories about the women in the room. It was like people watching gone wild.

"So, I hear you and Patrick exchanged the 'L' word," Paige whispered when Nora wasn't listening.

I could only smile.

"You know, I really shouldn't tell you this, however…"

"However, she has a big-ass mouth and she's going to anyway," Allyson teased.

Paige pinched her arm, causing both girls to giggle.

"Anyway, as I was saying…Patrick told Caleb that he fell in love with you the night he found you at the jazz club and you bit his head off about being called Legs. He said there was just something about you that called deeply to him."

I smiled at the memory of that night.

"I knew I'd fallen for him the day he found me at my sister's grave and asked me about my favorite memory. It was like he wanted to know her, as well."

"So, are you glad you decided to give him a chance?" Paige questioned, taking a sip from her cup.

"You know," I grinned lifting my cup as well, "I really am."

I listened as Nora told a story of how she and Thomas had tried to get away for a weekend when their children were little. She laughed and said that in the weeks leading up to the trip, every time Thomas would try to become intimate with her, one of the children would barge in.

"So finally, we're sitting in this lovely bed and breakfast, naked as the day we were born," she chuckled at her memory. "Thomas is thrusting like there's no tomorrow and the bloody phone rings."

She went on to say that it had been the uncle that was staying with the children and it appeared that Patrick thought it would be cute to 'launch' his little sister. She went on to explain the 'launching'. Patrick was on his back with his thighs touching his chest and she was to sit on the bottoms of his feet. He would then thrust his legs out and she would fly through the air. He was successful in not only projecting her straight into the air, but also in breaking her arm in three places and requiring surgery.

"We had to rush back so we could be there for little Paige."

I watched as Paige turned green from hearing that her parents were having sex.

"Oh, just you wait my darling daughter; have as much sex as you can now because once you bring those babies home, you'll never have it again until they leave."

The entire table erupted in laughter; well, except for Paige of course.

Being in this business for as long as I had, you got to see some pretty amazing things. Nothing could have prepared me for watching Paige open her gifts. From one of her aunts back in Ireland, she received this handmade lace handkerchief. Nora told me she would carry that during her wedding. Evidently, it had been made from the leftover lace from Paige's christening gown. I nearly cried as I heard the story. Thomas and Nora gave her an architect to build them a house. *A house...*

Caleb had sent over this absolutely stunning necklace that was covered in diamonds. Eileen closed her eyes and physically shook when Paige gushed over it. Apparently, it had been left to Caleb by Eileen's father. Nora whispered that it would have gone to Eileen if she would have married the man her father told her to.

Nothing could have prepared me for when Paige lifted a large, gold envelope from the table and read it out loud, "From Patrick and Christi."

She tore open the envelope as I sat like a statue in my chair. I watched as she took out an official-looking paper and began to literally squeal as she jumped out of her chair and ran around the table.

"Oh, Christi, thank you...thank you! It's the exact one I wanted. Oh, I'm so happy!" Her arms wrapped tightly around me, as she violently rocked me back and forth. I was helpless to do anything as she continued to vibrate with joy.

Once she finally let me go, she dropped the piece of paper on the table in front of me and then reached back into the envelope. It was at this point I noticed not only a picture, but a car title in Paige's name. Patrick had purchased her a Jaguar convertible.

"Nora, I had no idea."

She patted my knee as she leaned in and whispered, "Did you notice that Eileen gave her nothing?"

I looked at Nora with wide eyes. "You're shitting me, right? I mean, I got her a place-setting of dishes off her register, nothing huge."

Nora cut me off by placing her hand on mine.

"Yes, Lass, and don't think Eileen didn't notice that she received two gifts from you."

I whispered to Nora, "But I had no idea Patrick was going to do that."

Nora only smiled, "Yes, but neither did Eileen."

I didn't understand what was happening here and little did I know that I was about leave Eileen completely speechless.

Chapter Twelve

"Christi, come with me," Nora instructed as we watched Eileen getting upset with the hotel manager.

"…And the scones were at least a day old. You're bloody bonkers if you think I'm paying for them," Eileen hissed at the poor manager.

"Is there a problem here, Eileen?" Nora questioned.

"Oh, you know, Nora, stupid Americans, what do they know about English staples?"

Hearing her lashing out, not only at Edgar the hotel manager, but about everything she had seen today, finally got to me. I didn't even really think about what I was going, it just happened.

"I'm so sorry, Edgar. Here, let me take care of everything."

I hadn't given Patrick his credit card back from Shannon's party, so I quickly handed it to Edgar, who scurried away with it.

It was after he was out of sight that I caught the final price, eleven thousand dollars…great, there went a huge chunk of my savings.

I looked at the two ladies before me, Nora was standing tall, like the mother of a gold medalist. Eileen, however, wore a look of absolute shock and quite frankly, was a bit green around the gills.

"Yes, well, since that's all settled," Nora chuckled.

"Shall we have that drink now, Christi?"

"Wait! Let me…let me give you a check…you…" Eileen stuttered as she scrambled trying to open her Gucci purse.

I turned back to look at Eileen. I noticed then how her hands were shaking and fumbling to find her checkbook.

"Oh, Mrs. Montgomery, never mind the money. Us stupid Americans are more than willing to step up and help," I smiled at her and turned to join Nora in the hotel bar.

Nora waited until we were seated and had our drinks before she finally said anything.

"You acted like a Malloy today, I'm so proud of you. Wait until Patrick hears about this."

I lowered my head and let out a sigh. "What I did today was stupid. I disrespected her by jumping in the middle. My only reason behind that was to save my amicable connection with the staff here." Nora only smiled as she sipped her drink. I chuckled as I continued, "That was the most expensive lunch I've ever bought. It'll take me a while to recoup that money."

Nora quietly place her wine glass down on the table. "Do you think Patrick will even blink an eye at that credit card bill?"

I looked at her questioningly, "He won't have to. I'll give him a check tomorrow, along with an apology for using it without his permission."

Nora silently laughed as she continued to sip on her wine. I, on the other hand, chugged my martini.

"Lass, I think its time you were given a little more information on the people around you."

The bartender silently removed my empty glass and replaced it with a new martini. The bar was surprisingly quiet for the amount of people that were seated. I didn't notice any of Patrick's men and I did find that odd.

"Eileen Montgomery is a woman who lives with regret," Nora began to trace imaginary lines on the table with her perfectly manicured fingernail as she spoke. "You see, Christi, when she decided to leave Ireland and marry a non-Irish American, she had no idea of what was about to happen back home. She and Sherman had been married about a year and had Caleb's sister, Mia, when her only brother died suddenly."

I watched as Nora shifted her eyes from the table to my face.

"Family law states that in a case like that, the eldest daughter may inherit the family business when the father steps down."

My eyes went wide. I knew Eileen had refused to marry the Irish man her father had wanted her to, and because of that, she would have no claim to the family fortune.

"The same law states that she must follow the same rules and marry accordingly, which she did not. To make matters worse, she had a child by that American man."

The bartender placed a new glass of wine on the table and removed the empty one Nora had been toying with.

"Eileen's sister, Audrey, not only inherited the business when their father passed a few months later, but she married the man Eileen had run from. They now run the business and have six children of their own. Audrey wants for nothing, much as I do. That, however, is not the case for Eileen."

This was surprising as Eileen always looked so well put together and drove a Range Rover. Nora caught my shocked look and chuckled.

"Oh yes, Christi, Sherman Montgomery is nearly bankrupt. He's made one bad deal after another. If my Paige wasn't so completely in love with Caleb, I would've made Thomas break the marriage contract. Caleb has taken over the company, and with the help of Paige's dowry and Patrick's assistance, we expect to have a strong alliance very soon."

I was about to ask why, in this day and age, the exchange of money for a bride was still happening.

"Eileen thought that if she married Sherman, she would have the status you and I have."

"What status do I have?"

This wasn't my world and I had no real claim to Patrick or his family. I loved being with him, but that didn't change the fact that he could drop me like a bad habit and move on to the next girl. I had no status.

"Christi, I believe Allyson told you a little as to why Patrick's men don't look at you in the eye?"

"Yes, she said it had to do with honor and respect."

"Yes and no, it actually goes back further than we can really explain. I've been told it dates back as far as ancient Egypt and the Pharaohs. We give that same distinction to the wife or betrothed of our current king, so to speak."

If I was confused before, I was completely lost now. I wasn't betrothed to Patrick; we had barely begun to date.

"Okay, I get that it's an honor to be the king's wife or intended, but Nora, I'm neither. Clearly Patrick and I aren't married, and he hasn't asked me to marry him, so why do these rules apply to me?"

Nora rolled her eyes as she adjusted in her seat. "Jesus, Mary, and Joseph...God knows I love Allyson, but sometimes she fails to deliver the correct information; the bracelet, Christi." I looked down at my wrist, the diamonds glistening back at me.

"The bracelet is a complete circle, the diamonds, one of the hardest materials known to man. The platinum they're set in, strong and beautiful. It all means one thing. Patrick placed that bracelet on your wrist as a sign that you're his intended, and only you can break that bond by removing it. That's why he was so concerned that you'd removed it when I took you to the farmhouse."

I couldn't speak after her confession.

"Eileen has always wanted to have that level of respect. She's never wanted to be in a position of having to give it."

This was so overwhelming for me. I knew his feelings on getting married, but to be told that he was on that track.

Before I could ask Nora any more questions, Patrick and his men came charging through the bar entrance. "Oh, thank God! I've been tearing this hotel apart looking for you," Patrick said as he crossed the room and lifted me out of my seat, knocking my drink over in the process. He hugged me so tightly I thought he would break a bone. "Baby, please don't scare me like that again, I couldn't find you and no one knew where you had gone."

My face was crushed to his chest. I could feel his heart beating so fast I thought it was going to fly out of his chest.

"Patrick, I'm fine, I've been with your Mother the entire time."

He pulled me back to look into my eyes; I saw it then, relief.

I watched as Nora and Patrick looked at one another, silently saying something to each other.

The bartender was quick to come with a towel and a new drink for me. Patrick took a seat without a word and a glass of scotch was placed before him. He pulled me close and placed his hand midway up on my thigh, slowly making lazy patterns with his thumb; it was comforting and yet, a little erotic.

Nora began to tell him of the encounter with Eileen and how I had paid the bill. He smiled as he raised his glass with his free hand.

"I'm so sorry, Patrick, I'll have a check to you in the morning. I don't know what came over me," I shook my head as I apologized.

"No, you won't," his voice was firm.

I looked at him with alarm. "But, Patrick, I charged eleven grand to your credit card! You never gave me permission to use the card except for Shannon's party."

Patrick smiled as he lifted my wrist that had the bracelet wrapped securely around it. "This, love, is all the permission you need."

I could only blink as his words began to sink in.

"Listen, if this is really bothering you, then I can think of a way for you to make it up to me," he said with a low voice and I looked up into his dark, lusty eyes.

"Oh, I have no doubt that you do," I chuckled as I leaned onto his side.

"Patrick, love, I'm sorry to interrupt, but I wanted to tell you something before anyone else did," Nora's gentle voice filled the air. "Eileen didn't give your sister a gift —nothing."

Patrick shifted his entire body toward his Mother. I could feel his muscles tighten and I could see his hand grip the scotch glass firmly. "No lace or quilt?"

Nora could only shake her head.

I remembered hearing from my grandmother that in the old country, the Mother of the groom would make a quilt from the clothes the groom had worn as a child. It would be placed on the marriage bed for the first year as a good luck charm.

"No, love, not even a card from the corner grocery."

I didn't like the look that both Nora and Patrick had in their eyes. I couldn't describe it. It looked almost like one of betrayal.

"Speaking of gifts," I poked Patrick in the side with my index finger, "You bought your sister a car and then you added my name to the card." Patrick turned to face me, his devilish eyes locked with mine. The cheeky fucker pulled out the crooked grin just because he could.

"Amex wanted a Jaguar convertible she'd seen in a magazine. As far as adding your name, what's the issue?"

I rolled my eyes at him. "Well, a little heads up would've been nice. I'd already given her a place setting of her china."

He kissed my nose as he ran his hand along my thigh, slowly parting my legs and trailing his fingers between.

"I like it when you're feisty."

God, the things this man could do with his fingers…

"Oh, my love, you've not begun to see feisty," I moaned. He kissed my lips as his fingers went even higher. "Patrick," his name came out as a gasp.

"I'm sorry, I'll stop."

Unfortunately, he did. I knew Nora was at the table, but his fingers really did make my lady bits tingle.

"All right, you two, dinner is at our house. No excuses; and I expect you both," Nora began as she stood from her chair. Patrick followed her and helped to gather her things. Once he had her out the door, he turned and came back to the table.

"Well, so much for the plans I had for you later," he stated rather gruffly.

"Patrick, it's just dinner, we can always go back to your house after."

The smile returned to his face as he helped me out of my chair.

"I like the way you think."

"Oh, you have no idea the plans I have for you later," I stated as he took my hand in his.

"I look forward to each and every detail, trust me."

Dinner with Nora and Thomas was surprisingly relaxing. Seeing Nora go from her typical dress-to-impress style to her lounge pants and zip-up hoodie was refreshing, and I had to admit it was nice to just sit back and enjoy the casual atmosphere.

Once the meal was over and I had insisted on washing the dishes, we all found ourselves settling in the family room and enjoying a bottle of wine.

"So, how was the shower, ladies?" Thomas questioned as he shifted in his chair. He had not been able to attend and sit in the room next to ours.

"Eileen didn't give a gift, nothing," Nora stated with no emotion in her voice.

"Then it's true," Thomas responded, looking at Patrick.

I watched as Patrick nodded his head solemnly. No further words were exchanged and I was too nervous to question what they were talking about. I couldn't help but wonder why this gift issue was so significant.

Patrick didn't waste any time after we got back to his condo. I found my shirt on the floor and my bare back against his soft sheets. His strong hands were gentle on my skin. I made quick work of his shirt and ran my hand along his muscular chest, as his lips and tongue dominated mine.

I was so lost in his touch that I barely heard his cell phone ringing. Patrick ignored it and continued. It was seconds later that the house phone began to ring. Again, Patrick ignored it and continued. Barely a minute passed and the house phone rang again. This time Patrick jerked away from me, rolled to his side, and shouted into the receiver, "What?"

I couldn't hear what was being said on the other end, but Patrick's face began to soften.

"Brandon, she's a small woman, bust the fucking door down and get her out." Patrick was again quiet; his fingers found his hair and began to tug. I knew he was getting frustrated. "Fine, I'll be there in fifteen. Find the motherfucker who drugged her."

Patrick placed the phone back in the cradle and then turned to hover over me again. "I'm so sorry to do this to you." He lowered his forehead to mine, "Michelle has locked herself in the bathroom of some sleazy motel downtown. She refuses to come out for anyone else except me. Evidently, she went there with some guy and he roughed her up pretty good."

I knew Michelle had a drug problem. The situation made me think of my sister. If only Coleen could have had someone like Patrick to come save her, things would have been different.

"Babe, don't worry, go help her and then come back here. I'll be waiting for you."

He kissed me and then began to get dressed. With one final kiss and exchanges of 'I love you', he was out the door.

I laid there for hours after he had left. I began to think about how often this would happen if we were to marry. Would he miss baseball games and dance recitals for stuff like this? I guess only time would tell.

I felt him as I slowly came out of my twilight sleep. I was certain I had just drifted off. He was fresh from a warm shower and I turned to face him.

"Hey, you're home," I whispered, my raspy voice full of exhaustion.

"Umm hmm," he nuzzled his face into my hair and took in a deep breath.

I couldn't help but giggle. "Can you please tell me why you're sniffing me?"

He let out his breath and nuzzled in closer to me. "Because your smell is so much better than what I've just smelled for the past few hours."

I hugged him tighter to my body. I knew nothing sexual was going to happen between us tonight, he just needed me to be here.

"Did you get Michelle calmed down?"

"Yes, she'd barricaded herself in the bathroom. We never found the guy who roughed her up, but I have a few leads on him. I was able to check her into The Haven and get her some help for her drug addiction."

I smiled as I laid my head in the crook of his neck. "Allyson was right about you."

"How so?"

"At the end of the day, you really are a good guy."

No further words were said as I drifted off to sleep, wrapped in his arms.

CHAPTER THIRTEEN

When I woke up the next morning, I noticed two things. First, Patrick had the most annoying alarm. Second, the man could make a cup of coffee.

His alarm was a combination of a loud annoying beeping sound followed by all of the overhead lights coming on. Not to be outdone by the curtains on the window being opened and the bright sunlight nearly blinding me.

All was forgiven and forgotten, though, as soon as he handed me a huge steaming cup of liquid happiness.

"Mmm, good morning," I said sleepily as I kissed his lips.

"It is now," he said, his voice rather husky this morning.

Patrick sat beside me on the bed, his well-defined chest on display for me, his pale blue sleep pants hanging low and giving me just a hint of his chiseled 'V' that made me cross my legs.

I set my mug on the nightstand and began to make my way over to Patrick's lap. He had started a fire in me last night that he needed to extinguish. It felt like he was up for the challenge as he pulled my nightshirt off, tossing to the floor.

Before I could even get my lips on his neck, the loud banging of a door caused me to freeze.

"Patrick!" Paige's voice screeched down the hall.

I didn't even have time to climb off of his lap before she barged into the bedroom.

"Patrick, didn't you hear me calling you?"

Paige stood with her arms crossed and her foot tapping. She didn't seem to realize or care that I was sitting on his lap.

"Um...kind of trying to get laid here, Paige," Patrick stated as he continued to kiss my neck.

"Oh, would you forget about your stupid dick for one second. I need your help!"

Paige had no shame as she jumped into the middle of the bed.

"Dear Penthouse, Ever have one of those dreams where…?" I began as I removed myself from Patrick's lap and crawled under the covers, sighing as I pulled them up over naked breasts. Paige was totally unfazed.

"Christi, I'm so glad you're here. I need to talk too you."

Again, Paige had no boundaries as she picked up my cup of coffee and went to take a drink.

"Hold it right fucking there…" I snapped as I took my coffee out of her tiny hands, "I'll share a lot of things, my first cup of coffee, isn't one of them!" I cradled my cup of coffee as if it were the Hope diamond.

"Sorry, sorry, my mistake," she held her hands up in surrender.

"You said something about needing my help?" Patrick questioned, annoyance in his voice.

"Yes, dear sweet, Patrick. Did you know that Queen Bitch didn't give me a gift at my shower?"

Patrick took a sip from his cup as he leaned his back against the headboard. "I did hear something about that."

"No quilt, Patrick! No lace for my wedding…nothing." Her hands flew into the air, emphasizing her point.

"Trust me, Paige, that isn't *all* she failed to deliver at your shower."

Patrick went on to tell her the story of how I had pulled out his credit card and paid the hotel bill. Paige's eyes were huge as she looked first at me and then back to Patrick.

"Paige, this only confirms what we warned you about."

"She wouldn't, would she? I mean Ma said that when she spoke with Caleb's Aunt Audrey, the lace had been shipped weeks ago."

"It confirms they're broke, Paige; she took that lace and sold it to buy something."

Then it hit me. I felt so stupid for not catching this before. It was an old Irish tradition that when two families were being united by marriage, the mothers would get together and bind together pieces of their family's lace. Each piece of lace was extremely old, having been handed down through the generations, a sort of tangible genealogy. They were usually very intricate and handmade, and thus very valuable. This would continue down the line, and if I had to guess, Paige's piece of lace was hundreds of years old. It was done to symbolize the union of the two families. Many lace collectors would study these and could tell instantly where one family ended and another began.

A really intricate, well-made and well-preserved piece could sell for thousands. With that being said, it made perfect sense why Eileen would have wanted to sell hers.

My father had given Shannon the piece from our family. She had sent it to a lace maker back in Ireland who joined the piece that Dillion's mother had sent.

"Paige, let Ma handle this. Trust me, Eileen Montgomery will regret the day she messed with our Ma."

No truer words had ever been spoken. Nora could be a real piece of work, especially when provoked.

"So, um, Christi, do you still have his little black card?" Paige's voice changed as she asked and her shoulders came up to be even with her ears as if a child that was being coy.

"Yes, actually, I forgot to give it back."

I went to retrieve it from my purse, but Patrick stopped me by placing his hand on my shoulder, "Not so fast, keep that one until yours arrives."

I turned back to him and nearly fell off the bed, "What do you mean mine?"

Patrick gave me his signature sly smile. That usually worked to make my panties wet, but unfortunately this time it just pissed me off.

"I mean the one that my credit card company is sending for you. Don't even think about arguing, and have fun with it."

"Patrick Malloy..."

My words were cut off by his lips. He was really playing dirty now.

All right, Mr. Malloy, two could play this game...

~*~

In two short weeks, my sister would be a married woman. I was happy for her, thrilled even, and also completely jealous.

I wouldn't ever admit that to her, or to anyone else. It was just how I felt and I had every right to feel like I did.

Last night at dinner, Patrick told me he would be heading to Ireland soon. He said he had some business to take care of, but that he would be back in time for Shannon's wedding.

We were having her bachelorette party at *Smoke and Mirrors*, one of Patrick's clubs. He insisted on having it there and assured me he would take care of everything. I learned a long time ago to expect Patrick to be true to his word. When he said he would handle everything, he would handle *everything*. Thus, the reason I was sitting in the back of a stretch limo that was buzzing with very excited girls. Shannon had invited all of her friends from college and her bridal party; needless to say, it was quite loud.

We pulled into the valet area of the club and I listened as girl after girl screamed with excitement.

"Oh, my God, Shannon! How in the hell did you get into this club?"

I looked at my sister, silently asking her to keep quiet about me.

"I have friends in high places." She said with attitude.

Did I mention that I loved my sister?

Once we emerged from the limo, the blue lights that illuminated the outside of the building showed me two things; first, the line to get in was huge. Second, Allyson and Paige were standing beside three of Patrick's men, just outside the entrance.

I made my way over and hugged each of them.

"Patrick said he told you about his trip to Ireland?" Allyson had a glint in her eyes as she spoke.

"Yes, he said he'd leave early tomorrow and be back before the wedding. Some business he has to attend to."

Allyson and Paige gave each other a look that I honestly didn't want to know about.

The club was packed as we made our way through the crowd. Tonto was standing directly beside me and was ushering me to the back of the dance floor.

"Ms. O'Rourke, boss wants you to enjoy yourself." With his words, he gestured for my right wrist where he placed a silver Tiffany bracelet. I noticed that all of the girls in our party were given the same bracelet. "Just show the bartender this and you can have anything you want to drink or eat."

The area he had escorted us to was a huge section that looked more like a casual living room. It had several couches and small tables.

Posted outside the entrance of course were four of Patrick's men. It wasn't until I was seated on one of the couches that I noticed Nora sitting in the far corner. I was delighted to see her, so Allyson and I made my way over to her.

"Lass," Nora grinned and kissed us from her chair, wrapping me in a tight hug.

"Nora, I didn't expect you." I admitted, joy filling my voice.

"Well, she'll be my daughter and I wanted to help her celebrate."

Nora never stopped surprising me with her kind words. Considering the type of business her husband and son were in, you would have thought she would be a hard-nosed woman.

The DJ was wonderful as he played everything Shannon asked of him. The bartenders would get her on the bar and do body shots off her and her girls. I sat back and watched as none of them made a move toward me. I was getting used to not having jerks come up to me.

Everything was going really well when it happened...

I was dancing with Shannon and Allyson off to the side when a really big guy approached us on the dance floor. I had my back to him so I had no idea he was even there. Without warning, I felt tight hands gripping my hips. At first I thought it was Patrick and I tried to turn around. He wouldn't let me, his bruising grip tightening to the point of being painful. It was then I knew it wasn't Patrick. I could feel his hot breath on my neck and his erection grinding into my ass.

I again tried to turn around when I noticed Tonto plowing his way through the crowd. I looked at him and held my hand up, telling him to stop. I was finally able to pry the guy's hands loose enough to turn my body and look at the man. What I saw made my blood run cold.

He was huge, his eyes hooded and wild. I could barely make out his dark eye color as they were boring directly into mine. His massive shoulders rocked with the beat of the music as he began moving us away from the crowd, his hands never fully leaving my body.

"You need to step away!" I shouted at him over the music. He only snickered and jerked me back even closer, his grip tighter and more painful than before. I was sure I would be covered in bruises. The look in his eyes scared the hell out of me, but I tried to hide it and squared my shoulders. "Seriously, if you value your life, you'll walk away now!" I yelled trying to pull away from him.

It was then that he reached up and grabbed my face with one hand and jerked it to his, kissing me full on with his tongue shoved into my mouth as I fought to push him off. The guy was freakishly strong and I couldn't budge him off me. His other hand went up under my dress and grabbed a handful of my ass, pulling me against his erection again and grinding roughly into me. I felt my feet leave the floor then and suddenly we were moving towards the back of the club.

It all happened so fast that I wasn't sure if it was real. One second, the large man was on the verge of violating me with the hand he had begun using to roughly grope me between my legs, and then the next second he was three feet away from me.

I watched in horror as Patrick stood with the back of the large man's neck clenched firmly in his hands as he is repeatedly slamming the guy's face into a table. I watched as blood splattered everywhere, and what appeared to be teeth flew in different directions. Patrick's face was contorted in rage, his expression almost feral. It was all happening so fast that I couldn't process what Patrick was screaming at the man. With one final slam, the heavy table broken in half and the man fell to the floor.

"Get her the fuck out of here!" Patrick roared at Tonto.

I didn't wait for him, I turned and began making my way toward the doors. Once outside, I found the cold air of the night and a very anxious Angus began pulling me toward the car.

"I've got you, Ms. O'Rourke."

I didn't remember the ride back to my house, only that I couldn't get the mental picture of Patrick in an out-of-control rage out of my head.

Thank God for Angus, as he and Tonto helped me into my house.

"Ms. O'Rourke, boss wanted you to go to his condo."

"N...No, I want my bed, thank you."

I knew Tonto would be sitting on my couch all night; Patrick would have his head if he didn't. The next morning, my father was sitting at my kitchen table when I awoke. I knew Patrick would have called him, but what I wasn't prepared for was the story he had to tell me.

"So, I got a call from a buddy of mine that responded to a situation at a club downtown." *Okay...where was he going with this?* "It seems a patron got a little carried away and the owner had to step in." I poured myself a cup of coffee and then joined him at the table. "Normally, this wouldn't be a big deal, something that happens all the time."

"But...?" I coaxed.

"Patrick called me, Christi." I lowered my head. Half of me had hoped that last night was just a dream. "I know that what you saw spooked you." I didn't respond. "But you need to know the whole story before you go being afraid of Patrick. Have you ever heard the name Darius Vailer?"

The name alone caused a chill to travel down my spine. Darius Vailer was a man that had been convicted of murder and was sitting on death row, or he had been up until about a week ago when he had escaped by faking an illness. Darius had abducted thirteen women, most from nightclubs, and had strangled them to death after raping them. He would then remove different parts of their body as souvenirs, mostly ring fingers, but he was particularly fond of green eyes.

"Yes, he's that killer that escaped last week, right?"

"Yes, he's also the man that Patrick killed last night."

I watched as my coffee cup left my fingers and crashed onto the tabletop. "Oh, God…"

My father got a dish towel and began to clean up the broken china and spilled coffee.

"Patrick said he was upstairs watching you have fun with the girls and decided to leave you alone. He was just about to turn away from watching you when he saw Vailer move in and recognized him from his mug shot. Patrick said that animal was already trying to leave with you in his arms and was about two seconds from raping you on the dance floor with his hand. Christi, promise me you won't be angry with him for stopping that monster however he could. I know how you are."

My dad was right; had I not been told who the guy was, I would be thinking the worst about Patrick right now.

"I swear it, Dad."

"Good. Now why do you suppose Patrick went to Ireland?"

CHAPTER FOURTEEN

I didn't like the way my dad asked that question, "Why is Patrick in Ireland?" I instantly felt something was off, like he knew something and was just seeing if I knew it as well. I didn't have time to question him further, though, as the doorbell rang, followed by hard pounding.

Dad was quicker reaching the door and honestly, I was grateful. Once he looked through the peephole, he grinned as he unlocked the door.

"And it begins…" he said with a chuckle.

The door flew open and in marched a very excited Nora, Allyson, and Paige.

"Oh, my God, Christi! Are you all right?"

"Thank God my brother was there…"

"He has good form, doesn't he?"

All three were talking at once and I could do nothing but let them get out what they had to say.

Once they ran out of breath or shit to say, we all settled into my living room. Dad brought out a tray of coffee and then left for his own house.

"Okay, so I'm just going to just get this out of the way and deal with the elephant in the room." Allyson was always a "to the point" kind of girl. "Last night was the first time you saw his dark side…you doing okay?"

I pondered her question for a moment. "Honestly, when I first noticed the guy, I tried to warn him. I knew Tonto was close and I knew he would've pummeled the guy right there in front of us all. But I didn't want to ruin Shannon's night so I tried to just get him to go away peacefully. I had no idea Patrick was even in the room…"

My thoughts began to drift back to the music that was playing and the way everyone was laughing.

"Honestly, when I got in the car, I was on overload. I didn't know what to think, nor did I really want to." I tucked my legs under myself and took a large sip of my coffee. "I've never seen anyone as angry as Patrick was last night. I've never witnessed that kind of rage. It was like he was a different person."

The girls didn't interrupt as I continued.

"When I woke up this morning, I was fully ready to end my relationship with him. Seeing him lose control like that terrified me and I began to realize that he had an entire side I have no desire to know. But when my dad told me the guy's name…"

I began to feel strange, like I was becoming a new person, a better person.

"Is it sadistic of me to be thankful that Patrick was there, that he did what he did, and that I was able to walk away? What kind of person does that make me? What kind of person am I, so fucking happy that my boyfriend was willing to step in and beat the life out of someone? What kind of person am I that I'm so grateful that all I want to do is get dressed up in my naughtiest outfit, march over to his condo and thank him in ways that are illegal in seven states?"

Nora smiled warmly at me. "Christi, listen, you have every right to feel the way you do about Darius being dead and you being alive, that's human nature. I'm just glad to hear that you want to continue a relationship with my son."

I smiled as Nora crossed the room and wrapped me in her arms; this was what having a Mother felt like.

"I'm worried about Patrick, though. I thought for sure he would've come by the house when he found out I didn't go to his condo. He hasn't even called."

Nora took my hands in hers. Her hands were so warm and soft, like the feel of a warm blanket on a cold day. It was then that I noticed the slight bruising that was forming on her swollen right knuckles. I worried that she had gotten involved last night. Surely Patrick's men would have protected her.

"Lass, he couldn't. That's why he called your father. By the time the police left, he had to catch his plane."

I looked to her hand and then back to her face. "Nora, what happened to your hand?"

Paige began to giggle and Allyson bumped shoulders with Nora.

"I had to remind a certain future in-law that tradition cannot be messed with."

I gave her a curious look before Paige interrupted. "You should've seen it, Christi. Eileen was trying to say that she had sent the lace to the cleaners. The cleaners! Like you'd send a piece of priceless material to the same place you send your everyday drycleaning. Lucky for me, Ma knows a lot of people in this town. Eileen didn't even get a chance to spend the cash before they called my Ma with the lace."

My eyes went wide; Eileen had tried to sell the lace?

"Please say you're joking. She sold the family lace?"

"She tried, and for so little money," Nora shook her head in disgust.

"Can you believe this, Christi? For a lousy seventy-five hundred bucks, she tried to ruin the tradition." Paige was now the one to eye roll.

"Yes, but our Ma took care of that. Eileen won't soon be forgetting what's important in this family," Allyson piped up from the corner.

I then looked to Nora. She had the biggest look of pride on her face. She had protected the family and the rich traditions it held. It didn't take a genius to figure out that Nora had hit Eileen. My curiosity was in what Eileen looked like.

"So, back to Patrick, should I expect a call later today?"

Nora's face turned to mischief. "No, Lass. It'll be a while before you hear anything from him. His business is in a very remote area and he won't have access to any form of communication."

I was certain I didn't want to know anything. I would just say a prayer every night for his safe return.

"Enough about my stupid brother; let's get you dressed and hit some stores."

"Paige, some of us have work to do. Like, I don't know, a little wedding that's happening in a week," I gave her the bitch brow.

"Oh no, Christi, you owe me. You managed to get out of going shopping that day in Patrick's condo, you're so going now."

I then turned my attention back to Paige. I remembered that day a little differently. I remembered having my very sexy boyfriend all hot and ready, only to be interrupted by this evil sprite.

"Oh no, dear Paige, as I remember it, you owe me. I was about to get laid by your very sexy brother before you so rudely, and I emphasize *rudely* interrupted us." I then remembered that his Mother was still very much in the room as I quickly added, "Sorry, Nora."

Everyone giggled as Nora began, "Did something happen, Paige?"

Paige tossed her head back and huffed. "Oh, good God! I went over to Patrick's condo and these two were about to do the nasty," she said as she pointed at me and smirked evilly, "Just call me the resident cock blocker."

Nora tried to hold back her laughter. "Oh, Christi, you should make him wait until your wedding night anyway. It'd serve him right."

Paige was quick to jump up and began to raise her voice, "Really, Ma? Well, let's see, you married Da in November and Patrick was born the following April. If you do the math, it's obvious you so didn't wait till your wedding night and neither will Patrick."

Nora held her head up, but a hint of blush tinged her cheeks. "That's neither here nor there. The fact is, Patrick could use a good humbling and who better to do it than Christi? Besides, it'll set a good precedent as to who's really in charge. What do you say, Christi?"

I couldn't help but giggle and blush given this conversation was with his Mother of all people. "I'll think about it," was all I would commit to.

That seemed to be good enough for Nora. "Fair enough, Lass. So, now that we have that all settled, we have another important matter to discuss. Patrick's birthday is coming up."

It seemed that Patrick's birthday was the weekend before Shannon's wedding, a detail he had neglected to tell me. Patrick preferred to have just the family present to celebrate. Small quiet dinners were all he had ever allowed.

I had to give Nora credit; she was at least telling me this was a family affair so I didn't get upset when I wasn't formally invited.

"Um, all right, then I'll given him my gift either the day before or the day after, depending on when he returns from his trip."

Nora then looked at me with a questioning expression, "Why would you do that?"

"Because, you said it's just family."

Laughter erupted; well, they laughed, I just looked confused.

"Oh, Christi, I absolutely love your humor. You had me going there for a while," Nora chuckled as she took another sip of her coffee.

Guess I was considered family

All week long, the news was bombarded with the story of Darius Vailer's death and subsequent absence from the streets as a wanted and much-feared serial rapist. The person responsible for getting him off the street was considered something of a hero in the media. Patrick's name was never mentioned, but the reports stated that the person donated the sizable amount of reward money that had been offered to a battered women's shelter and I couldn't help but smile.

I expected to hear from Patrick at some point during his trip, but it had been four days without a word and I started to worry a little. I remembered how my dad had seemed to know a little more than he let on so I called him.

"Hey, Dad."

"Hey, Christi. Missing Patrick?" he chuckled.

"All right, Dad, cut the shit and tell me what you know."

He laughed even harder. "Well, it seems the apple doesn't fall far from the tree, you're just as questioning as I am. You should have become a detective like your old man."

"Whatever, Dad, what do you know. Why haven't I heard from him?"

"Sorry, Sweetheart, the only thing I can tell you is that he's in Ireland and he *should* be back in a few days."

"I don't like the way you say should, what aren't you tell me?"

"Oh, I'm not telling you plenty, you'll have to wait and hear it from Patrick."

Men...such useless creatures...ugh!

More days passed and still no word from Patrick. Thankfully, I had my sister's wedding to help plan, as well as Paige's. I had bigger worries on my mind, though. What do I get Patrick for his birthday? What did you get the man who owned nearly the entire town? He could buy anything he wanted, and then it hit me, the one thing he couldn't buy. I giggled as I began to put my idea into action.

Dinner was to be at Thomas and Nora's, family only, a very small affair. Most people would think that was maybe ten to fifteen people, but most people would be wrong. We are Irish after all.

There had to be at least sixty people sitting around three huge tables that were arranged in a horseshoe design. Everyone had a drink in their hand and was laughing and enjoying themselves. I scanned the room, but I didn't find the guest of honor.

"He isn't here," a voice sounded in my ear.

I turned to my left and found Thomas standing with a martini glass in one hand and a beer in the other.

I chuckled as I questioned, "Are we double-fisting it tonight?"

He laughed and then handed me the martini glass. "Patrick said this was your favorite and I swore I'd make certain you had one the minute you got here."

I took a drink and then smiled at him, "Thank you."

"Absolutely, let me introduce you to a few people."

"A few? Thomas, we have *got* to work on your definitions."

I met so many uncles, aunts, first and second cousins, that I was certain I would never remember everyone's name. Everyone, and I mean everyone, already knew everything about me.

I was well into my third martini when I had just about decided he wasn't going to show. Something had to have happened in Ireland. Maybe his plane had been delayed, or he had decided to celebrate in Ireland.

As I began to take the final sip of my martini before telling everyone goodnight, the front door opened and in walked a very gruff-looking Patrick.

Whenever I had ever seen Patrick, he had always been well-groomed and dressed impeccably and always in tailor-made clothing. His hair now looked as if he hadn't washed it all week, and his jeans were torn in several places. I finally noticed how quiet the room became as Patrick got closer to me. I found it odd that none of the men were greeting him. I took a look around the room to find that everyone had formed a circle around us.

"Uh, Patrick?" My voice shaky as I turned again to look around the room.

"*Mo ghra.*" (My love.)

"What's going on? Is everything okay?"

I was getting nervous. I hadn't seen him in a while and honestly, his current appearance was unsettling.

"*Na biodh eagla ort, le do thoil, beidh me ag insint duit goch rud*" (Don't be afraid, please, I will tell you everything.)

His voice was so calming and I watched as he motioned for me to come closer to him.

"Christi, do you remember the story I told you about the promise my great-grandfather made to my great-grandmother?"

I could only nod my head as I turned once again to scan the room. It was then I noticed my sister and my father standing beside Thomas and Nora. My father's arms were crossed and he had a look of pure joy across his face.

"Sweetheart, in my family, the men continue that tradition when they decide to marry. We go through a rite of passage if we want to prove to our elders that we're indeed ready for that step."

I couldn't speak. Here stood the man I had tried so hard to push away, telling myself and everyone who would listen that I could never be what he needed. And here he was telling me he had been proving to his family that he was good enough for me.

"I've spent the past week in the hills surrounding the very village where they grew up and fell in love. I cannot tell you what I've had to endure, as that's a secret I'll pass on to our sons."

I noticed my father chuckle at Patrick's words and Nora kissed Thomas's cheek.

"That first night I saw you, I watched you move around the room and I couldn't take my eyes off you. You had me spellbound from that moment on. You had such confidence and I just knew my father had been right when he said you were perfect."

My eyes then shot directly to Thomas, he simply smiled, and then shrugged his shoulders.

"Then you confirmed my opinion, when you showed up in my office and stood your ground." I blushed at the memory, not one of my better decisions. "But in the end, even knowing who and what I am, you gave me a chance and you let me show you who I could be. And even after you agreed to wear my necklace, you showed grace and courage, and you even called me out when I was acting like an idiot."

I watched as Patrick reached into his jeans pocket and removed a piece of lace cloth. As he unwrapped it, I noticed an appliqué of vines and letters. It was too small for me to make out from where I stood. He then held what looked like a green string.

"I told you he gave her a shamrock when he left her and came to America." He placed the lace on the table beside him. "I have a shamrock from the very same hill where he stood and promised to return to her."

I watched his fingers shake as he came closer to where I stood. His eyes locked with mine as he slowly lowered himself to one knee.

"Christi, I've loved you from the first moment I laid eyes on you. You've made me want to be a better and stronger, and I swear to you that if you'll grant me this one wish, on my birthday, I'll die a happy man. *A bheidh tu posadh liom?*" (Will you marry me?)

I could hear myself gasp as I looked into his deep green eyes. I looked to his outstretched hand that held the tiny shamrock.

"Yes," I heard myself answer as I felt the tears run down my face.

Patrick began to tie the end of the shamrock around my ring finger as the room was once again loud with laughter and applause.

I was quickly surrounded by the women of the room and engulfed in tight hugs. Patrick was quick to interrupt as he placed his dirty hands on my face and looked longingly into my eyes. He slowly leaned in and placed a soft kiss to my lips.

"Christi, as I was sitting in the middle of the shamrocks on the hill, I was asking myself over and over if I was really good enough for you. Then I looked down and I saw this. I think it was a sign."

His left hand was open flat and in the center of his palm was a very old, very distressed three-pence piece. I could barely make out the jack rabbit that sat in the center. I remembered seeing coins like this at my grandmother's house.

"I read somewhere that Irish brides carried a penny in their shoe on their wedding day. Since you've already said yes, I'd love for you to wear this as you walk down the aisle."

Tears were flowing down my face. Patrick was my home and my heart, my every wish come true.

"Patrick, of all the things you've given me, this is the one I'll treasure the most. This is priceless."

He gently kissed my forehead, "I'd hoped you would."

I raised my face to meet his, our eyes locked as well as our hearts, "As will our daughters."

We both smiled at that.

"I'm going to shower for the first time in a week, then I'll come back, and put your real engagement ring on your finger."

I didn't have time to say anything as he dashed out of the room.

"Here, Christi, this is to keep that shamrock in."

Nora then passed me the piece of lace that Patrick had placed on the table. I took a closer look and found it was a beautiful handkerchief. The green vines I had seen were dainty little shamrocks that surrounded the initial "M" embroidered into the lace.

"Her name was Christie, also. The villagers told her he would never return," Nora spoke into my ear. "She worked as a lace maker and when he gave her the shamrock, she made this to keep it in. It's now for you to keep and pass on to your sons."

I looked at the vine that was now wrapped around my ring finger. I could only imagine what it was like for her to wait for a man to make good on his promise while you heard negativity from all those around you.

"I wish that it wouldn't wilt, I'd rather have this, than all the diamonds in the world."

"Shush now, or he'll have a grove of these made so that he can get a fresh one daily. You hang on to it as I have mine. But, Lass, take the diamond he chose for you."

I laughed along with her as she placed the lace in my hand. I would treasure it forever, and if I was lucky enough to be blessed with sons, I would carry on the tradition.

Quicker than I thought possible, Patrick was back and tugging me away from his aunts.

"Are they trying to discourage you as their ancestors did for my great-grandmother?"

I sighed as I slid into his arms. I missed him so much and the feel and smell of my Patrick just made everything better.

"Nothing they could say could change how I feel about you."

"Well, I'm glad to hear that since I have this insanely beautiful ring I want to get on your finger."

I didn't want to move from the safety I found in his arms. I wanted to feel the warmth that radiated from him and bathe in the smell that was now a clean Patrick.

Far sooner than I was comfortable, Patrick released me from his chest and took my hand and carefully removed the shamrock he had so carefully tied around my finger earlier. I would never forget this day. I refused to have one detail removed from my memory.

As he placed the platinum band on my finger, I gasped at the sight of it. Patrick was correct; it was insanely beautiful. Three bands, all connected, with diamonds surrounding each one. The center diamond sat on four silver prongs that hovered over the three diamond-covered bands.

I watched as Patrick then placed a single kiss to the ring.

"Happy birthday, Patrick," I spoke only loud enough for him to hear.

"Best birthday, ever," he responded.

"Really, and I haven't even given you your gift yet," I responded with a wink.

"Oh, really? Saying yes was enough, I assure you."

"I wouldn't be so sure if I were you, Mr. Malloy," I spoke as I moved in closer, pulling his tie so that his body leaned closer to mine.

"I like how you think...Mrs. Malloy," he spoke as he placed tender kisses along my cheek.

Not going to lie...I liked the sound of my future name.

CHAPTER FIFTEEN

When I first thought of the perfect gift to give to Patrick for his birthday, I never once thought it would include saying yes to the most perfect proposal.

I had something a little more personal in mind.

Remaining seated last night was one of the hardest things I had ever had to do in my life. I answered a million questions and hugged and kissed everyone at least twice. Finally, we were able to bid our goodbyes and headed for Patrick's condo.

"So, is my gift bigger than a bread box?"

Patrick had been tossing out question after question as to what I had gotten him as a gift.

"No, it isn't bigger than a bread box, technically."

That was the last question I allowed him to have, before I excused myself to the bathroom. I had a little something to put on I was sure Patrick was going to enjoy.

I turned out the lights in the bathroom, slowly opened the door and peeked out to find Patrick sitting against the headboard. His chest was bare and he looked amazing in his black satin sleep pants, but they were going to be lying on the floor in about thirty seconds. Don't get me wrong, I loved it when he wore those things and walked around the house in them...just not right now.

He glanced up at me with his gorgeous green eyes and his chiseled jaw flexed, making me want to lick it.

I made my way into the light of the room, trying to be as sexy as possible. I watched his eyes as he looked at what I was wearing, the look of surprise spiking his brow as he took it all in. I watched as his pink tongue peeked out and licked his bottom lip...and then he burst out laughing.

"What...you think this is funny?"

"Oh, fuck, Babe, come here," he continued to laugh.

When I really got to thinking about what to get him, knowing he clearly had everything, I knew he couldn't possibly have this.

"Where did you find that?"

"On line, do you like it?"

He continued to laugh as I got closer to the bed. "I'm going to love it more when it's on the floor," his voice was husky and driving me crazy.

"Ugh, Babe. You have to read it…out loud," I said, curling my lip out. I was not certain who was having more fun with this, him or me.

"Oh, Jesus, not the pouty lip," he whined.

"Then read it to me," my voice sounded even whinier.

"Fine. '*Feck, yes, I'm Irish. Wanna see me shillelagh?*'"

"Why yes, Mr. Malloy. As a matter of fact, I do."

"Then by all means, let me introduce the two of you."

His lips were suddenly attached to my neck as he closed the distance between us. By now, Patrick would be able to feel that I wasn't wearing anything under this shirt.

"Is this a shirt you wish to keep?" he growled, his hot breath fanning across my face, desperation saturating his voice.

"It's actually the wrapping to your real gift," I whispered, my voice hoarse with need.

"Good, I never save wrapping paper."

I giggled as he quickly ripped the shirt down the front, pulled it off me and then tossed it across the room. I was suddenly on my back with Patrick's firm body pressed to mine, ending any additional giggles and allowing the moaning to begin.

He was setting me on fire with the feel of his hot skin under my fingertips, the hardness of his erection pressed against my hip, and his firm grip on my naked thigh as he hitched it around his waist, gaining a closer angle to my wet and wanting core.

"My God, you're exquisite," his gruff voice growled against my shoulder.

"Patrick," my voice came out barely a whisper as his thumb pushed between my folds. My lips found purchase on his neck, licking, sucking, and biting, marking him as mine. And after tonight, anyone who saw him would know.

His lips found mine as his tongue suddenly filled my mouth, capturing my own, and claiming it for his pleasure. The taste of him was almost overwhelming and yet I could not get enough. He wanted me as much as I wanted him. Having him gone had only increased my desire for him. This was how it was destined to be.

His left hand had made it to my enlarged clit. He began to circle and tease it, then he flicked it with the tip of his thumb. I cried out and jerked as he continued to circle and flick. Two of his fingers began to make slow and calculated massaging circles up and down my bare lower lips. My sudden climax was strong and nearly painful as my entire body lurched upward.

He moved his hand from my drenched folds and began to slowly trace his way up my body, stopping at my left nipple. With his hand firmly kneading my left breast, his mouth sucked wildly at my right. I would be shocked if he didn't leave a brand of his own. However, as I neared my next orgasm, I couldn't have cared less.

I could not move or speak. I could only feel; feel the moisture between my lower lips double as his efforts increased.

He switched breasts and began to attack the other nipple. Patrick knew exactly what he was doing. He knew what I needed without me asking, which was a good thing since I didn't have the ability to speak as my third orgasm ripped through my body. How many men could say they could give a girl an orgasm just from sucking on her nipples? Yes, my man was good.

"Oh, yes! Patrick…"

I felt his lips form a smile as he left my breasts and traveled slowly to my stomach, taking slow and deliberate nips at my lower pelvis. He raised his head slightly as he kissed just below my belly button, pausing to look at my stomach reverently.

"This is sacred, Christi. Someday it'll hold our babies as they grow."

"You seem very sure of yourself."

"I'm going to give you children, Christi. That's a promise I intend to keep."

He didn't let me respond as he tossed my legs around his neck and delved tongue first into me. My back arched off the bed as he probed even further inside of me, his tongue swirling around maddeningly as he searched for that mythical spot all women were rumored to have.

My reaction to his tongue was enough for him, as he added two fingers and with his free hand, he began to tease my clit. The added pressure of his fingers caused my next orgasm to hit like a tidal wave.

"Motherfucking…!" I couldn't finish as the next orgasm hit me just as hard. I was panting, sweating, swearing like a sailor, and I didn't give a flying fuck as Patrick continued to lick, probe, and suck me into oblivion.

His actions slowed as my legs began to quiver hard. With a final kiss to my clit, he made his way back up to my face. His eyes locked with mine as he hovered over me, his flattened tongue slowly licking my peaked nipple. He kissed each peak as he continued up to kiss my mouth. I had no idea when he had grabbed a condom, maybe he had expected things would lead to where we currently were. The gold foil glistened in the light from the table lamp.

"Didn't think I'd forget, did you?" his voice a mixture of lust and amusement.

I picked up the condom and smiled seductively. "Allow me."

I pushed on his shoulder, encouraging him to lay back. I crawled in between his legs as I grasped his very erect cock in my hand. Turnabout was fair play after all. With a wink and a smile, I ran my tongue from his base to his tip, circling the head and then plunging him deep into my throat.

"Sweet motherfucking…oh, God!" he shouted as I increased the pressure of my suction. I smiled around his cock as I continued to bob up and down, swirling my tongue as I went. Suddenly, his hand reached down and pulled my arm, and thus my body, back up.

"Babe, as fucking good as that feels, I want to be buried inside you for this."

I applied the condom and placed a firm kiss to the latex-covered tip. Placing my hands on his manly shoulders, I slowly lowered myself onto his cock.

All the times before Patrick were faint memories, as I began to grind myself up and down on his shaft. This was his birthday and I wanted him to enjoy this. I let go of his shoulders and placed my hands on my tits. Men were visual creatures and I wanted him to get an eyeful. While my right hand massaged and pinched at my nipples, my left traveled down to my clit and I began to rub it with slow calculated circles.

Patrick's hands firmly gripped my hips and I knew he was enjoying watching me when he began to actually lift me off his cock and slam me back down, his pace speeding up. I watched as his face contorted and I worried that something was wrong. However, my fear left just as quickly as it came as he shouted, "OH. MY. GOD!" Each word accentuated with a hard thrust in between before he came explosively, jerking uncontrollably beneath me before going limp and collapsing into the mattress. "So that's what heaven feels like."

I stayed atop him as he continued to twitch inside of me. I slowly kissed his forehead, loving the salty taste of him. I couldn't help myself and giggled as he began to lick a bead of sweat that was falling between my breasts.

"I love you," I smiled down at him. And I really did.

We were lying in each other's arms a while later when a question came to mind. "Patrick?"

"Hmm?"

"I need to ask you a question and I really want an answer."

"Yes, Baby, I'd be happy to go again."

I turned my face to look at him, "Later, this is important." I raised up to face him; I really wanted an answer to my question. "Why in the world did you call me Legs?"

He chuckled as he kissed my chin, "Truthfully?"

"No, fucker, lie to me. Of course I want the truth."

"The night of the wedding, you were standing talking to Charlotte and I watched you scratch an itch you had on your ankle. I followed that ankle to your knee and then to the hem of your skirt. You have the most beautiful set of legs I've ever seen," he smiled, his face so loving I could easily get lost in his eyes.

"That's seriously sweet," I kissed his chest. He began to chuckle. "And it's complete bullshit, isn't it?"

He was laughing now. "Fuck yes! I called you Legs because I wanted to know what was between them."

Before I could get angry with him, he flipped me on my back and dove back in tongue first between my legs. Well, now he had his answer. The man had a very talented tongue and I would gladly stand on the highest mountain and shout to the world that I was one lucky bitch.

Patrick and I stayed in bed the entire weekend. He preferred to take me in his bed, not to say he didn't pin me against the wall by the elevator yesterday after dinner was delivered, as well. I smiled at the memory of him waking me very early in the morning on Saturday by sucking on my nipple. As he slowly turned me onto my back, he reached for the condom that was conveniently lying on his pillow. I smiled as I shook my head and took the condom from him, tossing it across the room.

"No more condoms," I whispered to him.

The look of confusion on his face was nearly comical. However, that lasted long enough for him to quickly bury himself to the hilt inside me. I had forgotten how much a condom restricted and confined and I wasn't prepared for the sheer true-to-life size of Patrick. I almost felt like a virgin all over again.

As I crawled into my car on Monday morning, I winced as I felt the muscles in my thighs and nether regions protesting. It had definitely been a good weekend.

My sister would be dropping Abby off so she could go take care of some honeymoon preparations. I had embarrassed her to death last week when I asked Dillion if he preferred bare, triangle, or landing strip. He had looked at me confused while thought about my question. Finally, the light bulb went off in his head and he requested bare.

"Auntie Christi, look at what my daddy gave me!"

I was so lost in my thoughts that I didn't hear the door open. Abby was running full steam around my desk, her eyes were big and bright with joy. Once she was standing directly beside me, she showed me the beautiful shamrock necklace Dillion had given her.

"Isn't it pretty?" Her voice raised three octaves as she bounced in place. I couldn't describe the feeling I got when I heard Abby refer to Dillion as her daddy. But that was exactly what he was. That little girl had him so tightly wrapped around her whole hand, forget the little finger. She had taken total possession of his heart. "He says it's for good luck."

I smiled as I kissed her pink cheek. "It's very pretty, Baby."

"And look what Uncle Patrick gave me."

This took me aback. Patrick had given her something and he hadn't told me. However, there on her tiny wrist was a miniature diamond bracelet that matched mine and Shannon's.

"Uncle Patrick said I was his perfect princess and that all princesses deserved to have diamonds."

Uncle Patrick would certainly be hearing from Auntie Christi later.

"I think it's even prettier than mine, Abby."

She only giggled as she danced around the room.

Shannon and Frankie walked into my office together, laughing and whispering about something. Shannon took one look at me and her eyes went wide.

"Holy...S-H-I-T!" She pointed her index finger at me. With little ears around, Shannon and I had become very good at spelling out the bad words. It was comical when Abby would try it and just spout out random letters.

"Frankie, that's the face of a woman who's been well f-u-c-k-e-d, and by a man who clearly knows how."

I was certain my face was crimson, but I just grinned. "I'm certain I have no idea what you're talking about."

"Oh, don't play coy, Christi, if Dillion had given me a rock like yours, I'd still be riding him."

"Why would you ride Daddy, Mommy?"

Shannon had also become quick on the uptake, "Because he likes to play horsey with Mommy."

"Oh," her little brows wrinkled in the middle. "Is his horsey named Oh God, Mommy?"

Poor Frankie was doing everything she could to keep from bursting out laughing. Shannon was quick to keep a straight face as she responded, "He has a couple of names for his horsey, Sunshine, but they're a secret so let's not tell Daddy we know about his pretend horsey, okay?"

Abby shrugged her shoulders and went back to dancing around the room.

"Good morning, Ladies!" Paige shouted as she walked into the room.

"Good morning, Paige. How are you?" I smiled and rose to hug her.

"I hear a certain man is smiling from ear to ear this morning."

"He's not the only one," Shannon quipped with a smirk.

"I'm sorry, you'll have to excuse me, I have to go over the flower order for the wedding this weekend and I also have to meet with the Birches to finalize the cake selections for their wedding," Frankie smiled as she turned to leave.

"All right, Frankie. I'll be out of the office for a little while so call me on my cell if you need me," I instructed her.

"No problem, Christi, I'll be here." Frankie replied as she exited the room, winking at Shannon as she left.

"Auntie Christi, what are we going to do today?"

"Well, what do you want to do today?"

"Wait," Paige interjected. I looked toward her quick-moving form as she made her way to Abby, "How about you and I go have our nails done so Auntie Christi can get some work done?"

Thank God for Paige, Shannon's wedding was in six days and I still had several things to do.

Abby was so easily pleased as she ran around the room shouting, "Yeah!"

Two hours later, I had finished my remaining tasks for Shannon's wedding. Paige had texted me that she, Abby, and Nora were headed to lunch and then doing some shopping.

I had half a mind to see if Patrick was busy.

With my phone in hand, I was almost ready to hit send when I heard it, a thump coming from the room behind my office. I listened closely to see if I had been imagining it, when I heard it twice more. I slowly made my way to the storage room to investigate.

The door was wide open and the overhead light was illuminating two figures against the wall. I was so shocked at what I was seeing that I stood cemented in my tracks. The blonde-haired woman was shoved against the wall as the darker-haired man kissed her passionately. His hands cupped her face as he consumed her mouth with his. My hand went to my mouth to prevent any sounds of surprise from alarming the couple.

"*Shuu, caithfidh tu' a behith ciucin.*" (Shush, you have to be quiet.)

"Oh," The girl's quivering voice responded.

"*Mo ghra', fhois agat do mo challin cert?*" (My love, you know you're my girl, right?)

"I think you just called me your girl, is that right?" The blonde was now looking into his eyes as he continued to cup her face.

"*Caith me' dul, ta' me' garde Ms. Christi. Ba mhaith liom tu' roinnr a'it speisialta.*" (I have to go now, I'm guarding Ms. Christi. I want to take you somewhere special.)

"I have no idea what you just said, but my answer is yes. It'll always be yes." I had to hide my gasp as the couple parted and for the first time, I was able to see who they were.

I watched as Frankie reached up and gently kissed Shamus on the lips again, their hands falling as she moved to exit the room. I quickly and quietly went back to my desk. Frankie came in a half second behind me, startled as she came into my office, surprised I was still here.

"Oh, God," her eyes were huge as she realized the possibility that I had overheard what had just happened. "I...I..."

I could only smile at her. Shamus was a very handsome man. Even though he was no Patrick, he was easy on the eyes nonetheless.

"Sit, Frankie, we need to chat." Her face fell as she quietly took the chair that faced my desk, her fingers playing with an imaginary string on her skirt. "Frankie, would you mind telling me what that was all about?"

She continued to stare at her lap as if it held the answers to the mysteries of the universe. She slowly took in a deep breath as she began to lift her eyes to mine.

"Well, you see..." she crossed her legs and looked everywhere except at me. She was nervous, I fully expected it, but it was unwarranted. "Christi, he's so wonderful. At first, he was just trying to teach me Gaelic."

I looked at her bewildered. "Why?"

"Why what?"

"Why was he teaching you Gaelic? He barely speaks English."

"Because, I fell in love with him and I wanted to be able to tell him." I smiled as she continued. "He's always been nice to me, even when I was Harley. He never tried anything with me, like some of the other guys. He gave me a flower one night for no reason, just being sweet. He even rejected me when I tried to suck him off for doing it."

I remained silent as she continued.

"I don't know when it happened, but it did, I've been taking lessons from him for a while. He's never pressured me for anything and he treats me like..."

I watched as a single tear ran down her cheek. "Like what, Frankie?"

"Like a real lady," her words were slightly above a whisper as tears continued to roll down her face. I smiled as her words lingered in the room, her sniffles the only noise that remained.

My voice was soft when I spoke again, "Isn't that what you wanted, Frankie?" She nodded gently, her head still bowed. "Then what's the problem? Why are you crying?"

"Because it's probably going to get him in trouble with Mr. Malloy and me fired from my first real job."

"Why, Frankie? Has Patrick ever said you couldn't date his men?" She shook her head no. "Have I ever said you couldn't date on your own personal time?" She, again, shook her head no. "Then I fail to see the problem, my Dear."

Her head snapped up in my direction. "Do you mean that, Christi? I can still see him?"

I laughed as I nodded my head, "Of course, he's a wonderful man. You have my blessing, *and* my encouragement." Her smile now larger than life, her body vibrating.

"I was so scared that this was all a huge dream and I was going to wake up and still be the disgusting whore I was before."

It was my turn to shed a tear as her words hit my heart.

"You won't regret this, Christi, I promise. I'll be professional when I'm at work, I swear. You'll be so proud of me."

I smiled as I stood and rounded my desk, pulling her into a hug. "I already am, Frankie, I already am."

We stood for a few moments just embracing each other. She was a new person, a happy person, and everyone deserved a second chance. Frankie had taken that and run with it. She was finally a true lady. She let me go and said she had a million things to do. I smiled and waved her off.

"Oh, Frankie, one last thing before you leave."

She turned back to me, her face covered in a smile. "Yes, Christi?"

"He said you were his girl and that he wanted to take you someplace nice. I think you should call him and tell him, *'Dinne'ar ag se', i dont mo a'bheith de'anach."*

She looked at me confused, "What's that?"

"Dinner at my house, six o'clock, and don't be late."

She repeated what I told her and dashed off to her office.

Paige and Nora met Shannon and I with Abby at a restaurant a few blocks from Patrick's condo. Dillion stopped by and took Shannon and Abby home, as Paige and I were talking about her wedding. Nora was busy talking on her phone to someone back in Ireland, and by the tone of the conversation, it sounded like it was related to the lace incident.

By the time I got home, it was after eleven. I showered and then crawled into bed. Patrick had called me earlier and said he couldn't join us for dinner, but would see me in the morning.

As I lay in my bed, tossing and turning, my mind went back to the weekend I had spent in Patrick's bed. It was more than just the amazing sex; it was just being with him. After an hour, I conceded defeat, flung the covers back, packed a bag, and then headed to Patrick's condo.

All the lights were off when I got there. The rational side of me knew I should have called him first, he was a mob boss after all and he had guns all over the condo. But I didn't.

I made my way back to his bedroom where I found a sleeping Patrick flat on his back. The covers rested low on his hips, leaving me a clear view of his bare chest. I stripped off all of my clothes and slid into bed with him. I lay my head on his chest and felt his arm come around me, hugging me to him.

"Not that I mind this, but what brought this on?" His voice was pure sex and comfort rolled into one.

"I just needed to be near you," I spoke into his chest as his fingers combed through my hair.

"You don't need an excuse, you should just move all of your things over here and stay here every night."

I closed my eyes and contemplated how I would say this without pissing him off. "I don't want to live here, Patrick, I want a real home."

We lay in silence, my words hanging heavily over us.

"You're right, this isn't a home. Once Shannon's wedding is over, I want to start looking at houses. One that we can agree on, one that I can carry you across the threshold of, and bring our babies home to."

I smiled as his words resonated. He understood; this condo was his office, not a place to build our lives.

"Another thing, I want you to stop taking your birth control once we're married. I want babies with you, Christi, and I want to start trying before the ink is dry on the marriage license."

I smiled into his chest again, placing a kiss to his skin above his heart. "I can't wait to see how protective you are with our daughters."

Patrick took in a deep breath, "We're only having sons, twelve of them."

I didn't acknowledge his statement. I filled him in on Frankie and Shamus. I made certain to voice how happy I was with the couple and I hoped he would be, too. No more was spoken as I drifted off to sleep. My world was perfect and although I had fought against being with Patrick, I was glad I had lost.

CHAPTER SIXTEEN

"Oh, yes! Right fucking there..."

Patrick had woken me before the alarm went off. I didn't mind since he used his tongue.

"Oh...please...hunnnahh..."

With a mischievous laugh, he stopped licking my clit and asked, "Please what?"

I threw my head in his direction, my hair flying like a tidal wave across my face.

"Patrick Shane Malloy, you return that fucking tongue back to where you had it or so help me."

His laughing continued as he winked at me and then lowered his head back between my thighs. "You put a cheap ring on a girl's finger and she gets very demanding all of the sudden."

Three orgasms, a shower, and a blow job later, I was helping him tie his tie. "So, we never did set a date for this wedding you're forcing me into," he teased.

I locked eyes with him in the mirror and gave him the look. You know, the one that says be careful buddy, or your right hand is going to be your only friend for a while.

"No, we didn't," I responded as I cinched up his tie a little too snugly. "I called Father Murphy and he's ready to start Pre-Cana classes."

"All right, let's see..." I pulled Patrick's phone from the nightstand and touched the screen for his calendar, "Well, this weekend is clearly out...it's my sister's wedding." He only chuckled. "And your sister's is just a few weeks after, so the best day according to your crazy schedule is October thirteenth."

I then lifted my eyes from the screen to find him smiling at me, "October thirteenth it is."

I phoned my dad and asked him to meet me at our diner. With my wedding date now set, I needed to get a few minor details out of the way. I was surprised to find my dad hadn't arrived yet, but Patrick was sitting at our usual table. I couldn't help my smile as I made my way over to join him.

"Did you miss me?" I chuckled as I placed a kiss on his lips.

"Your dad invited me, actually, and yes, I did miss you"

Doris was on her game this morning as she placed a cup of hot coffee on the table in front of me.

"Your usual, Sweetheart?" Doris's friendly voice questioned.

"No, just coffee today," I smiled as I looked at her.

She then turned to Patrick and began to refill his cup, "Anything for you, Patrick?"

I was taken aback by the way she used his first name. I only knew of a handful of people who had.

"No, Doris, I'm meeting my future father-in-law, I'm a little nervous this morning," he chuckled as he winked in my direction.

"Oh, Patrick, that's not nice. Matthew's a wonderful man and you know it."

"Yes, Ma'am, I was only trying to rile Christi up this morning."

"Better be careful with that, she'll soon sleep beside you," Doris teased as she began to walk away. "Oh, before I forget, thank you again for your help with Ian," Doris added and then walked away.

I looked at Patrick who was sporting a happy grin; I had to know what that was all about. I wasn't certain how much he would tell me about his personal business, though. Patrick must have picked up on my curiosity and spoke before I could ask.

"Since you're going to be my wife very soon, you should know that I, or rather we, are helping Doris's son with his medical school tuition."

I could have been told the sky was green at this point and I would have had an easier time believing that, than what I had just heard coming from my fiancé.

"Are you kidding me?" I stammered before I could think.

"No…"

"So you're making like…like…one of those loan shark loan things? You know, all money plus interest, due in ninety days?"

Patrick began to laugh at me. Really laugh.

"Love, but not everything I do is for profit. I try to help out the kids in the neighborhood that are trying to better themselves. Ian was always helping out the other neighborhood kids, too. When Doris told me he'd lost his scholarship due to budget cuts, I stepped in."

I remembered Charlotte telling me Patrick donated millions every year to charity. I leaned toward him and beckoned him closer with my index finger. He smiled his signature smile as he leaned in.

"I think I just fell a lot more in love with you, Patrick Malloy." Then I kissed his lips.

"You know I'm only allowing that because of the ring you placed on her finger."

Even the sound of my father's voice could do nothing to make me break the kiss. I slowly backed away and proceeded to look directly into Patrick's eyes. I would always remember the way he looked at me— loving, cherished, devoted. He never had to tell me how he felt, his eyes told me everything.

"Good morning, Daddy," I said, my eyes never leaving Patrick's.

"Good morning," my father spoke as he sat down beside me, kissing my cheek as he settled.

Doris didn't miss a beat as she placed a cup of coffee on the table in front of him.

"Thank you, Doris," Matthew and Patrick stated at the same time.

I let my dad get a sip of his coffee before I began to question why he wanted Patrick here. I needed to talk with him about how we were going to pay for this wedding and honestly, I didn't want Patrick to hear this conversation.

"So, Dad, not that I'm complaining, but why does Patrick need to be here for our meeting?"

I took another sip of my coffee as Patrick reached across the table and took my free hand in his. Something was going on, and by the looks on their faces, I might not want to hear it.

"I asked Patrick to join us because I have some news and I'm not certain how you'll respond to it."

Patrick gripped my hand tighter as I tried to turn my body toward my father. I could feel the anxiety begin to travel up my chest and into my throat. Was something wrong with my father? Was he ill, or had he gotten into trouble?

"For the past year I've been seeing someone—romantically."

And just like the minute you get your period after having had unprotected sex, relief washed over me and I let out the breath I had been holding.

I smacked my father on the arm as I scolded him for worrying me. "Don't you ever scare me like that again! I thought you were dying by the way you were talking."

Both men began to chuckle as I took another sip of coffee.

"Well, you may want to kill me when you find out who it is."

Cue the return of the anxiety. *I think I'm going to kill him…she's married.*

"Before I tell you who it is, I want you to know that I…we didn't plan on falling in love, but we did and I've asked her to move in with me. She isn't ready to get married just yet, but I'm willing to wait for her to be." I looked to Patrick and he squeezed my hand tighter. "She wanted to come today and be here with me, but I told her this needed to come from me."

Doris chose that moment to bring my father his breakfast plate.

"Thank you, Doris."

I watched as my father looked at his over-easy eggs, took a deep breath, and then turned his face to me, "For the past year, I've been seeing Charlotte."

I could have sworn I heard him say Charlotte, but that was crazy…

"I love her, Christi. She makes me feel good, she makes me want to live again."

I loved my father and I loved Charlotte. I began to really think about the past year. Had Charlotte acted any different? She didn't really talk about her personal life, now I knew why.

"She wanted to tell you so many times and I asked her not to. If you're mad, be mad at me, not her."

"Babe, you're not saying anything. Talk to me, please," Patrick spoke gently to me.

I took in a deep breath and then winked at Patrick where my father couldn't see. My father was a grown man and if Charlotte made him happy, then who was I to stand in their way. That didn't change the fact that I was about to give him shit because he had scared me earlier.

"Dad, are you kidding me? Charlotte is my age. You're old enough to be her father for Christ sakes."

I looked to Patrick who was trying very hard to keep from laughing. He knew I was just playing with my dad.

"I know, and don't think for one-second that I didn't fight these feelings I have for her, because I did. I mean she may want to have children someday and I can't give them to her. My girls are grown for Pete's sakes."

Okay, so that pulled at my heart a little, not going to lie.

"I've given myself a thousand reasons why this relationship is a bad idea, but the one thing neither one of us could ignore was our love for each other."

I looked at my dad for a second, really looked at him. He was happy with one of my best friends in the world and I knew she would take care of him.

"Dad, honestly, I'm happy if you are," I leaned over and kissed his cheek just as Patrick's phone began to ring.

"Well, I'm certainly glad you were wrong about her reaction, Matthew," Patrick chuckled as he tossed some money on the table and stood up. "I'm sorry to leave, but I have an issue that needs my attention. Can we have dinner tonight? My place?" He leaned over and kissed my lips.

"Dinner sounds great," I smiled at his beautiful face. "I love you," I said kissing him again.

"I love you, right back," he grinned and returned my kiss.

"All right, all right. I have my limits, even with that ring," my dad teased as Patrick continued to kiss me.

I watched as Patrick walked away and toward the door. He stopped briefly and gave Doris a kiss to her cheek. She laughed at something he said and then he was out the door with a wave and a wink.

It struck me as so odd how it wasn't that long ago that I had thought the worst of him. I had judged him by society's standards and that wasn't fair. I was not naive enough to believe that he was this wonderful all of the time. However, I just chose to concentrate on this side of him and let the other show only to the people who needed to see it.

"So, Patrick tells me you start Pre-Cana classes tomorrow."

And just like that, my father was ready for a new subject.

"Yes, we set a date of October thirteenth so that doesn't give us a lot of time."

"And Father Murphy is all right with that?"

"Dad, you should never doubt the kind of charm Patrick has."

"I wouldn't know firsthand, but I've heard in passing," He chuckled as he gave my shoulder nudge.

"So what was your reason for needing to see me this morning?"

I took another sip of my quickly cooling coffee. Doris lifted the pot she was holding, silently asking if I needed a refill. I nodded my head and she began to walk toward our table.

"Well, I know you're less than a week away from your first daughter's wedding and then I announce that I'll be getting married in a few months."

Doris arrived to fill up my cup.

"Thank you," I told her as she was about to walk away.

"Yes, so what's your point?"

I sighed and set my cup on the table. The thought of what I needed to discuss with him had kept me awake for most of the night.

"Well, I have a good idea of what Shannon's wedding is costing you, I also know that with me marrying Patrick, the cost of ours will make the cost Shannon's seem like pocket change."

My dad lowered his own cup and looked at me like he knew I had more to say.

When I didn't continue, he probed me. "I don't get what you're trying to tell me."

I looked at him like he had three heads.

"Dad…my wedding is going to cost both arms and legs. The guest list is going to be huge. Even with my connections, this is going to cost us a ton of money. Now, I've got some money saved up…"

"Stop right there, Christi. If you think for one second that I can't give *both* of my daughter the weddings of their dreams…"

"No, Dad, this isn't going to be the wedding of my dreams, it's going to be the weddingI'm required to have. I won't know most of the people there, and the majority of them will have a record that's longer than the guest list," I said the latter in a hushed voice.

"Christi, how much money do I have in my pocket right now?"

I looked at him with confusion. "I…I have no idea."

"That's right, you have no knowledge of my financial status. I could have millions in the bank and you'd never know. Don't decide things for me that aren't your decision to make."

My father again correct. I had assumed he couldn't afford things. I left for my office that day with strict instructions to have anything I wanted for the wedding.

Shannon's wedding was in less than a week and there were so many details that remained unfinished. As her maid of honor, it was my job to get them completed. I was just about to call the florist when a knock at my door sounded. Frankie stood with her clipboard in hand and grimace on her face.

"Sorry, Ms. Christi, but you have a visitor."

I looked to Frankie.

"Who is it?" I questioned her softly.

"Sophia Porchelli."

What in the world could she want?

"Thank you, Frankie, send her in."

I rose from my chair and checked my makeup. I had no clue why I felt the need to look pretty for her. I knew she had a history with Patrick. I didn't have details and honestly didn't want any.

I expected Sophia to be dressed to the nines and be either drunk or stoned, based on past history. She didn't disappoint as she swept into my office. Her red suit was definitely not off-the-rack, and her shoes and handbag I knew had to cost more than my car. Her beautiful long hair was bone straight down her slender back and moved as she walked. Sophia Porchelli was without a doubt a beautiful girl.

He oversized sunglasses hid her eyes from me as she continued into the room, only removing them when she set her handbag in the chair. I needed to be careful with this one. Just because her tongue didn't fork didn't make her any less of a snake.

"Christi, I just heard the news and had to come over and give our congratulations."

In all my years of working alongside Charlotte, I had developed a sixth sense, if you will. I could read people with pretty good accuracy and tell if they were sincere. Sophia was after something and it didn't take a rocket scientist to figure out what she wanted…Patrick.

All right, bitch, you want to dance, let's dance.

"Oh, thank you. We're so excited and we can't wait for our big day."

She stepped closer and wrapped me in a hug. The smell of her overpriced perfume was barely covering the smell of whatever alcohol she had drunk this morning for breakfast.

"I'm so happy that Patrick has chosen such a beautiful girl to marry. I was worried for a while that he'd never settle down, always with a different girl. Now that'll all change, at least I hope he changes…for you I mean."

Ladies and gentleman, there it was, the snake in the grass. She had just taken her first strike. But I had dealt with my fair share of snakes.

"Well, I certainly hope he never changes. I like him just the way he is."

I could see the shock in her eyes. I was giving her a challenge.

"Really, Christi, you'll turn a blind eye…"

"And let him have a goomah? Well, considering he *is* Irish, that would be a mot, but…"

Her face was priceless. She actually believed I would let this happen, perhaps let her warm his bed or polish his knob on occasion.

"I'm certain you have some personal experience with that." My words flowed like honey, dripping sticky and sweet.

"Oh, you misunderstood me..."

"Oh, no, I hear you loud and clear. You came here today hoping to plant a little seed of doubt in my head. Perhaps tell me how you had this long, torrid love affair with Patrick, which I know is bullshit by the way."

I remained calm as I continued to fire holes in her plans. She wouldn't scare me, she was nothing to me.

She began to backpedal.

"Christi, I only came to congratulate you. I would never speak of intimate things that happened between Patrick and I, that's water under the bridge."

"Sophia, is your ass jealous of the shit that comes out of your mouth? Did you seriously think I'd believe you had any kind of relationship with him?"

You could see the fury building in her eyes. She honestly thought I would cower in the corner at the possibility that he had been with her.

"No, I understand you perfectly and I do appreciate you stopping by, but as you can imagine, I have a long list of things to accomplish today and I really need to get to them."

"Oh, yes, but of course."

I watched as she gathered her purse and replaced her sunglasses. I walked with her to the front lobby of my office. Just as she was about to open the door to leave, she turned and asked one last question.

"When is the wedding by the way?"

"October thirteenth," I gladly replied.

"Hmm, Friday the thirteenth? You seem to play with fate. You do know that's considered a bad luck day?" She smirked as she turned and walked out. I was suddenly regretting being unable to slam the door. It would have looked amazing smacking soundly off her overly-rounded ass.

As I sat in the middle of Patrick's living room, I poured us each a glass of wine. Dinner was amazing and I loved being with him like this.

"So, I forgot to ask, how was your day?"

Patrick had brought takeout from the deli around the corner. We were both so hungry that we ate in comfortable silence.

"Well, I got a visit from Sophia today."

Patrick looked to me quickly, shock on his face.

"Sophia came to your office?"

"Yep." I popped the 'p'. "She wanted to congratulate us."

I gave him a look of...I got this.

"What kind of bullshit did she spew?"

"I didn't let her. She's a snake, Patrick. I know this. Her visit was pointless."

Patrick took my glass from my hand and gently placed it on the end table. His face was filled with pride as he slowly wrapped his arms around me and lowered me to the floor. Our eyes never left each other's as he gently caressed my face.

"My father was right, you are perfect for me."

CHAPTER SEVENTEEN

With Paige's bridal shower in my rear view mirror, I took my planner hat off and put on my sister-of-the-bride hat. Patrick assured me he would look after Dillion during his bachelor party. Shannon was worried it would end up like the movies, complete with the hangover from hell. Patrick gave his word he would keep things tame. I told him he was full of shit...he only chuckled back at me.

Shannon chose to stay with me that night. We wanted to have one final night of sister time. So with pajamas on and old eighties movies in the DVD player, we made a huge pallet in the living room floor and had margaritas. I had never laughed or cried so much in my entire life.

She told me how much she admired my free spirit and my dedication to our family. She also told me to never change when it came to Patrick, not to let him wear the pants alone.

It was shortly after one o'clock in the morning when my cell phone began to ring, scaring me. I answered trepidatiously. "Hello?"

"Babe, what's wrong with me?" Patrick slurred into the phone.

"Patrick...what is it? What's wrong?"

"I'm surrounded by naked women and all I can think about is how they don't look like you."

"Patrick, are you drunk?"

"Oh, Love, I passed drunk a long time ago."

I could hear cheering in the background, "GO! GO! GO!"

"Do I even want to know what you're doing in a room full of naked women?"

"I'm missing you, that's what."

"Babe, you just saw me this morning."

"So? Doesn't take away the fact that I miss you, can you just be in my bed when I get home?"

"Not when you've just left a room full of naked women."

"I love you. Do you know how much I really love you, Christi?"

"I love you, too, Patrick."

I said goodnight and ended the call. Shannon had fallen asleep while I was on the phone with Patrick. I pulled the blanket off the couch and covered my sister's sleeping body.

~*~

I was determined that Shannon's wedding day be perfect. I had everything planned out. First, she would soak in a tub filled with bubbles and rose petals. Second, she would have her own hairstylist and makeup artist; I didn't want her to feel rushed.

Shannon had chosen red and white as her wedding colors. All of her bridesmaid's dresses were red with very dainty white appliqués. Shannon's dress was pure white with a red sash that wrapped around her waist. She chose a cathedral-length veil and red roses to carry in her bouquet. I was honestly shocked as her favorite color was pink.

Two of Shannon's attendants tried to get into a heated argument, but I put a quick stop to it. I had worked my ass off to make sure everything was perfect and nothing was going to tarnish this memory for my sister. When we began to plan this day, Nora tried to get a close friend of the family who was a wedding planner to do it so I would be free to just enjoy the day, but she was already booked. She assured me that she would plan mine so I wouldn't have to do it myself.

As I stood in front of my sister, making sure her dress was just right, I looked into her eyes. She was happy, truly happy, and that was all I had ever wanted for her.

"I love you, never forget that," Shannon whispered.

"I love you, too."

I felt a soft hand brush my bare shoulder and I turned my attention to the owner of that hand to find Frankie standing there. "I'm sorry, Christi, but there's a situation in the front of the church you need to come see," Frankie whispered with the look of pure panic. I motioned for her to lead the way as I told Shannon's bridesmaids to keep Shannon inside the room.

As I made my way to the front doors, I passed a number of Patrick's men; I had never seen any emotion on any of their faces until this moment. As I placed my hand on the door, I heard it.

"I'm her fucking Mother! I demand you let me by!"

It had been too many years to count since I had last heard that voice, but it was one I never forgot. There standing at the bottom of the concrete steps was the woman who gave birth to Shannon and me, Morgan.

Poor Shamus and Tonto stood still as statues as she continued to hurl swear words at them, demanding to be let in. Dillion had been very firm on the guest list. He wanted this day to be perfect as well, although neither one of us thought *she* would make an appearance.

I placed my hand on Shamus's broad shoulders and asked, "*Cad cosu'il le bheith ar an bhfadhb anseo?*" (What seems to be the problem here?)

Shamus turned to face me and responded, "She say she Mother."

I did a double take at Shamus; he had spoken English. Granted, it was broken, but it was English nonetheless.

"Shamus, I'm so proud of you!" My screaming egg donor was momentarily forgotten as I leaned over and kissed his cheek. His smile was electric and he blushed as he ducked his head.

My smile faded as I turned back to the issue. "What are you doing here?" I spoke through clenched teeth.

"Don't you use that tone with me, Christi. I'm still your Mother."

I closed the distance between us, my nose less than an inch from hers as I snarled my words at her. "Oh, no you fucking don't," my hazel eyes locked with hers. "You don't get to claim that fucking title. You gave it up a long fucking time ago."

My chest was heaving with my panting breath; I could feel the heat of my anger rising from my very soul. "Where the fuck were you when she was sick with the chicken pox and didn't get to see the lunar eclipse?"

When we were little girls, we loved to watch the stars and at one point, Shannon had wanted to work for NASA. Dad had bought us each a telescope and we could tell you anything you wanted to know about the planets. When Shannon got the chicken pox, she couldn't go outside and it just so happened that a solar eclipse occurred. She was inconsolable.

"Where were you when she had to get ten stitches from falling out of a tree when the neighbor's dog chased us?"

The dog was huge and it got out of the fence one day. Mr. Fitzpatrick was so scared that he had called an ambulance for her. Her treatment had been delayed because dad was on a stakeout and we had no other parent available to give permission for treatment.

"How about when she got her first period and hid under the kitchen sink because she thought she was dying....tell me, where the fuck were you!"

My breathing was labored and I was shaking from head to toe. She had left us—no goodbye, no kiss my ass, nothing.

"Where were you when she screamed in labor with her first baby for sixteen hours? Where were you when we buried our big sister? You remember her, don't you? Did you go to the hotel and identify her dead body? Did you?" I screamed at her.

"He gave me money, did he tell you that? Your father, he gave me a lot of money."

Her words were slurred, she was drunk, I caught the stench of it in that moment.

"But you took it, didn't you?"

Her expression was one of shock, she couldn't respond.

"Christi, is everything all right?"

I turned to see Patrick standing beside Shamus and Tonto. As I looked past him, I noticed quite a large crowd had gathered on the steps. Allyson and Paige stood side by side glaring at Morgan, while Frankie had kicked off her shoes, ready to throw down if necessary. My girls had my back.

I looked back to Patrick, "Yes, just let me get rid of this piece of trash."

As I turned back to her, I noticed a black sedan sitting parked across the street. The windows were rolled up, but I could clearly make out someone sitting inside.

I raised my left hand, my engagement ring glistening in the bright sunlight. "Morgan, do you see this ring?" I moved my hand closer to her face, her eyes grew huge as she took in its size and brilliance. "I'm going to marry the man who gave me this ring, and I'll give that same man children." I lowered my left hand so she had nothing to distract her from hearing what I had to say. "I would kill him with my bare fucking hands if he *ever* tried to take my children from me."

She tried to speak, but I cut her off.

"He's one of the deadliest men in this fucking town and I would kill him dead if he ever tried to separate me from my fucking children," the last three words were pronounced very sharply and with emphasis on each word. "There isn't enough money in the entire world that would be enough to pay me to stay away from my children. You sold me and my sisters like we were nothing, and now that's exactly what you are to me, nothing. Tonto, get this piece of shit out of my face and make certain she doesn't return. She's not welcome here."

"Yes, Ma'am."

I didn't listen when Morgan tried to respond. I heard the sound of a car engine start and I turned just as Morgan got inside the black sedan.

"Follow it," I heard Patrick command as I grabbed his hand and walked back into the church.

I watched my father walk Shannon down the aisle. Huge tears rested just on the edge of his eyelids as he kissed her cheek, and then placed her hand in Dillion's. It was then I noticed Patrick sitting on the second row. His eyes locked with mine, *I love you* silently spoken, and a wink to seal it.

As I looked around the church, I smiled as I remembered Charlotte's scolding that I hadn't attended mass in a very long time, while Patrick and his family were faithful mass attendees. That had changed for me as well; I was now sitting on Patrick's left every time we attended together.

Father Murphy had done an amazing job, and as I watched my sister turn to face her guests, I could only smile as I thought it wouldn't be much longer until it was my turn.

As we posed for picture after picture, I couldn't stop looking at Patrick, who sat patiently across the courtyard. I remembered the first time I saw him in a tux, how he carried himself, how he had owned the room.

Once the final photo was taken, Dillion asked to have a few minutes alone with Shannon before the reception. I made use of the time by crossing the yard and launching myself into Patrick's awaiting arms.

"Mmm, you do know that it's tradition for the maid of honor and the best man to hook up later?"

I chuckled as I pulled back. "Is that so? Well, that's a tradition I'll be breaking. Did you see the best man?"

Travis was Dillion's older brother and his best man. Last night at the rehearsal dinner. he had told me, in no uncertain terms, that he was very interested in me. Patrick of course had made it known to everyone that I was not available. Not that I would have gone for Travis, he was just…gross.

"Good thing, I'd be breaking him otherwise," Patrick's husky voice vibrated in my ear.

"I think after last night, the entire city knows we're together."

He openly smiled at that.

"Christi, this dress is absolutely beautiful on you." His fingers danced across the top of the delicate flowers that were stitched on the side of my right breast. "It'll be even more beautiful on the floor of our condo later," he whispered as his teeth came down sharply on my earlobe.

I dug my nails into the material of his tux and closed my eyes as I pressed my torso into his chest. "You have no idea how dangerously close to losing control I am right now," My voice shook with want.

"Your office is three blocks away; I think you left the coffee machine on this morning." His husky voice suggested in my ear.

"I think you're right, that could be very dangerous."

The lights in my office were off when we stumbled through the door. We didn't waste time in correcting that as my back was slammed into the wall behind my desk.

"Babe, my sister will kill me if I ruin this dress before the reception."

Patrick sucked in a huge breath as he lifted me onto my desk, scattering all the papers that lay in his way. "These won't matter then." I gasped when he ripped my panties off my body. "Babe, I can't be gentle, I need...need you right fucking now," he hissed, his words rushed and spoken between clenched teeth.

"Who said you had to be?"

The next thing I knew, my back was against my filing cabinet and I could feel the cold metal against my bare shoulder. Patrick's cock was suddenly buried so deeply that I cried out in surprise. His thrusts were hard and he was bouncing me against the filing cabinet, but I just couldn't make myself care. I wanted this, I wanted him. I didn't need gentle right now, I needed pure raw fucking. Patrick certainly didn't disappoint.

"Oh, yes, Baby! Come on, Christi, fucking come!" He demanded as his hips continued to pound into mine.

I could feel that wonderful tidal wave building and just when I thought he would come before me, he shifted his hips and began thrusting at a different angle.

I cried into his ear as I came hard.

"Wow, I'm never going to look at my office the same," I said between pants.

"Oh, yeah? Mine is next."

Waiting to go into the reception, Travis took the opportunity to try,one last time, to make certain I knew I had options. I took one look at Tonto and Brandon who stood in the corner. Tonto had a hold of him in less than a second.

"You were warned, Sir."

I watched as Tonto took Travis outside and Brandon wrapped my hand around his arm, "I always knew I was the best man." We both chuckled. Dillion looked at Brandon and only shook his head as he kissed my sister on the forehead.

As the DJ announced my name followed by Brandon's, I was shocked that the news had traveled so fast. I looked around the room to find Patrick talking away on his phone. He didn't look angry, although he was pulling at his hair. You would have thought there wouldn't be any left after the way I went at it only minutes ago.

Brandon made me laugh as he began to twirl me around the dance floor. The crowd cheered and I was laughing so hard I nearly lost my breath.

Once Shannon and Dillion were announced, Patrick wasted no time in claiming my hand. Brandon's dancing was nothing compared to my Patrick.

"Please tell me Travis will be able to give his best man speech."

"No, I'll be delivering that one."

"Oh, Patrick, you didn't kill him, did you?"

"No, *croi milis*."

Patrick had started calling me sweetheart in Gaelic since returning from Ireland. Honestly, I loved it.

"Don't you sweetheart me! I'll be pissed if you ruin this wedding."

"He's being attended to as we speak."

No more was said about Travis and Patrick stood graciously and announced that he was feeling under the weather. With a gleam in his eye, he gave the most amazing speech I had ever heard. I just couldn't wait for this man to be my husband.

"I was so proud of you tonight," Patrick whispered into my ear as we lay in bed later that night.

"I just did the reception."

"No, I was talking about your..."

"Morgan," her name left my lips with disdain.

"Yes, her. I can't imagine what it was like for you and your sisters. All the little things that Mothers do for their daughters."

I burrowed deeper into his chest.

"I meant what I said; I would kill you if you tried to separate me from my kids."

Patrick actually chuckled, "You'd be in line behind my Ma. She loves you and she'd kill me if I did anything stupid like that."

We both smiled wide. He was right, she would.

As I closed my eyes, I began to go over the events of the wedding. So much had happened, yet Shannon was none the wiser.

My last thought, before I let the darkness take me was who was driving that black car?

Chapter Eighteen

"Christi, clear your schedule for three weeks from tomorrow for your engagement party."

With Shannon far away on her honeymoon, I had plenty of time available. I still smiled at Nora as she flipped through her desk calendar and began writing with fury. Nora wanted to handle everything about our engagement party. I wanted to make her happy, so I didn't argue.

Nora had wanted me to meet with a friend of the family who owned a prestigious event planning company. I had never worked personally with Makenna Gilbert, but I had heard she was very good at what she did. Up until the Connor-Donnelly wedding, she had done purely corporate events.

I had only seen her across the room as Charlotte handled the actual meetings. I knew she was beautiful and commanded a room, but that was all I knew.

"Is Patrick going to meet us at Makenna's office?"

Nora had spoken to Makenna the second I said yes to Patrick's proposal. Makenna had assured her that if she had something else scheduled on the day of my wedding, she would reschedule.

"He said he'd try, but he did have a meeting he couldn't get out of." Patrick had been very busy since the wedding and I had barely seen him. I already knew that he would tell me to pick out what I wanted. However, I wanted him to have a say in things as well.

"Have we decided on colors yet?"

That was probably the easiest answer I had today. I wanted to have the Malloy family plaid, like the yellow sash and blue plaid kilt that the gentleman wore in the picture that once hung in Patrick's old office.

"Yes, the Malloy family colors."

You would have thought I had just handed her the golden ticket, her eyes instantly became bright and I watched as a single tear fell down her cheek.

"Nora?"

"Oh, I'm sorry, Lass, I just expected you to want something trendy."

Nora dried her tears as we made our way to the waiting car.

"Good morning, Angus," I spoke as I sat in the back seat of the Mercedes.

"Beautiful morning, Mrs. Malloy, Ms. O'Rourke," was his nodded reply.

Angus had grown on me. There was just something about him that was very comforting to me. He never smiled, but he was always polite and always a step ahead.

The drive to Ms. Gilbert's office wasn't far, but with the morning traffic, it was a time-consuming trip. We arrived to find Makenna's office was housed in a high-rise building just off Michigan Avenue. Once inside the lobby, I was shocked to find how cold and sterile it was decorated. No pictures on the wall or comfortable chairs to sit in. It reminded me of an emergency room waiting area.

In the corner of the room sat a desk with a dark-haired girl nestled behind it. Once we approached, she raised her eyes from her computer screen to Nora's face. I recognized her immediately as the young girl who had run down Patrick's stairs that night at the strip club.

Michelle looked great, it seemed rehab had done her some good. Her face was fuller and she had a genuine smile on her face.

"Mrs. Malloy, good morning. Let me get Ms. Gilbert for you."

The young girl was up and out of her seat before I could even blink.

From the door that she so quickly disappeared into came a very beautiful blonde. Her light blue dress clung to her like a second skin and she looked like she had just stepped off a Milan runway. She cleared the space between us very quickly yet remarkably gracefully. She immediately engulfed Nora into a tight hug.

"Oh, Nora! I'm so excited for you. Two children in the same year!"

Nora and Makenna began to exchange the customary pleasantries as she ushered us into her office.

The decor in Makenna's office wasn't much better. A single desk and two hard plastic chairs were about the only things there. Not once did she offer us anything to drink, not that I would have accepted, but it was customarily polite to offer.

The longer I looked at her, the more I just didn't feel right. I couldn't put my finger on anything specific, but I just knew I had seen her before.

"Oh, Makenna , I nearly forgot to introduce you to my new daughter. Makenna, Christi. Christi, Makenna ."

I extended my hand out to her, and just as she brought her hand up, that was when it happened. It was the motion of her hand that caused my mind to flash back to that night in the parking lot. This was the over-processed, hooker wanna-be with Patrick that had flipped me off.

"I've wanted to meet the person who's taken our Patrick off the market."

Our Patrick? Bitch, please...

The sound of Nora's cell ringing stopped me from saying what I really wanted to.

"Lass, I'm sorry, but this is Thomas and I have to take it."

She gracefully rose from her plastic chair and left the office.

"You're not at all what I expected," Makenna's facade dropped and the demeaning tone in her voice did nothing but piss me off.

"Funny, you're meeting all of my expectations," I sneered back at her.

"What the fuck is that supposed to mean?" She threw back at me.

"Don't think for one minute that I don't remember you," I spoke as I leaned in her direction.

"Whatever. I've never..."

"Gino's parking lot, you got out of the car with Patrick and decided he was paying too much attention to me and decided to flip me off. Ring any bells?" I spat, giving her the bitch brow.

She could only glare back at me.

"See, it wasn't that you did that just to me, my four-year-old niece was in that car and she could have seen you..."

"Who gives a fuck about your niece? You do realize he's only marrying you because he and your father have a contract?"

I didn't believe her for a second. Makenna was no better than Sophia. They would say whatever they had to in order to hurt people.

"Well, that and the fact I can fuck his brains out."

I could tell by the look on her face that I had hit a nerve. She and Patrick had obviously never been together, but that clearly wasn't by her choice.

"You wouldn't know anything about that, fucking him I mean."

She didn't get the opportunity to respond as Nora came back into the room. She wasn't alone, she had Thomas and Patrick on each side of her.

I rose from my seat as I crossed the room to greet Thomas. With a quick hello and a kiss to the cheek, I turned my attention to Patrick as he pulled me into his arms.

"*Chaill me` dathuil tu`.*" (I missed you, handsome)

"*Chaill me` dathhil tu` croi fresinin milis.*" (I missed you, too, sweetheart)

Out of the corner of my eye, I could see that Makenna had not one clue what was just said. She may have had an Irish name, but she didn't speak a word of Gaelic.

"Oh, Thomas, remember when we were like that?"

"What are you talking about, my love? We're still like that. I love you very much, my Nora."

As I peeked at Thomas and Nora staring at each other, I questioned if Patrick looked at me like that. Directing my attention up to his beautiful face, I had my answer...oh, hell yes.

"I was just discussing with Christi the plans for your upcoming wedding, Patrick," Makenna purred, batting her lashes. Seriously?

"Oh, and what did you decide?" Nora questioned, her face still glowing.

"Yes, Makenna, what did we decide?"

I had already made up my mind about her planning my wedding. The second I knew it was the same trashy woman from the parking lot, I knew.

"Well..." she muttered uncomfortably, "She has, um..." *Keep digging.* "I thought..."

Patrick's arms were still wrapped around my waist and he was softly moving his thumbs in a circular motion on my hips. I couldn't take her stupidity anymore. She had no idea how to handle a situation like this. She could spew venom, but that was about it.

"Makenna, allow me," I said interrupting her rambling.

The look on her face was of relief, but that was about to change.

"You see, Nora, Makenna here has somewhat of a history with *my* Patrick," I said removing myself from his very talented fingers and then encouraging him to sit in my chair. "She showed her true colors one night when they were out together."

I looked to Patrick's face, he was confused.

"I had been eating dinner with my father and my niece when I saw Makenna, standing in what would be described as 'prostitute' attire." I looked directly at Nora as I continued, "Makenna here, didn't know me from Adam, and when she decided that Patrick was looking at me too long, she flipped me off. Thankfully, my niece didn't see the gesture."

The look on Nora's face was one of concern.

"Now, I have pretty tough skin when it comes to those things, I simply thought she wanted me to know her IQ."

Thomas let out a snort of laughter, Nora shooting him a look, leaning into his arm, a smile beginning to form.

"However, as a professional, I would've never acted toward any of my clients as she has toward me while you, Nora, were out of the room just now."

Nora looked to Makenna and then to Patrick.

"Patrick, Makenna simply cannot believe you're marrying someone like me. And informed me that you are only doing it out of a contractual obligation between our fathers."

Before Nora or Patrick could question, I dealt my final blow.

"I realize that Makenna is a friend of the family, but if you want me to marry you, Patrick, it'll have to be planned by someone who doesn't want to climb up your dick, cutting my throat on the way."

You could have heard a pin drop in that room.

"But…we had a deal," Makenna's voice now sounded desperate.

I turned back to face her, "What deal?" I demanded. No one spoke, as Makenna looked desperately at Patrick. "I said, what deal?" My voice a little louder.

"Makenna owes the family quite a bit of money and this was how we arranged for her to pay it back," Thomas finally answered.

It had nothing to do with me and I could've care less who she owed money to. She was not getting anywhere near my wedding. I pulled my phone from my purse and dialed Charlotte's number.

It rang three times before she answered. "Sick of Makenna already?" She chuckled into the phone.

"Cut the shit, Charlotte, I need a name."

"A…all right," she responded startled.

"I want someone who's new to the business, who'll be more interested in the planning of my wedding than bedding my husband," I looked directly into Makenna's ashen face. "Oh, yes, and I need her to be Irish. The wedding will be mostly in Gaelic and I don't want her confused."

"Wow, I'm having a proud moment here. You're cutting her where it matters. Excuse me, I'm feeling verklempt."

I ignored Charlotte's sarcasm; I was mad and I wanted to stay that way.

"Maggie Callahan. She's been trying to get her business rolling, but she's still wet behind the ears."

I looked at Nora as I responded, "It's a good thing I'm registering for towels then."

Charlotte gave me the number and I made a point of calling while I was still sitting in Makenna's office. I wanted Makenna to know she had messed with the wrong woman when she pulled her little stunt.

Maggie was available immediately and lucky for me, so was Patrick. I said a quick goodbye complete with a 'go to hell' smirk to Makenna, and out the door we went.

Maggie's shop was only a few blocks from Saint Josephine's church where Paige and Caleb, as well as Patrick and I, would be married.

I knew Maggie's was the place we needed to be when we pulled up to the shop. There was nothing cold or sterile about it, it was night-and-day different from Makenna's.

Maggie was a young, beautiful woman; I would have guessed her to be in her late twenties. She was a little taller than I was, with beautiful red waves of hair falling around a pale face that was sprinkled with freckles. Her bright green eyes twinkled excitedly. She was the poster child for all things Irish.

She invited us into her shop that was so welcoming. Her furnishings were all soft and neutral. The music that played quietly in the background was pleasant and not too disturbing. But the best thing was the wonderful smell of freshly baked Irish scones. Walking into her shop reminded me of visiting my grandmother when I was a little girl.

"Please, have a seat, I have the tea on. You can't have a good conversation without a proper cup of tea and a good scone."

I looked to Nora, who had already fallen in love with Maggie.

I let Nora take the lead and do the introductions.

"Ah, Lass, so I'm betting that you'll be using the Malloy colors, yes?" Maggie's thick Irish accent questioned.

"Yes, Ma'am," I responded.

"Ah, fine, fine." She nodded her head in agreement.

"And will you be using the Gaelic?"

"Yes, Ma'am, I want it to be a traditional Irish wedding, down to the Jameson whiskey at the bar."

As we continued to sip our tea and get a feel for the type of wedding we would have, the better I felt about having Maggie work for us.

"Maggie, I only have one question for you," Nora's soft voice filled the table.

"Yes, Love, what worries you so?"

"I'm concerned that you're so new to this and have no connections. You do realize the size of the wedding?"

I watched as Maggie chuckled softly to herself. "Aye, I know what you're getting at, but the bigger question is, Love, do you have the quid to pay for it?"

Yes, Maggie would do just fine.

CHAPTER NINETEEN

"Christi, can I ask you a question?"

I looked up from my computer screen and into Maggie's green eyes. "Of course, is something wrong?"

Choosing Maggie as my wedding planner had been the very best thing I could have done. She had everything mapped out for me and even went as far as to contract a company in Ireland to make the traditional fabric I would use for accent pieces.

Although, I wanted to use the Malloy colors, I didn't want to go overboard. Patrick refused to wear a kilt and I agreed, as long as he wore one for me when we were alone. He had agreed with a cocky grin. He knew that I wanted to answer that age-old question for myself and find out what he wore under it, if anything.

"Nothing is wrong, per se, I just have a delicate situation that I don't know how to handle."

I scooted away from my desk and made my way over to the electric teapot I had behind my desk. I made a pot and then settled back into my chair. "The tea will be ready shortly, but go ahead and tell me what's on your mind."

Maggie took a deep breath and then squared her shoulders. "Angus asked me to supper."

I waited patiently for her to finish, but she seemed stuck.

"And...?" I finally gestured with my hands for her to continue, drawing out the word.

"Well, I don't want to do something inappropriate."

I couldn't help but smile. This was mine and Nora's doing. After our initial meeting, Maggie had followed us out to the car where Angus stood holding the door open. I noticed that his usually stiff stature was suddenly off kilter as he looked at her. Nora had nudged me and I could only respond with a quick, "uh huh."

That night, we set about a plan to introduce the two. I, being who I was, aka the fiancée, did what any woman in my position would do, I called Patrick.

"Hey, Babe," I cooed into the phone.

"Hello, *croi freisin milis.*"

"I need a huge favor."

"Of course, anything."

"I mean I'll make it worth your while."

"You don't have to bribe me, Love. Just ask me so I can make it happen."

"But you don't know what I have to bribe you with, you might like it."

"All right, ask me and then tell me what you're willing to trade."

"Okay, I'll give you a repeat performance of your birthday gift, if you tell Angus that it's fine to ask Maggie out."

There was silence for a short time and then I could hear chuckling. "Did he put you up to this?"

"No, I noticed him looking at her and I thought since they're both just-off-the-boat Irish, they might enjoy each other's company."

I knew that Angus had left his home in Ireland to work for Patrick, and I also knew Maggie had left when she couldn't find work.

"I'll drop the hint."

When I talked to Maggie later about Angus, she looked like she wanted to protest.

"Do you not like Angus, Maggie?" I didn't really look at her reaction to his ogling. Maybe she didn't care for him.

"That's the problem, I like him—a lot. I just don't want to cause problems."

I smiled at her as I began to pour each of us a cup of tea. "So, what are you going to wear on this date of yours?"

"I'm not sure. I guess it'll depend on where he takes me."

"Oh, I have a pretty good indication it'll be over the top, so dress nice."

"I think it'd be better to wait until after your wedding, though."

"Oh, no you don't, Maggie. You call him right now and tell him you'll go out this week."

Maggie looked at me with big eyes and quickly donned a bigger smile. She followed my direction and called Angus. Their first date would be tomorrow night.

Later that evening as I was trying to get ready to leave, I was finding myself quite distracted. "Patrick Shane, if you don't let me finish getting dressed, we'll miss our own engagement party."

Patrick only continued to nip and lick my earlobe and neck. If I knew we could get away with not going, I would have taken this to a new level, and a more horizontal surface, but we had a room full of people waiting for us.

"Besides, I'd let you deal with your Ma all by yourself."

That was the proverbial ice bucket as he pulled away with a deep groan.

Our party was being held at *Pieces,* the club I had gone to with Patrick on our first date. It seemed only fitting to have it there as that was where he had revealed his intentions.

Maggie had joined Nora in planning this event and as we made our way into the bar, the cheers rang loud and the music stopped temporarily.

Thomas and my father were standing at the bar as we greeted everyone. I kissed my father and then hugged Charlotte. Having my dad and Charlotte together turned out to be a wonderful thing. I could tell they cared for each other and it wouldn't be long before they would also be celebrating an engagement.

Maggie had found ribbon and paper products made in the colors of my wedding. Each table had a flower arrangement and as I looked closer, I noticed smatterings of shamrocks around the bottom. All of the drink napkins were of the Malloy plaid with 'PMC' monogrammed in gold in the center. Yes, Maggie was perfect. Paige had continued with the theme and had my shoes covered as well.

The drinks flowed and the laughter sounded as story after story was told. I learned that Patrick was such a *Superman* fan, that he had worn a cape around his neck until he was six. He learned that I took tap lessons for three weeks and then was expelled from dance school.

Nora had a collage of photos that were currently being shown on the large flat screen. It was fun to watch as photo after photo of both of us growing up was displayed. Honestly, even as an awkward teen, my Patrick was hot.

As Patrick held me, pressing his chest to my back, a picture of me dressed for my first communion flashed on the screen. The crown of flowers that encircled the top of my curly hair and the white dress that was so delicately covered in lace, made me smile at the memory.

"I want all of our girls to look just like their mother," Patrick's gentle words whispered into my ear.

"I hate to disagree, but I want all of our children to look just like their dad."

Patrick excused himself to go to the restroom and I took that opportunity to head to the bar. The night had been perfect and I couldn't have asked for anything better.

"Christi, I finally get to offer my best wishes," a slurred voice sang in my ear. I turned to my left and came face to face with none other than Sophia.

"Fuck, me! What security guard did you blow to get in here?"

I was having too good of a night to let her ruin it.

"My, my, such words coming from a so-called lady."

I didn't want to even dignify her with an answer. She was the true spawn of Satan and I wanted nothing to do with her.

"Listen, I think you should know that in time, Patrick will get tired of this Pollyanna image you have going on and want a woman who will do very dirty things to him, and you know what? I'll be waiting."

Maybe it was the three martinis I had already had. Or maybe it was the fact I hadn't eaten since breakfast, but what I was certain of, was the fact that Patrick had taken his place behind her, listening intently to everything being said.

"Really, Sophia? And what makes you think I don't do really dirty things to him already?"

Patrick only smiled and wiggled his eyebrows, he knew I had this under control. He was going to enjoy the show.

"Oh, dear little Christi, we both know you'll enter your wedding chamber pure as the driven snow. You most likely haven't even seen a naked man up close." She took another drink from her wine glass. "Patrick is the type of man who needs a woman who's comfortable with her sexuality. You, my dear, have not even discovered yours yet."

The bartender had handed me my drink at that point and I turned to her again. "Sophia, I may not have frequent flier miles on my bed sheets, but I do know how to make Patrick very happy. As for him running to you for those dirty things, well, we'll have to see about that. Right, Honey?" As I said the latter, I looked directly at Patrick.

"Not a chance, *Croi freisin milis*, you know all my dirty secrets." He moved past Sophia and lifted me by my hips and placed me on the top of the bar where he kissed me good and deep.

The catcalls from around the bar caused both Patrick and I to chuckle, thus breaking the kiss.

"We're definitely finishing that kiss later."

Had I not been so distracted by Patrick lips, I would have overheard Sophia call someone to say, "Va bene, sto cazzo dentro." (All right, I'm fucking in.)

CHAPTER TWENTY

I loved Patrick. I couldn't say it enough. After all the pushing him away I had done, I found myself just loving everything about him. Last night at Paige's rehearsal dinner, he sat beside me with his entire body gently wrapped around mine. Even as the toasts were made and the gifts handed out, he kept at least his fingers touching mine. Even when Sherman stood and made a slurred drunken toast, Patrick only snuggled closer to me. It was still a mystery how Eileen got the large yellowing bruise on her chin even makeup couldn't hide. Well, a mystery to those who didn't know Nora.

Patrick even laugh as we watched Eileen pouring leftover wine from the tables into empty bottles, and then slipping out to her car. She must have had at least a case of wine in the trunk of her car by now.

"Some things just never change," Nora whispered into my ear.

We both giggled as we watched her begin to shove leftover bread into napkins and then into her huge bulging purse.

Muscles was red-faced with laughter as he sat beside Patrick. "What has him so giddy?" I questioned Patrick.

"He just told me he made it a point to let a good dose of backwash back into the bottle from their table, followed by half of the salt from the shaker."

I couldn't help it, I began to laugh as well. To see the look on Eileen's face, when she discovered the tainted wine.

Patrick insisted I stay with him at his condo. He had been doing that a lot, actually. In the past few months, he had gone to great lengths to get me into his bed every night. He even broke out the pouty lips on occasion. Who knew a man that carried a gun and had the status of Patrick could pout like a three-year-old child, it made me smile.

Patrick had found us the perfect house. It was huge, and I had decided not to argue with him on this one. He wanted to give us something nice, in a safe neighborhood, and I wanted that as well. So with a heavy heart, I placed my house on the market. I didn't even get the sign all the way into the ground before Angus wrote me a check. I handed over half to Shannon, and as soon as she returned from her honeymoon, I would have all my things moved into my new home.

Today was Paige's wedding and I was happy to announce that my dad would have two dates, myself and Charlotte. She made him happy, and I meant face numbing from grinning happy. We had a long talk about it after dad told me, we cried and hugged, and she swore she would never make me call her mom. I still loved her to death.

Frankie was in charge tonight. We had been slowly making that transition. Patrick and I had decided that starting and raising a family was my top priority. The baby-making efforts would begin on the honeymoon, so no condoms, and no pill.

I had no doubt that Frankie would do a perfect job. She and Shamus were so good together. He was just what she needed to help her cross the finish line. I always knew she would make it.

Patrick insisted on sending a car for us. I told him it was too much, but there was just no arguing with him on certain things.

Charlotte and my father were already in the back seat of the limo when Angus held the door open for me. I greeted him with a kiss to his cheek; I had grown to love Angus. He and Maggie were perfect for one another.

"Well, Charlotte, are you ready to see what our Frankie is made of?"

"No, I'm ready to watch you fidget as she handles everything perfectly."

Charlotte was right, I was having a very hard time letting go. Maggie had been amazing. She had made friends with Frankie and together, they made an incredible team.

"Listen, I'm going to enjoy myself. I want to kick up my heels and dance with my two favorite guys," I leaned over and kissed my dad's cheek.

"One hundred bucks says you won't last fifteen minutes before you'll be checking on the food."

I extended my hand out to her and we shook on it.

I didn't care how many times I had seen Patrick in a tux; he took my breath away every time. He was waiting as I tried to get out of the limo. I said tried because the dress I was wearing wasn't cooperating. I had found it one day while I was shopping for another event. It was hanging in the display window and the second I saw it, I just knew it was perfect for me. I had worn my hair up, at Patrick's request. The man loved my neck and I loved when he loved on my neck.

"My God, you're gorgeous," he said as his arms wrapped tightly around me.

"Well, hello to you, too, Handsome."

Patrick's eyes were devouring me. I felt positively naked under his intense gaze. Not in an inappropriate way, but in a loving and desired way. He would do anything for me and truly loved me without conditions. He could go the rest of our lives and never tell me he loved me again, so long as he looked at me like he was right now.

"Okay, no lingering around after the reception, I have plans for you."

I could only smile as my thoughts reflected his words.

I noticed security was even tighter than the Connor wedding. I held firmly to Patrick's arm as we passed suit after suit. I couldn't imagine how many guns were here today.

Saint Josephine church was one of the most beautiful churches in Chicago. It was built in the early nineteen hundreds and was on the national historical list. Its stone bricks and wooden doors reminded me of a castle from medieval times. The beautiful landscaping was heightened with a pond and fountain that sat majestically at the entrance.

However, nothing could compare to the interior. It was breathtaking.

"Christi, how lovely to see you." My ogling was interrupted by Eileen's words.

"Oh, goodness. Congratulations on such a wonderful day," I replied honestly.

Paige and Caleb were perfect for one another. Patrick had told me Caleb had gotten his business back in the black for the first time in years. Sherman was even given a small job so that he could continue to support his family. Things were definitely looking up for them.

We continued to say hello and make our way to the massive wooden entry doors, I paused at the first step, my mind wandering back to Shannon's wedding. No way in hell would Morgan show her face here today, although the mystery car had remained just that, a mystery.

Once inside the doors, and after doing the sign of the cross across my chest, I noticed Shamus was waiting patiently with his elbow extended in my direction.

"I have to go play my part, but Shamus will not leave your side," Patrick whispered as he kissed my temple.

"Well, this is my lucky day then," I smiled as I spoke, addressing both Shamus and Patrick. "How many girls can say they have two incredibly handsome dates to the same wedding?"

Shamus could only smile as his eyes were clearly on my chin and not my eyes. After all this time, I was still having a hard time with that.

"Yes, well, he's only my stand-in. I get you back."

He eyed Shamus with his silent warning, although it was a wasted look as Shamus was head-over-heels in love with Frankie. Nora had informed me that he had given her a bracelet, not a diamond one like ours, but a gorgeous bracelet nonetheless.

"Are you ready?" Shamus's question this time was in perfect English.

"Shamus, God love you for trying so hard for her."

His face was all smiles as he began to lead me down the aisle.

"I love her. She's good with me."

"Yes, Shamus, she is good with you."

I couldn't help but cry as I watched Paige's entrance into the cathedral. Her dress was breathtaking, as she gently glided down the aisle. The detail of the lace that rested on the hem and then gradually faded as it went up the dress, was spectacularly intricate. My favorite was the sheer lace shrug that covered her shoulders, the veil trailing behind her just as gracefully. Nora was on her left and Thomas on her right. I watched as Paige graciously smiled and made eye contact with as many people as she could, as she made her way to Caleb.

Turning my attention to the front of the church, a single tear began to fall. The little ring bearer had decided that his place was next to Patrick. He stood in all his little glory, all proud and tall, hanging on to Patrick's hand with one hand and the ring pillow with the other. For a brief moment I imagined our son doing the same, feeling important and safe.

Due to the fact that the Montgomery family was not from Ireland, the ceremony would be entirely in English. I leaned over and told Shamus that if he didn't understand something, to tell me and I would say it in Gaelic, but he never did.

I looked on as Nora wiped her eyes and Thomas raised Paige's veil, kissing her cheek. He leaned into Caleb and whispered something into his ear, I was certain it wasn't congratulations, as no smile appeared on his face.

I watched in awe as they exchanged their vows. I couldn't help but smile as I thought about my own wedding being not that far away. I looked to my right and noticed Maggie looking around. That had been another change; since the Makenna incident, Maggie and Charlotte had entered into a partnership. Maggie was being recommended for all the events that came through Charlotte's office.

"What God has joined together, let no man put asunder."

With those simple words, Paige was now a Montgomery, and it was time to celebrate.

Since Patrick was in the wedding party, he had to ride with them to the reception. Angus drove me and Shamus, and Dillion and Shannon decided to tag along since neither one of them wanted to avoid drinking. As we pulled up to the venue, Shamus tried to discretely adjust the gun that rested in the small of his back, while Dillion did the same. My father looked in the other direction.

I knew Patrick's guys carried; I just didn't realize that Dillion did as well.

This was it, the moment I had been waiting on. We had worked so hard getting this just right and I silently prayed that Paige would be happy.

Due to the sheer number of guests at the wedding, we rented a local concert hall. We had to hire an additional three hundred wait staff to accommodate the nearly nine hundred guests. Paige was just as picky as Allyson when it came to her guests being happy.

"God, I missed you."

Patrick wrapped his arms around my waist as I was leaning over to sign the guest book.

"Shit, Babe, you scared me."

I turned and met his gaze. I followed his line of sight as he was looking at my signature. His eyes had a hint of sadness and pain.

"What's wrong, Sweetheart?"

"You signed it O'Rourke," his voice was hoarse.

I placed my hand on his cheek and tilted it toward mine, "Honey, that's still my name."

"I know; I just want to see Malloy instead."

I smiled as I stroked his cheek. "Soon, now come and buy me a drink, Handsome."

Patrick escorted me to my table, my dad and Charlotte were already seated. I noticed they were having one of those silent conversations that couples who were in love often had. She was good for him and he deserved to be happy. Hell, everyone deserved to be happy, even Makenna and Sophia, just not with my Patrick.

Speaking of Sophia, where was she? I knew for certain the Porchelli's were invited to the wedding, but for the life of me, I couldn't remember seeing them at the church. But then again, there had been a full house.

As I took my seat next to Charlotte, I made it a point to Motion toward my wrist, "Pay up, Babe."

My dad chuckled as Charlotte rolled her eyes. "All right, so you lasted longer than fifteen minutes. Double or nothing says you won't last through the cutting of the cake."

I smiled at her only because I knew Maggie had suggested that the cake be cut as soon as they walked in, that way it would be out of the way and the staff could cut it and box it up.

"All right, twisted sister, you're on."

Less than a minute later, the man Maggie had hired to act as master of ceremonies announced the arrival of Mr. and Mrs. Caleb Montgomery. I then sat back and gloated as the cake was rolled to the middle of the dance floor. Paige had gone with a traditional white cake. Her cake was a huge five-layer geometrical design, with her beautiful peacock blue ribbon around one of the layers. It was truly a work of art.

Since this was such a large event, Charlotte had hired a company to come in and set up massive big-screen televisions so the people in the back could see what was happening at the head table, which I had to admit was brilliant.

I watched as the camera guy stood beside the three photographers to capture the moment. Once the cake was wheeled away, I placed my hand palm-side up, parallel to Charlotte's face. The entire table erupted into laughter as she slapped it away.

Charlotte should have bet how long it would take before Patrick found his way to our table. Paige had wanted only eight people per table, but Patrick made his place known beside me.

"I don't like being in the same room and not being able to touch you," he spoke into my shoulder.

Glasses around the room began to clank as forks touched them. I smiled at Patrick and whispered, "Let's practice for our own wedding."

He smiled and kissed me gently. "As long as we get to practice for the honeymoon later, I'm all for it."

Dinner was served and I couldn't help moaning as I tasted the grilled lamb chops. The garlic mashed potatoes added just a little something. The food was so good that I wanted to lick the plate clean. I didn't, but I wanted to.

Once all the dishes were cleared away and the toasts were given, it was time for the dancing to begin. Nora had hired a team of Irish dancers to come in and get things started. Although I had witnessed theses dances many times, I was still in awe of the speed in which their feet moved.

Once the dancers finished, it was time for the traditional wedding dances to occur. I watched as Patrick glided his cousin around the dance floor. Her name was Shannon and she was attending Harvard school of Medicine. He told me she would return to Ireland and work for the government as payback for the tuition she had received.

Once the bridal party left the floor, the music for the dollar dance came on. I watched as Paige's face lit up and she began clapping. The dollar dance had been around for as long as I could remember. The bride was placed in the middle of the floor and she danced as her guests threw money at her.

Patrick dug into his pocket and handed me a wad of cash. He took my hand and we joined the other guests as Paige began to dance. I didn't know who had more fun, Paige dancing, or me throwing twenty-dollar bills at her.

Once my wad of cash was gone, Patrick leaned over and asked if I wanted a drink. I fanned myself and said yes and told him I would meet him back at our table. I kissed him and he told me he loved me.

I hadn't taken three steps when Douce came rushing toward me.

"Christi, I'm so sorry to bug you, but I didn't know who else to get." The look on his face was one of pure panic.

"Douce, what's wrong?"

"It's Harley, err…Frankie. She's in the back room crying. She said she was going to get in big trouble, but she won't say why."

I looked around, but I couldn't see Maggie or Charlotte. It was a good thing I had already won that bet. "All right, Douce, show me where she is."

I motioned for him to go ahead of me as he headed toward the kitchen. The music had changed and it was now the electric slide. I looked and saw Paige motioning for me to come dance with her. I mouthed in a minute and continued to follow Douce.

The room was so crowded it was hard to keep him in sight. Once we reached the hall to the kitchen, Douce pointed to the door at the end of the hall.

"She's behind a shelf in the stockroom."

"Thanks, Douce. Now, go tell Patrick where I am and that I'll be back as soon as I can."

I could hear my heels clicking on the tiles of the hall floor and the clattering of dishes as the kitchen staff was working on clean up. I reached the door and turned the knob. The room was dimly lit, and I tried to feel along the wall for a light switch. Switching it on, I called out for Frankie, but heard nothing.

The storage room was large and had a number of rows of metal shelves. I continued further into the room, moving around the maze of shelves, until I heard sniffling. I quickened my steps and then rounded the corner, only to stop dead in my tracks.

"What the fuck are you doing here?"

CHAPTER TWENTY-ONE

1 had entered hell, a hell that I deserved. Sins of my youth had presented themselves to haunt me, to destroy my very soul. It had been six weeks. Six weeks of scouring the city, six weeks of no word, no clues, not a single lead. It was as if she had just vanished into thin air. I had been over that night a hundred times in my head and it always ended the same, with her gone.

I had watched as she crossed the floor with her glass of wine. I think she was only carrying it to make people think she was merely a guest. She was too much of an amazing business woman and friend to leave things in just Harley's hands. She had been making subtle inquires all night. She thought I didn't see her, but I did. Why didn't I keep better eyes on her?

I had failed her, I was supposed to protect her, care for her, love her, and I had most certainly failed her.

When she wasn't at the table when I got back that night, I had gone looking for her. I asked everyone if they had seen where she went, but no one had seen anything. I sent Douce and Tonto to search the room and I had Charlotte go see if she was in the ladies' room.

I would never forget the absolute panic I felt as I saw her shamrock pendant lying on the dirty floor, not far from her broken shoe. I hadn't been entirely truthful with Christi when I told her the story of the significance of this pendant. Hell, none of the men in my family had completely admitted the truth. The ladies in our life simply thought it was carrying on tradition, however it was so much more than that. Years and years ago, we started having them fitted with tracking devices. Only the men in the family and members of our security team knew that. This pendant was designed to protect her, but judging by the manner in which I found it, it only served to make her a target. It was clear to everyone she had put up a fight. Whoever had taken her had suffered some damage as well. It would be nothing to what they would receive when I got to them, their death would be slow and excruciatingly painful.

I'd held onto her shamrock ever since I had found it on that floor. The chain was broken, and skin and blood were found in the links, her blood, my Christi's blood. They had ripped it from her beautiful neck. I would be breaking theirs.

Matthew had called in every available cop in Chicago to look for her, even the commissioner got involved. Christi had helped a lot of people when she had planned their events, making many friends. The commissioner had called in the FBI and their forensics experts. They had turned up nothing, not even a blood splatter or a fingerprint.

The first week I didn't sleep a wink, I couldn't. I began to search every abandoned house and warehouse in this city. I questioned every hooker, drug dealer, and homeless person, but no one had seen a thing. Even after I announced a ten million dollar reward, I was no closer to having her back with me.

I decided that God was punishing me. Not just for the crimes I had committed, but for the dishonesty I had shown Christi. There was still something she didn't know. She was so innocent and didn't deserve this.

When I turned sixteen, my parents told me that I needed to start thinking about my future as head of this family. I had internally rolled my eyes. I didn't want a wife, I wanted to have women throw themselves at my feet. I wanted a different girl every day, no strings attached.

When I was seventeen, my dad had again brought up the subject. I was no closer to accepting his demand that I take a wife. He told me he had a girl he wanted me to meet. He told me everything about her and I wanted nothing to do with her. However, in this life, even when you were at the top, you still didn't get to decide everything for yourself. I knew I had no choice but to get married; legitimate Irish-born children were a must.

However, I did decide that if I had to marry and have these children, I would do it on my terms. So even before I met this girl, my seventeen-year-old arrogant ass decided I would be married in name only. I would have my different girl every night and this farce of a wife of mine would just have to deal with it.

My father took me to a popular mall here in Chicago. I watched as groups of giggling girls walked passed us. I learned a long time ago that a quick lick of my lips and a wink would get amazing responses.

"There she is, Son. The young lady in the blue shirt."

I turned my attention to the bench that sat outside of a popular teen store. The dark red-haired beauty was sitting with her back to me. Suddenly, she stood up and grabbed her bag from the floor, effectively giving me a complete and clear view of her face.

My world literally stood still, as I watched her slowly stand. Her perfect hair, kissable lips, and skin were so flawless they had me spellbound. I stood there as my heart and soul left my body, they were now hers. The beautiful nameless girl held my heart in the palm of her perfect little hands.

"Her name is Christi O'Rourke. She's the daughter of a good friend of mine."

My eyes never left her as I questioned my father. "She isn't one of us then?"

"Not in the sense you're referring. She knows nothing about you. You'll have to win her on your own merit."

My father's words were like a rushing river, effectively drowning the fire that had begun to rage in my soul. "What do you mean, by my own merit?"

My father only smiled as he wrapped his arm around my shoulder. "I mean the arrangement her father and I made specifically states that *she* must choose *you* and not the other way around."

I turned quickly in shock, as this was never the norm. The girl I would marry would have been raised to serve me and would be expected to come to me willingly.

"Her father isn't in the family as a member, he's an asset. He keeps me informed of the Porchelli's criminal activity."

I looked at my father and waited for him to finish.

"I helped him out several years ago. His wife was heavy into heroin and threatening to take his girls and run."

"Girls?" I questioned.

"Yes, Christi is a twin." He pointed to a red-haired girl that was beside her. I looked to the girl who looked similar to Christi. Although she was her twin, I felt nothing in my chest as I took in her smile and body.

"So did he sell his daughter to you?"

"Patrick, you may be seventeen and well on your way to leading this family, but watch your tongue, I will not hesitate to beat you to a bloody pulp."

My father never made an empty threat. He would most certainly beat me for being disrespectful.

"She's beautiful, Da."

I continued to watch as she spoke with one of the groups of girls that had passed me. Was she talking about me? Would she want me?

I watched as a large man approached the group of girls. His smile was huge as he wrapped his arm around Christi. It hit me like a wrecking ball. What if she already had a boyfriend? What if she didn't want me? What if she found out about my life and ran far away? I knew what this feeling was inside my chest. The more I thought about it, the more I wanted nothing to do with it. She was beautiful and she would only break me. Besides, I wanted a wife in name only. I wanted a different girl hanging off my arm and my dick every night. I wanted to be the heartbreaker, not the heartbroken.

"That big guy that's with her is her father. He agreed to meet here to do a formal introduction. Are you ready to meet your future bride?"

Even though I knew the man that had his arms around her was her father, the hurt was still there. I decided then that Christi was not for me.

"No thanks, Da, I'll find a girl on my own."

Famous last words. I left that day determined to forget about Christi O'Rourke. I saw her about three days later waiting in line to purchase movie tickets. I swore I would forget about her, even though I made my friend go over and buy a ticket. I had him tell her he had an emergency and couldn't stay to watch the movie and give it to her.

The next time I saw her, she was holding hands with Mikey Fitzgerald He was a decent enough guy. He could give her a normal life with a house with the white picket fence and fill it with kids. That was what she needed, not a guy like me who wanted to play with her emotions. It didn't lessen the hurt I felt as she laughed at something he said. I was done with Christi O'Rourke. I would go away to school and forget she ever existed—I had to.

I had been invited to a back-to-school party at a friends house. I decided it was a fine time to start breaking some hearts. I sought out a girl who looked the most unlike Christi. It didn't take long before I found her. She was a bleached blonde with too much makeup and not enough common sense. I barely uttered a simple 'hi' to her and then led her upstairs.

I was so pissed when I couldn't finish and stormed out of there. The girl was none the wiser, as I was certain she was faking her enjoyment.

Not going to college wasn't an option for me. My ma was quite clear on the subject. She told me it took more than a shiny gun and a few threats to run our family. She was right. I had seen firsthand how Velenci and Sherman had made far too many bad business deals due to a severe lack of sound education based know how.

I also knew that having that kind of distance would put Christi out of my head for good. So, off I went to Yale. I went to every party I could find for the first two weeks. After several additional failures, I called my da, who flew out, and took me to a specialist. When all of the tests came back normal, my father and I had a long talk about what he thought my problem was.

He told me that even in the best of men, the most feared and ruthless, there was one thing that could bring them to their knees. For me it appeared to be Christi. My da said he had no doubt that the reason I couldn't be intimate with those other girls was because my heart wasn't mine anymore, it was still back in Chicago with her. I didn't want him to be right.

I was trying to study one afternoon out in the quad, when I overheard a couple of girls talking about how they would give their boyfriends blow jobs instead of having sex. For whatever reason, I stopped listening after I heard that part. Later that night, I went to another party and this time I let the blonde go down on me. Having a girl between my legs that I didn't have to be face-to-face with wasn't sex for me. I could hold her hair and imagine it was whomever I wanted. It worked; I was able to finish and so began my way of getting a release.

I finished school in three years, but didn't wait around for graduation. I had more important things to do than walk across a stage and have my picture taken. I returned to Chicago and began to take the reins from my father. The transition was a slow and tiresome process. I had to make examples out of a number of people. By the time my father was completely ready to step down, my ma had begun talking about a wife and kids for me...again.

I hadn't seen Christi O'Rourke in nearly four years when my ma made her position on her desire for me to marry abundantly clear. I asked her if I could just go back to Ireland and pick out a woman. She gave me the one look that no son wanted from his ma. My father informed me that Christi was still very single and he was happy to arrange a meeting. My ma jumped head first into that discussion by informing me and my father, that Christi was working with Ammo on her reception.

That night as I stood inside my condo staring into the Chicago skyline, I made a decision. I was tired of running from my feelings. My heart had belonged to Christi all this time. It was time I manned up and tried to win hers. I called my father and asked him to arrange a meeting with myself and Matthew. My next call was to my Ma.

"All right, Ma, you were right, I'm going to try and win Christi's hand."

Christi certainly didn't make it easy for me. She fought me at every turn. Sophia Porchelli had certainly tried to complicate matters, as well.

It wasn't until that day at Christi's sister, Coleen's, grave that I felt like I had a real chance. I made inquires to find out who Jimmy was, the asshole that had supplied Coleen with the drugs that had killed her. There wasn't much out there to go on and so I had let it drop.

I knew I frustrated Christi with all the women that ran in my circle. However, I never suspected Makenna would turn out the way she had. She and I were strictly business associates, at least on *my* end we were. Christi was quick to call her out and put her in her place.

But now I was being punished. I had tried so hard to get her out of my system and now she was paying the price for my stupidity

It wasn't even a week after Christi disappeared when Sophia came slithering into my office. Christi was right when she had called her a snake. I didn't trust her. So when she entered my office with her fake concern, I played her. I made her think I was glad to see her and even accepted her help in finding Christi. I knew better, she was feeling me out. She hoped that if Christi didn't return, that I would turn to her for comfort. What she didn't know was that there would be no one else. Sophia was someone who would never warm my heart nor my bed.

Once Sophia made her fake offer of help, she slithered her way back out of my office. I picked up the phone and put Douce on her tail. I reminded him that he had better do his job this time or he would be dealing with me, personally. Douce was already skating on thin ice with me as it was. Once I found out about Giggles, I had given him the opportunity to come clean. It wasn't long before more and more women came forward, claiming their children were his. Not all were, but an additional three turned out to be. I reminded him that if he was man enough to climb into bed with a girl, he should be man enough to accept the consequences and responsibilities. He was working harder now to support those children. They all deserved the best and I assured Douce that he would be providing that.

Christi had been missing for ten days when Tonto came into my office. He had been beside me the entire time I scoured the back alleys and shady hotels. He offered to have his brothers come out and see if they could turn up anything. He informed me that his brothers were a group of bounty hunters. They had been known to travel outside of the law when they needed to. It was rumored that they had exceptional abilities and could find anything and anyone. I told Tonto that I would cover their expenses and whatever else they needed, I would make certain they had it. That afternoon, Beck, Dustin, and Russell arrived. They went to Christi's house and searched. They came to my condo and did more searching. Five days later, they got back on the plane after turning up nothing. Whoever had taken Christi had been thorough in hiding their trail.

At the two-week mark, Harley came into my office. She was visibly upset as she offered to return to the streets and see if she could get anything out of her old contacts. I rose from of my chair and gave her a hug. "Frankie, you know Christi would be pissed at us both if I let you do that."

That was the first time I had ever called her Frankie, but it wouldn't be the last. She had proved herself. That same week, Maggie informed me that she was continuing to plan the wedding. She told me she just knew Christi would be home soon.

My ma made it a point to attend church every day and light a candle. She prayed twice a day for Christi's safe return. I joined her in the evening. Even with all my money and connections, I still had nothing.

So here I sat, six weeks later and I was no closer to finding her than I was the minute she was taken. The sun was barely starting to rise when I heard a firm knock on my office door. I didn't sleep anymore; there was no point. Images of Christi would flood my closed eyes.

"Enter!" I shouted as the knock sounded again.

I didn't even turn to look at who had walked through the door. I didn't care. Unless they had Christi by the hand, I had no use for them.

"Boss?" Angus's deep voice called. I didn't answer him. I didn't turn around, I just kept looking at the horizon. "I know this is trivial, Boss, but the alarms down in the cavern over at *Clair's* started going off a while ago."

My father had installed an alarm system inside the caverns a few years ago. Before that, I had to have someone go down and physically take a look around. It was a waste of manpower since it took nearly an hour to get a look in all of the rooms down there. Now, if too much water was detected, an alarm would sound and tell us which room was flooding.

Angus was right, it was trivial. They could fill it to the top with water and it wouldn't bring her back.

"Boss, I want her back as much as you do. I remember the first time you took her to *Clair's,* you promised her you'd take her on a tour when she was ready."

I remembered the conversation he was referring to. I remembered the promise I had made to her, I also remembered how she smelled and how she was still against being with me then.

"When Ms. O'Rourke gets back, I want the caverns to be ready for her. She'll be upset with me if she knew I let them flood and she missed seeing them. I owe her so much. I wouldn't have my Maggie if it weren't for her. She always treats the guys with respect and we all love her."

Angus was right. She would chew us both out and I knew they all loved her, just nothing like I did.

"I called Douce, but he didn't pick up and the alarms keep going off."

I turned to Angus and looked him in the eye.

I remembered when Christi called me and said that she wanted me to set Maggie and Angus up. Little did I know that she had already put the ball into motion. Christi wanted everyone around her to be as happy as she was.

"You're right, Angus. Go check on the caverns and let me know what you find. I'm going to keep my promise to take her down there."

Angus turned to leave when I called to him.

"Oh, and have Douce call me when you finally talk to him."

Angus nodded his head, and then turned and left.

The more I thought about it, the more I began to question Douce's whereabouts. When I gave him instructions to follow Sophia, he would tell me that she wasn't doing anything out of the ordinary. He would tell me what clubs she visited and what stores she shopped at. Nothing apart from the norm he would say.

Except that Sophia was a New York girl. Even with all the shopping and clubs Chicago had to offer, it was nothing compared to New York. Or so my sister had told me. So why was she staying here? Douce needed to call me. I wanted, no needed, to find out the answer to that very question.

The shrill ringing of my cell brought me out of my thoughts. The sun was now high in the sky and nearly an hour had passed since Angus had left. I grabbed my phone and didn't bother to check the screen.

"Yes," I spoke into the phone.

"Boss, I found her."

CHAPTER TWENTY-TWO

Moldy, stale, wet dirt.

The smell engulfed my senses and made me want to vomit. Where the hell was I? Why did my body hurt so much?

As I tried desperately to open my eyes, I began to remember. Paige's wedding, the storage room and then...oh, God...Jimmy. Jimmy was leaning against the wall, arms crossed over his chest, that sinister smile across his evil face.

"What the fuck are you doing here?" I remembered questioning him as he only glared back at me, like he was enjoying himself.

I turned to my left and saw two more figures that crept slowly forward. Sophia slithered her way towards me, her smile calculating and without joy.

"Do you know how long I've waited for this moment?" she sneered.

It was then that I noticed Anthony Porchelli, dressed in an Armani tux, much like many of the men present at Paige's wedding.

"Well, well, well, we meet again, Christi," he cooed, his face stoic and evil.

I turned to leave. I knew this wasn't a good group to be alone with. Jimmy was nothing but bad news, he was heavy into drugs and I was certain, other illegal dealings. I had to find my dad, tell him Jimmy was back in town.

As quickly as I turned, I felt a hard shove to the middle of my back, followed by the pulling of my hair, causing my neck to bend back as I tried to grab onto the shelf that stood to my left. Whomever had a hold of my hair only pulled harder, freeing it from its up-do and I felt myself falling backwards. Instinct kicked in and I tried to scream, but a hand quickly covered my nose and mouth. I began to flail my arms and legs. My hem had been too long, but the alteration lady told me it would take away from the dress if I had too much removed, so I had worn very high-heeled shoes to compensate. If I could get my spiked heel near whoever had me, I knew I could do some real damage.

I tried over and over to stomp my heel behind me. I must have made contact, because I heard Jimmy yelling, "Stupid bitch!" in my ear, but he didn't stop and neither did I. At some point, my shoe gave out and before I could reach my other heel back, I felt myself being lifted off the ground.

I could feel the metal of the shelves as I was slammed repeatedly against them. My vision started to blur as I closed my eyes and began to pray. "Please, God, let Patrick find me."

With a final blow, I felt a sharp sting to the back of my neck and then everything went black.

Finally, after who knew how long, I was able to open my eyes. The room, if you could call it that, was very dimly lit. I could hear the dripping of water as it hit a puddle somewhere off in the distance. I tried to sit up, but a wave of nausea hit me causing me to lie back down, darkness engulfing me once again.

"Wake up, you lazy cunt!"

Jimmy...that voice would haunt me forever.

Before I could react, I felt a sharp blow to my ribs. "I said wake the fuck up!"

His kick was so hard that I began to cough. My vision blurred and this time I began to throw up uncontrollably. Minutes passed while I continued to vomit. Suddenly, a stream of ice cold water hit me square in the chest.

"Knock off that puking shit and wake the fuck up. You're even more pathetic than your fucking bitch of a sister."

I struggled to sit up, leaning my body against the uneven texture of the wall behind me. Where the hell was I? The wall felt like stone, cold and hard.

"Jimmy, why are you doing this?"

My words managed to set him off. "My fucking name isn't Jimmy, you stupid fucking bitch, it's Jeremiah! I told your ignorant cunt of a sister that, but she couldn't get it right either."

I began to shake from the cold water I was now sitting in. I could feel it dripping off my face and down my back. I reached up to wipe my face when suddenly Jeremiah grabbed my left hand.

"I'll be taking this."

He held my wrist with one hand while he tore my engagement ring from my finger. I watched as he began to carefully examine it, and then he tossing it up in the air, letting it fall back into his waiting hand. "Bet you had to suck a lot of cock to get this from him, didn't you?"

I chose to say nothing, Patrick preferred me not to go down on him. I could count on one hand in the past six months the number of times he had allowed me to do that.

*You're too special to me, Christi...*his words echoed inside my head.

I heard the clicking of heels as the door to the room swung open and in walked a very put-together Sophia.

"She isn't needed for that anymore, he told me I do it better."

Sophia's eyes never left mine as she crossed the short distance from the door. She knelt down and continued to look into my eyes. "That's right, little Christi, Patrick has forgotten all about you. My mouth on him is all he can talk about now." I began to wonder just how long I had been out. It could have been days, weeks I doubted. "I can tell you, he's happier than he's been in years."

Her face showed no dishonesty, no lack of sincerity.

She leaned in further as she continued, "He's the best fuck I've ever had." I watched as her dark lips formed the words, her teeth touching as "the best" left her mouth.

"In the future, when you hear someone talking about me, no matter who it is, ask me before you do anything."

Again, his words filled my head, he had told me to come to him after that day in the cemetery.

Before I could respond, Sophia grabbed my wrist. "He said he wanted this back, it's for me now."

She quickly removed my bracelet and placed it on her own wrist. She was trying to break me, telling me he was with her, taking away his promise. She thought she was hurting me, but she was wrong. The bracelet was only a symbol, I had his heart, and I knew I always would.

Sophia stood to leave and I took in a painful breath. "Sophia, wait." She turned and met my eyes again. "You say you're with him now?"

Her smile was big, as she longingly looked at my bracelet, that now rested on her wrist. "Yes, I'm going to meet him after I leave here. Jealous?"

I wanted to laugh, I wanted to say that she was bat shit crazy if she thought for one second that my Patrick would ever consider being with her.

"Tell me, when you're in his bed, riding him, calling out his name, does it bother you that you're in the same bed where he promised me forever? The same sheets where he made me cum over and over?"

The smile dropped from her face.

"Secondly, if it's true and you're warming his bed every night, what is it that hangs over his bed on the wall?"

The smile returned as she made her way back to kneel in front of me. "A painting, but I never have time to really look at it, if you know what I mean."

I began to laugh, my ribs hurt like hell, but it was worth it to watch her face as I delivered my final blow.

"You're so full of shit, behind his bed is a window, you dumb bitch, and further-more, he doesn't let me go down on him because he says only whores are allowed to kneel in front of him. I guess you know where you stand with him."

I never saw Jeremiah's hand until it connected with my face and the room faded to black.

"Looks like the princess has been dethroned." If I could just keep my eyes closed, maybe he would go away. "You should've taken me up on my offer, you know."

Luck was clearly not on my side. I had no clue what day it was or what time. I knew it had been a while because I could smell myself. I had lain in the same place, on the cold stone floor long enough to know which area stayed dry and which one had moisture on it. I couldn't remember the last time I had eaten, if you could even call it that. Once in a while, the door opened slightly and someone threw in a piece of food—usually stale moldy bread or half-rotten fruit. At first, I tossed it in the corner, but now I ate the parts that were salvageable. Right now I was so thirsty I was ready to lick the wet floor, which wouldn't be the first time, either.

"Why am I here?" My throat stung as I questioned the man standing in front of me.

"Oh, my Christi. You wound me, you're here because I want you."

I opened my eyes to find that the face indeed matched the voice, Anthony. What could he possibly want from me?

"How does it feel to want, Christi?"

I was so tired; fear was something that had left me a long time ago. I knew Patrick was trying to find me, and my dad would never give up looking for me. But I just didn't know how much longer I could hang on. My body showed me all the signs, I hadn't had to pee in a very long time, and I hadn't cried since the last time I was fed stale bread.

"Oh, you do make this a fun game."

I watched as he reached out and cupped his hand around my cheek. I couldn't have stopped him if I'd wanted to, and, God, did I want to.

"Even drained of all your spirit, you're still breathtaking."

It was then I realized the news reports were correct. He was a very sick person. He played with his victims before he killed them.

"You'll learn to love me, Christi."

I closed my eyes again as he continued to traced my cheek and throat. "That's where you're wrong, I'll never love you." It took all of my remaining strength to turn my head, removing his hand from my skin.

"Oh, I think you will. It's either that, or I'll let you die."

Death sounded so good right at that moment. How long had I been here? A week? A month? I had no clue.

"Then take that shiny gun you have and just shoot me now."

He began to laugh, not with a normal that-was-a-funny-joke laugh, but a laugh that caused me to shiver. "Oh, Christi, you have so much to learn about me."

I opened my eyes once again. He lowered his entire body so that he was sitting directly opposite me. He took my dirty hand in his pale, cold one and I noticed he had a large ring on his index finger. It was silver and in the shape of a cobra's head, the eyes were rubies. My memory flashed back to the engagement party, his guards wearing the same snake on their suits. I watched as he slowly ran that finger up and down my own.

"When I first saw you at that party, you have to know I wanted you. I watched you for a long time, and when you tried to hide from me, you only made me want you more."

He shifted in his position. He was remembering that night. The smile that adorned his face told me it was obviously good.

"I followed you home that night. I stood outside your window and I watched as you removed that dress you had on. I watched you as I touched myself. You gave me the best orgasm I've ever had, continue to have, actually." The thought of him jacking off outside of my window made me want to vomit. "You made it so easy, you're far too trusting, I stood inside your house for hours as I learned about you, about your family. That idiot Patrick began to call you, but I pocketed your cell phone because I wasn't ready to leave. Then you destroyed my gifts."

I had to smile as I remembered tossing the flowers in the trash. "They were shitty flowers," I croaked out. Not bothering to address him being in my home. The missing cell phone had become a stepped over memory.

"I wanted to take you then, but Malloy was always around. Then between Malloy pissing off Jeremiah and trusting the wrong people, I was finally able to take my opportunity. Imagine my surprise when Jeremiah told me he knew you."

Had Jeremiah been there that night?

"Malloy didn't know how much he helped me when he turned down my sister, or you when you told her off. And then there's...ah, but I digress. No need to worry about family problems now. They'll all be resolved soon no doubt." This conversation was more in his twisted mind than in this room for me to hear. His eyes were black as coal as he continued to translate his memory.

"When I was in prison, I told everyone that I was going to find a girl and settle down. My father wants me to go back to Italy and run things there, and I will, but first things first. Malloy is beside himself with worry about you, you know. He's weakened, and he's distracted right now. He'll be so easy to get rid of, but don't tell Sophia. She thinks she's going to get him to want her, so let's just let her have her fantasy while she can, hmm? As long as the liquor flows freely and the drugs are plentiful, she'll be content enough, eventually," he grinned, making me cringe. He really was nuts.

"Yes, once the Malloy's are taken care of, the Porchelli family will be free to do what they will and we can go about our business. I know you'll come to see things my way, Christi, and you'll love Italy. Once you're there, you'll submit to me. You'll want me as much as I want you, and I want you there with me as my own."

I wasn't worried about making the trip, I knew at this rate I would be dead soon. But what he was saying about the Malloy's had me scared.

"You may not be Italian, but it matters not to me. I rather like Irish women, well, most of them. Some are just so...rapacious. I can be very patient, though, Christi. I've waited this long for Malloy to leave you alone. He's had his time with you, now I want what's mine. I plan to collect that reward he has out for you, ten million dollars, before he dies. We'll have fun spending his money. I plan to take you over and over again, lying on a bed of his money. I'll video it and send it to him, let him see you spread out for me, hear you screaming my name while I fuck you every way I please as he dies slowly while watching."

Internally, I was smiling; Patrick was stronger and more cautious than Anthony bargained for, and I knew he and his family were looking for me, even though Anthony was a delusional psycho thinking he could kill them. I was looking at a dead man.

"I've watched you, my Christi, and I have to say, you certainly know how to impress a man with your wit and charm. Where did you get that from, my Christi? It was certainly not from your Mother."

That got my attention.

"Oh, yes, my Christi. It was too easy to find your Mother, and she was more than willing to help me. I don't know what she was more excited about, seeing you or the bag of coke I gave her. Never have I watched someone so delighted to snort a line of coke. Too bad she didn't get to enjoy the whole bag. She was too clingy, too willing to do anything I asked of her. She begged more for the coke than for her last breath."

I closed my eyes as the reality began to set in, Morgan was dead and Anthony had killed her.

"So you see, Christi, I *will* get what I want. Whether it's you by my side or watching you slowly die, I win either way. Call me selfish, but my winning is all that matters to me. The rest can tend to their own agendas. With the Malloy's dead and you gone with me and out of the picture, we all get what we need. See? Things work out if you're patient."

Time continued to pass. I was given water a while after Anthony left; not much, but at least it was clean. Just when I was getting weaker again, Sophia came back. She was dressed to the nines and carrying her designer purse. She took one look at me and turned up her nose. She opened the door and shouted for someone to get inside. Never in a million years would I have guessed who was waiting outside of that door. Douce. My mind instantly went back to the night of Paige's wedding. Douce was the one who had told me Frankie was upset. He had betrayed me, and Patrick. I began to pray that I did survive this so I could watch as Patrick returned the favor.

"Kevin, you need to clean her up. Anthony is almost ready to take her out of here. He's talking about heading back to Italy early."

"How the fuck do you suggest I do that?"

Sophia pulled out her cell phone and began to push buttons. I imagined she was texting someone. "I don't care how, just get it done! You can smell her from upstairs." She tossed her phone back into her purse and then directed her next words to me. "I'm late for dinner with *my* Patrick."

She was so full of shit, I knew this, but my heart was beginning to question my brain. I wanted to laugh at her and tell her that she likely was about to die and I wanted to watch, but I was too weak to even speak.

Douce ran his hands through his hair several times. He would look at me and then ponder again. He quickly turned and left the room. I tried not to think about what his plan was. He clearly was involved and wouldn't care what happened to me.

He returned a short while later with what appeared to be a water hose. He came further into the room, before he turned on the hose and blasted my already tired cold, body with freezing water. I didn't have the energy to fight. I lay lifelessly against the wall as the water continued to pelt my ravaged skin for what felt like forever, the water chilling me to the core.

I was helpless to do anything. It felt as if he had used every last gallon of water in the city of Chicago. When he finally shut the water off, he leaned over my shivering body.

"I'll be back in a little while, Christi. I want my turn before he takes you away. I want to see if you're as tight as your sister was. Right now, it's time to go and collect," he sneered then muttered. "She damn well better have it this time."

He then kissed my chapped mouth, turned, and left the room.

My skin was wet and raw from the high-pressure hosing off Douce had given me. I prayed that I would not be here when he returned. Although I wasn't certain which would be worse, Douce or Anthony.

I closed my eyes and began to pray. I prayed that Patrick would be safe and that he would go on and have a long and happy life without me. It was important that he have a wife and children, even if it was with someone else. I prayed that Abby would grow up to be a self-confident and happy young lady. I prayed that Charlotte would take care of both, my dad and my sister. But mostly, I prayed for death to be quick and preferably before Douce or Anthony returned.

But God wasn't listening as I watched the door slowly open. I shut my eyes tight as I prepared for Douce to follow through on his threat. My breathing picked up as I waited. My heart was hammering inside my chest and I silently hoped this would be enough to finish me off.

I was so wrong, God had been listening. As I opened my eyes and took a good look at the person standing at the open door, I felt all the tension leave my body and the silent sobs took over.

"Ms. O'Rourke!" Angus's manly voice sounded loudly in the caved room.

I tried to call out to him, but my voice was gone. Angus rushed across the room and knelt by my side. I watched as he took his coat off and wrapped it snugly around me, the heat from his body feeling like a hot flame against my freezing cold skin.

I watched helplessly as he took his phone from his pocket and pressed it to his ear. Just before the blackness took me, the words I heard him speak were like the finest symphony being played, in the best hall.

"Boss, I found her."

CHAPTER TWENTY-THREE

I slammed my car into park as I skidded into the valet lane at *Clair's*. I didn't even waste time in shutting off the engine. Let someone steal it, I didn't give two shits about that car, my Christi had been found and I had to get to her.

After Angus called me, I jumped out of my chair and ran down the stairs. As I ran to my car, I had called Matthew, but I only got his voicemail. I left him a message to meet me at *Clair's*.

I prayed over and over for Christi to be alive. I didn't care what she looked like, what they had done to her, I would still love her. I would get her the best doctors in the country and help her in any way I could. If she had been raped, I would be patient with her. I would continue to honor her as a husband should.

As I passed the door that led to the caverns, I was hit with the most putrid smell I had ever encountered. It was a combination of human waste and rotting food. I held my breath as I flew down the stairs and into the room where Angus had said he had found her.

I slammed full force through the door that separated me from my Christi. What awaited me was a sight I would never forget.

What had they done to her?

Christi was lying in Angus's lap, his jacket wrapped around her lifeless body, his gun pointed at my chest.

"Sorry, Boss, I didn't know if it was one of them coming back to finish her off."

I crossed the floor, ignoring the horrid stench that was clearly coming from this room. As I dropped to my knees, I noticed she was still in the same dress from Paige's wedding. It was now black with dirt and grime and her hair was a filthy, matted mess. There were huge purple circles around her beautiful eyes, the sockets badly sunken in. She looked like one of those starving, African children they showed on the television, little more than a skeleton.

"She's alive, Boss. Barely, but she's alive."

I looked to Angus who had begun to hand her off to me, and I took her willingly. Her eyes slowly opened and she began to recognize that it was me.

"Patrick?" Her voice was so frail and small.

I wrapped her wet body closer to mine as I began to cry with joy and relief. I placed gentle kisses around her beautiful face.

"Yes, Babe, it's me, I've got you. You're safe, Christi."

"Not with Sophia..." she began to mumble.

I slowly pulled my face back to look at her, her eyes remained on me. I searched her eyes, waiting for her to say it again.

"Not Sophia," she whispered again.

"Christi, love, who did this to you?"

Christi's eyes were closing again and I quickly felt for a pulse, it was there, but just slightly.

"She said it was Douce and Anthony Porchelli, and some guy named Jimmy, Boss."

I didn't have time to react to Angus's words as the door busted open again and my father and Matthew stood in the doorway. Angus again had his gun pointed at them.

"Christi?" Matthew's voice trembled.

"She's alive, Matthew. She's severely dehydrated and clearly malnourished, but she's alive." Angus answered.

Angus was a trained medic. During his time in the Irish military, he'd had to undergo training for events such as this one. I knew he was telling the truth, and I trusted him.

"Has anyone called an ambulance?" I questioned as I began to kiss her face again.

"Angus, are you certain nothing is broken?" Thomas questioned as he crossed the room.

"Yes, Mr. Malloy. She pretty badly bruised up, though, and she needs a doctor badly." Angus instructed.

"Patrick, give her to me, it'll take too long for the ambulance to get here in this traffic. I can have her at the hospital before an ambulance can even get here," my father promised.

The words were barely out of his mouth when I heard shouting coming from outside the door, "Patrick, it's Ma, I'm coming in."

My ma was a smart woman. She knew if she opened that door unannounced, at least one gun would be pointed at her.

The look on my ma's face was enough to bring me to my knees again. She shoved Matthew out of the way and took Christi's pale face in her hands. She began to place soft kisses along Christi's sunken eyelids and was whispering soft words in Gaelic, her words meant for only God and Christi, as I couldn't hear what was said.

She stood abruptly and looked directly at me. "You make certain you kill whoever did this to my Lass." Her words held venom and her green eyes bore into mine. I knew if I failed to follow her instructions, she would take matters into her own hands. My ma wasn't someone to be played with.

I simply nodded as I began to pass Christi's lifeless body to my da. My mother captured Christi's pale hand in hers. It was then I noticed her engagement ring and bracelet were missing. My ma noticed as well.

"We'll replace them, Patrick. She's alive and that's all that matters."

She was right; I would buy Christi a thousand rings if it would keep her close to me.

"Are you coming with us, Son?" My da questioned as he shifted Christi in his arms.

Running my hands through my hair, I knew he would fight me on my answer. "No, I want to be able to tell Christi when she wakes up that Douce is dead and can't hurt her anymore."

Before my da could argue, the door again swung open and a very nervous-looking Douce came running in with Tonto right behind him.

"Fuck, boss, I just heard," Douce stammered as he ran closer to Christi and my father.

It took everything I had not to cross the distance and slam him into the wall repeatedly until his bones disintegrated. I wanted to kill him with my bare hands, drain the life from his body as he had tried to do to my Christi.

My ma interrupted and brought me back to reality, "Remember your promise."

I looked to Tonto as I spoke in a hushed voice, "Tonto, close the door."

Douce's eyes became huge as they darted between me and Tonto. "Why are we standing around? We need to go after whoever did this. Show them that they can't mess with our family."

His words were like acid on my skin. How dare he refer to anyone in this room as his family!

Tonto didn't question me and placed his body in front of the door, his arms crossed over his massive chest.

Douce continued to look around at the men in the room, no one said a word as they watched, waiting for me to calm down enough to not just kill him outright.

"Tell me, Douce, was it all worth it?"

"Wh...what are you talking about, Boss?"

"You lied to me, Douce. You betrayed my trust." I took a step closer. So did Angus to my left.

"No, Sir, I haven't missed a payment since you told me."

"You think this is about child support?"

Douce began to look around the room at each of the men. He was trying to play us off, act as if he knew nothing, then run like the coward he really was.

"Listen, guys, we're wasting time..."

"Tell me why you did this!"

Douce's body began to shake. He was at least smart enough to know when he was caught.

"I...I sh...sh..." His body was fully trembling now.

"Did you really think you'd get away with this?"

Angus and I took another step closer. "Here's what we're going to do, you're going to start telling me everything you know or I'm going to start shooting parts of your body off."

"Allow me, Boss. Save your bullets for the finale," Angus spoke from my left.

Douce began moving his feet side to side, looking like he was about to piss himself.

"Who are you working with?"

Several seconds went by and Douce remained silent as he continued to shuffle. The sound of a gun being fired and the distinct sound of a bullet lodging in the stone wall was evidence that Angus had grown tired of the silence. "That was your one and only warning shot."

Douce began to tremble in earnest and then the sound of water dripping started. At first I thought it was the leftover water from where Christi had lain, but as I looked at Douce, the distinctive darkening of his pants proved otherwise. He actually had pissed himself.

"Now, I'll ask you again. Who are you working with?"

"J..Jeremiah and A...A...Anthony Porchelli. S...Sophia is in on it t...too."

"What was the plan?"

Silence again followed. This time the sound of a gunshot was heard from behind Douce. Tonto stood with his gun pointed at Douce's ass. "Boss asked you a question."

Douce was now crying out in pain. This was nothing close to what he was going to suffer. "All I know is…I was to get her to the storeroom…so that Jeremiah could bring her here." Douce gasped out between pants of agony.

"When are Jeremiah and Anthony Porchelli due back here?"

I watched as he closed his eyes; a small puddle of blood had joined his puddle of piss.

"Sophia said they're planning to take Christi back to Italy soon, Anthony Porchelli wants Christi to be his. He gave me instructions to only feed her dirty water and garbage a couple of times a week, and never two days in a row."

My hand tightened around the handle of my gun. He had intentionally starved her, breaking her down so that she would do anything he asked by treating her like a sewer rat.

"Sophia told her that you're with her now. I don't think Christi believed her, though."

Trying to break her spirit, my Christi was too smart for that.

"So what was your payoff?"

Douce looked at the ground and then slumped to the floor. The puddle of blood was larger now and his skin was turning pale.

When he didn't answer, I raised my gun and fired two shots into his right knee. His screams did nothing but piss me off. The only thing keeping him alive right now was my need for more answers.

"Boss asked you a question, Douce," Tonto prodded.

"Once Christi was gone and you followed her, I wouldn't have to make my child support payments anymore. Things would go back to the way they were before Christi," he gasped out.

Listening to Douce tell me how he only wanted Christi out of the picture because of a few dollars he had to pay for the care of his children was the straw that broke me. Giggles was my niece, she loved her Aunt Christi and would be devastated if something would have happened to her. Douce didn't deserve to have the privilege of calling himself that beautiful child's father.

My next move shocked even me. I found my foot planted in the center of Douce's chest, slamming his back flat to the cold stone floor, my gun pointed between his shocked eyes.

"You don't deserve that child," I growled, my foot shoving harder into his chest. "You need to know that after today, you'll only be a faded memory to the mother of that little girl since you were too much of a selfish son of a bitch to get to know your own daughter. Giggles' true daddy will be there for her instead." My foot pressed harder into his chest.

"Her daddy will take her to the park and buy her ice cream. Her daddy will bandage up her scraped knees and help her with her homework. Her daddy will comfort her when her first crush breaks her heart, while Uncle Patrick crushes his skull. Her daddy will clap for her at graduation and drive her to college. He'll walk her down the aisle at her wedding and hold her first child with tender care. Her daddy will love her Mother like the most precious thing in the world that she is. But you, you'll be rotting like the piece of worthless shit you are."

Removing my foot, I bent down so that my face was only inches from his. "But first, you're going to call your buddy, Anthony Porchelli, and tell him to get over here quick. Tell him there's a big problem with Christi. Don't worry; you won't be lying."

Douce's breathing was rapid but this time he didn't hesitate as he reached into his pocket, retrieved his phone, and dialed. "Dude, you gotta get here quick. I think the bitch is dead," he said and hung up.

I steadied my breathing as I let his words settle. Looking him square in his face, I spoke the final words he would ever hear. "No, she's not, but you are."

I could see the flash from the bullets being fired into Douce's skull. Blood and brains were splattered in all directions. No one said a single word, as the smell of gunpowder lingered in the room, the final shell casing was spinning on the floor. Douce was dead and I could now tell my Christi that he could never hurt her again.

Now to wait for Anthony Porchelli. His death wouldn't be so quick.

"Angus!" I heard Shamus shout from outside the door.

"In here, Brother!" Angus shouted back.

The door slowly opened and in walked a pissed off-looking Shamus, followed closely by a tired-looking Frankie.

"Angus, I've been calling you for hours," Shamus said as he took a look around the room, his eyes finally landing on a dead Douce. "Is that…?"

"Yes, it's Douce, although it's a good thing he won't be having a funeral. Even his mother couldn't identify him." Angus explained.

Shamus shrugged as he continued to look at the faceless man that lay on the ground, "Guess he pissed you off once too many, huh, Boss?"

No one said a word as every eye was now on me. "He assisted in the kidnapping of Christi."

Shamus's eyes were now bulging. "Did he at least tell you where she is?"

I closed my eyes and pinched the bridge of my nose, the memory of her lying in Angus's arms still fresh in my mind. "He had her here on the cold wet floor, she was still in the clothes from the wedding and he'd starved and beat her. My father took her to the hospital."

"Is she...?" Frankie's tiny voice spoke from behind Shamus.

"She's alive, just barely," Matthew spoke from my right.

"Boss, can I ask why you two are still here? I mean shouldn't you be at the hospital?"

I looked at Shamus, but Matthew began to speak before I could. "Patrick and I are waiting for the ones responsible for this. He made a promise that he'd take care of them so she won't be afraid when she wakes up. I'm waiting to see if one of the men is the man who's responsible for the death of my oldest daughter. If I'm correct in my suspicions, I want to deal with him myself."

I turned to look at Matthew, "You think this Jeremiah and Jimmy are the same? The man that killed your Colleen?"

"I'm fairly certain of it. Christi said Jimmy is what Colleen always called him."

"What are you doing here?" Angus questioned Shamus.

"I got your message that you were going to check on the caverns. When I didn't hear from you and you didn't answer my pages or calls, I got worried. I told Frankie I'd take her to lunch, so I thought I'd kill two birds with one stone."

It was only seconds later that we heard the distinct sound of feminine laughter, followed by the clicking of high heels. Shamus moved himself and Frankie away from the door as the laughter got louder.

The door opened as three figures entered. They were laughing, talking, and joking about the stench permeating the building, as if it were funny. I was going to make certain this was the last time they would ever have anything to laugh about.

My eyes met Anthony Porchelli's first. His expression was one of shock at first, but then a huge smile spread along his thin lips. The man that stood beside him tried to turn and run out the door. I recognized him as Jimmy the Mooch, the low-life that had wanted to work for me years ago. Tonto was quick to slam him to the floor and then pointed his gun in his face.

Anthony Porchelli's eyes never left mine as I cleared the distance between our bodies. His eyes dropped from mine long enough to take in Douce's dead corpse.

"Ah, I should thank you for that. Less cleanup for me, Malloy."

Sophia stood like a deer caught in headlights with her purse on her arm and her phone in her hand. I would deal with her later.

"That's nothing compared to what's in store for you, Porchelli."

He began to laugh as he moved toward me. "Don't think for one moment you can touch me. My father would have his men after you in a second," he hissed, his eyes dilated, spit coming off his teeth as he spoke.

"Not if he can't prove anything," Angus interjected. "No one will ever find your bodies."

"My father is an ignorant old man who's ruled by his foolishness of the past, but he does have his sources. They've been handy in getting me my Christi," he grinned.

He was either trying to piss me off or he was telling the truth, but either way, Porchelli was a dead man.

"What's that on your arm?" Frankie screeched at Sophia.

Everyone in the room turned to see what Frankie was yelling about. I looked directly at her left arm and there it was; the bracelet I had given Christi, Sophia had clearly stolen it from her.

"It's mine!" Sophia shouted as she drew her arm against her chest. "It should've been mine from the start, but that stupid, ugly girl got in our way, Patrick!" She whined as she began to walk toward me, like a cat in heat.

"Stop right there!" Frankie warned jumping in front of her. "You stole that from my friend and where I come from, there's a punishment for stealing."

"Get out of my way, you washed up whore. Don't you know Patrick only used you to get what he wanted? He never loved you, he was supposed to be mine, but that tramp got in the way!"

I took a quick step back as Sophia attempted to take yet another step around Frankie, lunging toward me. Frankie was quicker and using her left hand she took the gun that rested in the waistband at Shamus's back, and fired two shots. Sophia stumbled back hitting the wall behind her, sliding down, and then coming to rest on the dirty floor in a sitting position.

Frankie walked over to where Sophia sat dying, staring up shocked at Frankie's angry face. "You don't fuck with my family!" Frankie reached down and jerked Sophia's wrist up, removing my bracelet from her arm before she spit in her face.

Sophia looked up at me as she took her last breath and then slumped onto the floor.

"I never cared for my sister, you know. She was such a spoiled brat, and quite daft, too," Porchelli said with a shrug.

My attention now focused on Porchelli. He was looking at his dead sister with no emotion. Had that been Paige, I would have torn every man in this room apart for hurting her. Porchelli only looked at her as if she was a dirty piece of gum on his shoe.

"How can you say such a thing? She was your sister!" Matthew questioned.

"She was weak and worthless."

"She was still your sister."

"Perhaps…"

I was sick of this. I needed to get to the hospital, back to Christi. I had to be there when she awoke so that I could assure her that she was truly safe.

I raised my gun and steadied my grip. "I promised *my* Christi the responsible ones would pay. I always keep my promises to her."

My finger was steady on the trigger as I watched Porchelli's eyes grow bigger. By the look on his face, he knew I was deadly serious.

"If you kill me, Malloy, you'll never know…"

I cut him off. I was sick of his games, sick of him taking up air that good people like my Christi needed to breathe. "I already know all I need to know; I know that you won't be able to hurt her anymore."

I didn't give him a chance to respond as I unloaded my magazine into his chest, my last bullet hitting him squarely between the eyes. I watched as his hand came up to his heart as he gasped for his last breath, the force of the bullets propelling him into the wall. With a hard thud, he lay dead in a pool of quickly flowing blood. His eyes still open, a trail of dark blood descending down his face.

I couldn't remove my eyes from his body. I had killed my fair share of men in my days, but this one was personal. He had dared to touch the one thing that was forbidden, breaking the unwritten rule that wives were off limits. Velenci would be powerless to enforce anything and as far as Sophia was concerned, she would just be a causality of the drug war.

"You killed my daughter," Matthew's voice invaded the quiet that was present after the gunshots stopped.

I looked to see Jimmy, who could only smile as I began to reload my gun. "Here, Matthew, use mine," I told him as I tried to hand him my gun. Matthew looked at me, and then at the gun that was offered. "It's a clean gun and we'll dispose of it when we're finished here."

He looked from my gun to my face, and then turned back to Jimmy. "A bullet is too quick for this son of a bitch. He needs to suffer." The smug smile on Jimmy's face disappeared, replaced with pure terror as he looked into Matthew O'Rourke's eyes boring into him with the anguish and rage of a grieving father. "You took my daughter from me. You left her to die, naked and alone in a seedy motel room."

Matthew began to walk closer to Jimmy, never taking his eyes off him. "She wanted to be a teacher, did you know that?" It wasn't really a question, more of a thought he had that passed his lips. "She wanted to teach kindergarten, she had her whole life ahead of her. But you changed all that. You stole her bright future, traded it for drugs, and death."

Matthew was getting closure. He needed to share his memories with the man who had taken away his daughter.

"You took my beautiful daughter and made her into a broken, hateful person who would stay gone for weeks. She no longer cared about her sisters or her father. She only wanted her next fix."

Matthew stayed quiet for several minutes and surprisingly, so did Jimmy. Finally, Matthew raised his head and turned to Jimmy once again. "Did you know that in the time of King Henry, VIII, when someone offended the crown, they were given the most severe punishment?"

Again, this wasn't a question.

"When my girls were little, they loved to play princess, especially Colleen. She looked just like a little fairytale princess with those red flowing curls and her porcelain skin. They would dress up so cute and want me to play the role of the King." His eyes showed me he was seeing his little girls dancing around him, free and innocent.

The warmth from his memories faded from his eyes as he looked back at James. "You took away my princess." The look that followed that statement was one I hoped never to receive from Matthew O'Rourke. He was no longer in control of his actions and Jimmy would be paying the price.

"Patrick, can you instruct your men to assist me, please?"

I didn't have to say a word, Shamus and Angus stepped forward to flank Matthew.

"Gentlemen, strip him of his clothes and hold him to the wall." Jimmy was clearly too terrified to say a word. My men wasted little time as the sounds of clothes ripping filled the room, the strips landing in a pile at my feet. On a chain hanging around Jimmy's neck was the engagement ring I had given my Christi. Matthew was looking at it as well, but would leave it there for now as a reminder of what he had done to his other daughter as well. This wasn't just for Colleen anymore.

"In that time, the King would order the offending person to be drawn and quartered. Since we have to adjust due to the circumstances, we'll just be drawing."

Jimmy didn't know what had hit him as Matthew pulled a razor-sharp switchblade seemingly from nowhere and made a large deep slash across Jimmy's lower body. He screamed out in pain as blood began to pour from the wound. However, Matthew wasn't finished as he drew the blade through the cut again, and this time the gash opened and what looked like James's intestines fell out, splattering onto the floor as he watched.

"See, in the days of the King, your intestines would been pulled out and burned at this point, but I don't want to end your suffering quite that quickly."

This time the blade coming down sliced off Jimmy's manhood and I would admit that even I cringed.

The pool of blood at Jimmy's feet was growing at an alarming rate, enough that I had to take a step back to avoid getting it on my shoes.

Matthew crossed the room and took a seat on the floor as he continued to watch Jimmy die a slow and excruciating death.

I watched as Shamus and Angus held tightly to Jimmy's naked body, pinning it to the cold stone wall. Moments later, a bubbling sound was heard from Jimmy's and then the contents of his bladder and bowels, fell to the floor, followed by Jimmy's head dropping forward, a sure sign of his death.

Matthew stood and walked over, unclasping the gold chain from around Jimmy's neck holding my Christi's ring. "Let him fall, Gentlemen," Matthew's voice said softly as he sighed deeply and backed away. "Rest in peace now, princess," he sobbed, his voice full of emotion and it was all I could do to not join him.

Matthew inhaled deeply and then turned to me, taking my hand and placing the ring in my palm, "It's over, Son. Let's go tell our Christi the good news."

CHAPTER TWENTY-FOUR

The waiting room at the hospital was full of family when I arrived. My ma rushed over and threw her arms around me. "Dr. Bradshaw is in there now, please tell me you…"

I leaned in close so that no one else could hear. "Yes, she has nothing to fear."

"Patrick." I looked up to see Amex making a quick b-line for me. She and Caleb had returned from their honeymoon two weeks ago. "They won't let us back there," she whimpered, her arms going tightly around my neck. Amex released me and immediately pushed me away, "Oh, crap, Patrick what is that horrible odor?" she groaned as I noticed my father entering the room with a man in a white lab coat following close behind.

"Christi's prison," I told her as I removed her arms from around my neck and made my way over to my father. The man in the white coast's pocket read Dr. Kenneth Bradshaw, MD, Emergency Medicine.

"Da?" I called out.

Thomas's head snapped in my direction, "Patrick, you're here." I continued to make my way closer, as the room grew very quiet. "Son, this is my good friend, Dr. Bradshaw. He's been attending to our Christi."

I held out my hand to him, grasping his firmly and making direct eye contact. "Sir, I'm Patrick Malloy, Christi's fiancé."

Dr. Bradshaw was an older man, with round glasses and silvering hair. If my dad trusted him, then so did I.

"Yes, well, I have to tell you, we were very lucky you got to her when you did. I've run several lab tests and the good news is it doesn't appear that she's suffered any permanent damage. Her liver enzymes are in an acceptable range. My only concern is that when we started a catheter on her, nothing came out. We've put her on a rapid infuser to get as much hydration into her as quickly as possible, but I'll feel a lot better when her kidneys start showing some output."

I had a question that was burning a hole in my gut. I had to know, not that the answer would change anything between Christi and I.

"Dr. Bradshaw, was there any evidence of…sexual assault?"

Dr. Bradshaw placed his hand on my shoulder as he responded, "No, Patrick, there were no obvious physical signs of a sexual trauma. However, we'll have to ask her when we wake her up to be certain."

I looked at him perplexed, "Wake her up?"

"Yes, we've given her medicine to make her sleep. It's better for her body to heal if she doesn't have any outside stimulation right now."

I nodded my head as I silently thanked God.

"When can I see her?"

Dr. Bradshaw only smiled as he responded, "The nurses are cleaning her up, give us an hour and I'll have one of them come and get you."

I shook his hand and thanked him for everything he had done for Christi.

My da came over and gave me a tight hug, "Is it finished?"

I nodded my head as we separated.

I noticed Matthew had joined us and had heard everything Dr. Bradshaw had told us. For a second, I felt guilty for not making certain he was there, he was her father after all.

I turned and headed to where my ma and Amex were sitting. I hadn't noticed that Sherman Montgomery was in the room. Sherman and Eileen had stayed in Chicago after Caleb and Amex went on their honeymoon so Sherman could make certain Caleb's business interests here were taken care of.

I needed a distraction. Christi was the one person who could calm me down, no matter what the issue was. I needed her, but she needed me more right now.

Ma handed me a cup of coffee as Sherman began talking to me. "Patrick, my God, when Caleb called me, I couldn't believe it and rushed right over. Christi is a dear thing and I've been praying for her every day. Is there anything you need, Son?"

I knew I was going to get asked that question a lot today.

"Thank you for coming, Sherman. I'll let you know if I need anything."

He patted me on my back as Caleb made his way over to us. "Eileen will be happy to hear that Christi has been found." He noticed me looking around for Eileen, but she wasn't in the room. "She's due back next week from her vacation with Mia," he sighed.

I looked to Caleb confused; I would never go on a vacation without my wife. Caleb only shook his head, silently asking me not to question it. Apparently, this was a sore subject.

I noticed Matthew standing beside Sherman. "Matthew, this is Sherman Montgomery, Caleb's father." I then gestured to Matthew, "Sherman, this is Matthew O'Rourke, Christi's father."

"Matthew, I just can't imagine what you're going through as her father. I can't imagine what I'd do if that happened to my Mia."

"You have a daughter?" Matthew questioned.

Sherman retrieved his phone and began to scroll through his pictures, finding one of Mia and showing it proudly to Matthew.

"She is a beautiful girl, Sherman."

Sherman continued to look at the screen. "She takes after her mother in the looks department."

Matthew chuckled as he responded, "I think every father gives the credit for the beauty to the mothers, but I'll say I'm an exception to that rule."

Sherman looked to Matthew, but didn't question.

"Patrick, you remember my Mia?"

I smiled as I took his phone from his hand and politely glanced at the picture quickly before handing the phone back to Sherman. Mia seemed to be a very beautiful girl with her long dark hair and model-perfect face. "She's beautiful, Sherman."

The conversation quickly ended as a feminine voice called out, "Patrick Malloy?"

I turned my attention in the direction of the voice to find an older woman in white scrubs, standing with a clipboard. Her glasses perched lower on her nose. "Yes, I'm Patrick Malloy."

She smiled as she motioned with her free hand for me to follow her. "Come with me, dear, she's ready for you to see her. I'm Nurse Casey and I've been assigned to Christi today."

I followed her through a set of doors, passed the nurses' station, and then down to the end of a long hallway. "Mr. Malloy was very specific about Ms. O'Rourke's accommodations," she said as she stood outside a set of double doors.

Books was standing outside the room. "I guess I'm not needed anymore if you're here?" Books asked as I grabbed him in a hug.

"No, the situation has been handled. Go home to your wife and daughter."

Books nodded his head in understanding, "Call me if you need me, I'll bring Smiles up later." I smiled at him and nodded before I followed the nurse into the room.

The room looked more like a suite at the Ritz than a hospital room. I knew I had my parents to thank for that. Only the best would ever do for their kids, and that definitely included my Christi.

She was nestled in what appeared to be a queen-sized bed. Her dark hair had been pulled to one side, as if it had just been combed. Her face now looked peaceful, despite the circumstances she had been found in only a few hours ago. Above her head was a machine that held what looked like a flat screen, where I could see numbers and lines, her name was written across the top. Upon closer look, a white heart was flashing in the corner above the number seventy-two.

"Her vitals all look really good," the nurse spoke softly. "Feel free to hold her hand or face, you won't hurt her."

I made my way around her bed, taking in the paleness of her skin and the still-sunken-in appearance of her eyes.

An overstuffed chair sat beside her bed and I took a seat, taking her hand in mine. Her fingernails still had bits of dirt under them and were chipped and tattered. Christi rarely wore nail polish, but her nails were always neat.

Lifting her hand to my lips, I kissed each knuckle and fingertip. I could still smell the horrid odor that had been present in that cavern. Now it was mixed with that telltale smell of hospital disinfectant.

"Sponge baths only get them so clean, Mr. Malloy."

I continued to look at her, so pale and so fragile. "She won't like this. She's always been so particular about being clean."

I felt the nurse's warm hand on my shoulder, "You can bring her things up and we can have them ready when she wakes." I nodded in understanding. "Her IV is nearly ready to be changed. I'll be just down the hall if you need me."

I could just make out the sounds of the nurse's shoes on the tile floor as she turned, the soft thud of the closing door telling me she had left.

I got up from my chair and leaned over Christi's still body. I began to place soft kisses over her face, including her eyes and lastly her chapped lips. I pulled back to look at her; I could see remnants of tiny stones in her hair as well as scaling skin and clumps of dirt. I retrieved my cell from my pocket and sent my ma a text.

Send someone to get her things, she isn't clean enough.

Pocketing my phone, I nestled back into the empty side of her bed. "You scared me," I whispered into her ear. "I swear I won't ever fail you again, just please come back to me."

Running my hand along her cheekbone and down her chin, it didn't take a genius to see that she had lost a sizable amount of weight. I had no doubts ma would reverse that in a minute once I got my Christi home.

"Our wedding is in a few weeks, so you need to rest and get better so you can walk down that aisle to me."

I had no intention of postponing our wedding. Even if she had to be pushed down that aisle in a wheelchair, we were getting married.

"Our house is finished and I had ma order those sheets you liked. I know you said they were too expensive, but I plan to conceive twelve children in that bed so it needs to be comfortable."

I had told Christi I wanted twelve boys, truth was I didn't really care, as long as they were healthy.

"I've loved you for so long," I whispered quietly into her hand closing my eyes, holding back the tears that begged to escape. I pictured her young face in my head the first time I saw her. If I would have only followed my heart that day as a teen, she could have been mine much sooner. Instead I let my pride and ignorance make my decision. "You'll never know how long I've loved you."

There was no point in telling her my sins of the past, it wouldn't change anything. I didn't want her to think for even one second I didn't want her always. After what she had been through, she only needed to know that I wanted her more than anything.

"From the first moment I saw you, you've owned my very soul. My heart has continued to beat because of its longing to be close to you." I finally let the tears fall. They needed to be set free, give me the closure I needed. "I want you back in my bed, I don't like you here. I need to know I can wake up in the middle of the night and you're right there beside me. I watch you sleep, I know you don't know that, but I do."

I couldn't count how many nights I had lain next to her and watched her sleep. The light from the moon as it illuminated her face; it fascinated me, as did her quiet sighs as she dreamed. I wanted it all back.

I must have fallen asleep, since the next thing I knew, I was being shaken by my ma. Standing beside her was Ammo and Smiles.

"How is she?" Ma's soft voice was music to my ears.

"Well, having Patrick here was good for her," Smiles pointed to the bag that hung from the side of the bed, a small amount of dark amber fluid present. "Her kidneys are working."

I had never been so happy to see pee in all my life.

"Patrick, I want you to go clean yourself up. I know you won't leave the hospital, but I brought your things as well. You need to be fresh when she wakes up."

I wasn't even going to attempt to protest. My ma would throw me into the shower with my clothes on and scrub me herself and not think twice about it.

"I brought the girls to help me give her another bath and clean up her nails. She'll be upset if she sees them like this."

My ma knew her well. Christi was a strong person, but at the end of the day, she was a beautiful woman and she was always clean. She loved to soak in the tub at the condo, and she always showered twice a day.

I only nodded, as I accepted the bag from her and headed into the adjoining bathroom.

The hot water felt amazing as it cascaded down my body. My Christi was safe and back where she belonged, no more worrying about who was out to get her. She would be free to go about her day without a guard outside of her door. She would be thrilled to hear that.

By the time I was clean and dressed, ma had Christi's hair and body thoroughly washed and her clothes changed. Leaning over her body to kiss her forehead, she once again smelled like my Christi. Ammo was at the end of her bed rubbing her lotion on her feet and legs. I had to smile as the memory of the last morning we had spent together came to my mind.

Christi had a ritual of rubbing lotion all over her body after her shower; I would usually come in the room with her coffee and watch her as she slathered her legs in lotion. She would always look at me and smile, asking me if I was enjoying what I had termed the lotion rub-down. She knew it was one of my favorite things to watch.

The fresh feminine smell of her lotion permeated the air. I was so glad that rancid smell was gone. I knew it would upset her when she woke if she could still smell it.

Four days.

Four long days of watching my Christi sleep. Watching as the fluid in the bag went from amber to pale yellow. Dr. Bradshaw said that all of her labs were looking very good, so today he would be stopping the meds that made her sleep. He couldn't give us a timeframe of when she would wake; she would do it in her own time.

That was true Christi fashion. She did everything in her own time.

Matthew and I had taken shifts sitting with her. Neither one of us wanted her to be alone when she finally woke. I found him on more than one occasion telling her stories from her childhood. One night I found him whispering that he was sorry for deceiving her. He admitted that I had given him the credit card she was using to pay for things for our wedding. Matthew was a proud man, but he knew what was important, and he knew when to ask for help. We had agreed that she never needed to know that he didn't pay for his daughter's wedding, some things just weren't important.

I was no better. I had told her every secret I'd ever had in the hopes she would sit up and slap me for doing half of it.

I had contacted the jeweler that made all of the Malloy jewelry and had him repair her shamrock necklace. Nurse Casey had encouraged me to place it back around her neck.

Shamus brought me the bracelet that Sophia had stolen off of Christi's arm; I took it downstairs and dropped it into the donation box of the hospital chapel, after lighting a candle. I wanted nothing that woman had touched to be anywhere near my Christi. I had a new one made for her. I would wait until she woke up to place it on her wrist.

I had her engagement ring in my pocket. Ma had gotten it cleaned, but I wasn't ready to place it back on her finger after what had happened. Ma told me to let Christi decide if she wanted that one back or not. I hoped she didn't, as I didn't want it to hold any bad memories. I was sure the priest wouldn't mind finding another piece in the donation box.

It was just after midnight, day five that she had been asleep. I had to catch up on some much neglected paperwork. Caleb had sent me an email stating that he needed me to look at some discrepancies in his books. He told me that of course they could wait until Christi was well, but I needed a distraction for a while.

I had just opened the spreadsheet on the expenses of *Whiskers* when I heard it. The sound I had waited weeks to hear. The sound that made my heart race every time I heard it.

"Patrick."

CHAPTER TWENTY-FIVE

Warmth…Softness…Comfort.

Death was a funny thing. I had heard stories of people seeing their lives flash before their eyes. However, I heard voices. My father telling me of the time I had climbed a tree when I was seven because the little boy next door double-dared me, this resulting in the breaking of my left arm and the little boy getting spanked all the way home by his mother.

Patrick telling me how he had switched his mother's sugar and salt when he was ten. She had baked several pies that day and wouldn't let him have any, this being his retaliation. She caught him before any additional inedible pies were made. Needless to say, he couldn't sit for a week either.

Nora telling me she was so glad that I was going to be all right as she caressed me with her warm hands. The warmth was my favorite part of death. I had been cold for so long. I snuggled further into the softness and let the comfort engulf me.

Tap…Tap…Tap…

Some said that hell was different for everyone. Clearly, my hell was having to listen to someone typing on a keyboard. Maybe if I asked nicely they would stop. Part of me was afraid that if I opened my eyes, I would lose the heat and the comfort. But the tapping wouldn't stop and it needed to stop, like now.

Slowly, I began to open my eyes, waiting for the cold to come rushing back, my hell to return. But it didn't. The room was dimly lit by a single lamp that sat in the corner by what appeared to be a desk. The bed I was currently resting in was so lush and soft, and did it smell nice in here. A clear bag hung over my head, half full of fluid, clear tubing descended down, ending in my hand.

Tap…Tap…Tap…

Scanning the room, my eyes finally found the source of that annoying noise...
Patrick. Even as an angel, he was seriously handsome. The glow from his computer
screen illuminated his pale features. The dark circles that lined his still beautiful eyes
made deeper by the darkness of the room. He looked so exhausted.

I had to tell him I loved him, that it was fine to go on without me, find love again
and be happy.

"Patrick," I managed. My voice was barely above a whisper, husky and deep,
sounding foreign to my ears.

I was startled by the loud crashing sound of his computer hitting the floor, not that
he seemed to care, as he sprung from the chair and onto my bed beside me.

"Christi, Baby."

His hands and eyes were exploring every part of my face, his lips leaving gentle
kisses as they trailed after his fingertips.

"Patrick?"

"Shhh, don't talk, save your strength. You're safe, I swear it this time."

I looked to him in confusion, safe?

"Am I...dead?"

Patrick began chuckling, "No, my Love, you're not dead."

"What happened to...?"

"All taken care of, Douce, Sophia, Jimmy, Anthony, all gone. They'll never hurt
you again."

I closed my eyes at the relief of his admission. I would never have to worry about
looking behind me and wondering if they had found me.

Patrick began to tell me how Douce was actually responsible for Angus finding
me. Had he just cleaned me off with a bucket of water, I would either be dead or sitting
in Italy as Anthony's captive right now. I shuddered at the thought.

"Anthony was a very sick man, Patrick."

"Yes, I know. But he can't hurt you from where he is now."

My eyes shot open, was he sitting in jail?

Patrick seemed to sense my panic and wrapped his arms around me, settling me on
his left arm, his chin resting on the top of my head. "He's sitting in Hell, right alongside Douce, Jimmy, and Sophia."

Closing my eyes in relief, I let sleep take over.

·

Over the next two days, several things occurred. First, Dr. Bradshaw removed all the IVs and had me start eating. You would think I would have just dived in and ate till I was full, but that wasn't what happened. We started small and I filled up quite quickly. Nora brought homemade chicken broth and had me sip it. It warmed me from my head to my toes. She told me it was an old family recipe that she would share once I got home. It did wonders for me.

Second, Dr. Bradshaw insisted I speak with a therapist. Dr. Nancy Green was about my age, she had also been a victim of a kidnapping. She told me some of the feelings and emotions she expected I might feel. She explained that she thought it would be a good idea to meet in her office a couple of times a week and I quickly agreed.

After eight days in the hospital, I was finally released. I had gained four pounds and could handle solid foods.

Nora and Patrick insisted that I stay at Nora and Thomas's house; I chose not to argue as I did tire easily. Patrick and I agreed to continue planning the wedding that was scheduled in just over a week. Nora assured Patrick that she would do the majority of the work and make me rest.

True to her word, that was exactly what she did.

Patrick needed to handle some neglected business decisions and I insisted that he go and take care of them. Nora had me resting in an overstuffed chaise lounge, with the softest throw I had ever felt. It was heaven.

"I'm just a phone call away if you need me," Patrick told me for the hundredth time, kissing every part of my face he could find.

"Patrick, I know, I'll be fine. Maggie is coming over later and all I have planned is to sit here and be spoiled by your mother."

"Son, I have plenty of experience taking care of sick children," Nora said sternly from her place in the doorway.

"I know, Ma. I just don't want to be away from…"

"But Caleb has been very patient and he needs you, now go…she'll be fine."

I watched as he walked across the carpet, stopping to kiss Nora's cheek as he left the room.

"This was hell for him, too, Christi. Not to the extent of your hell, but hell nonetheless."

"I know, Nora, I'm just so glad this is finally behind us."

CHAPTER TWENTY-SIX

1 sat in my car for at least fifteen minutes. Every fiber of my being was begging me not to leave her there, to go back in that house and curl protectively around my Christi.

My business head finally kicked in as I started my car and headed to my condo. Twenty minutes later, I was standing in my elevator, replaying memories of the conversations that had followed Christi's awakening. Holding her hand as she told her father that Anthony had killed Morgan, how he had played on the other's weaknesses for his gain. Hell was far too good for Anthony.

One mystery that still remained for me was who had been driving Morgan the day of Paige's wedding. All fingers pointed to Anthony, but until I had solid proof, I would always worry. I would find out who was driving that car.

The ding of the door opening brought me out of my memories.

I walked the distance to my office, rounding the corner to find both Shamus and Caleb sitting around my desk. Shamus was already busy typing away on the keyboard as Caleb was talking in whispers on his phone.

"Morning, Boss. How is Ms. O'Rourke?" Shamus questioned in nearly perfect English.

I smiled as I took my seat behind my desk. "She's doing much better. Chased me out of the house today, which is a good sign."

He smiled and began typing away again on his keyboard. Caleb quickly finished his phone call, leaning back in his chair.

"Sorry, that was my father." The look on his face was a mixture of confusion and anger.

"Everything okay?"

"Yes, just family drama."

I didn't pry, this was clearly another sore subject, and the look I got from him at the hospital came back to mind.

"No Angus today?" Caleb questioned.

"He's taking Maggie to the doctor, she's been very ill the last few days," I informed.

No one questioned the reason for the illness. He would tell us if he thought we needed to know, although I knew Angus would be thrilled if Maggie was indeed pregnant.

"Caleb, I had Shamus come today just in case we needed to get into any systems and have a look around." Caleb gave me a puzzled look. "Shamus hasn't found a firewall that he can't break."

Caleb only nodded in understanding. He leaned forward and placed three large file folders on my desk as he began. "When I took over for my father, I had our accountant give me a current financial overview. I changed all the passwords and encryption as you'd recommended." Caleb began to open the files and arrange them. "Then I began doing random audits on the accounts as you'd suggested."

He took a deep breath and then sat back in his chair as he continued. "Everything was fine for months," he sighed and crossed his left leg over his right, his ankle resting on his knee. "When I got back from our honeymoon, the first thing I did was run an audit report. It was fine."

His phone began to ring, but he silenced it.

"The next night, I was suffering from jet lag and was restless. Since I was up, I decided to run another audit; this one was less than twenty-four hours later, but as you can see, the numbers are hugely different."

I began scanning over the paperwork, seeing that he was correct. On all three accounts, the numbers were thousands of dollars different.

"Shamus, run these accounts." I gave him the numbers and his fingers began to fly across the keys. "Caleb, are these the only accounts that show these large withdrawals?"

He pondered for less than a second, "No, my Visa card had an unusual charge on it, too, but it was taken care of by the company."

"Sorry for interrupting, Boss," Shamus said getting our attention, "Mr. Montgomery, who you know in Montepulciano, Italy?" he questioned again in broken English.

Caleb rose from his chair and made his way to the desk that Shamus sat at. "Montepulciano is the place my mother always travels to when she visits Italy. She's been going there for years."

Where had I heard that name before?

"She actually just got back from there."

I remembered Sherman saying Eileen was away and how I wondered why he would have chosen to let her vacation alone.

"Does she always go alone?"

I was not certain why I questioned this, something just wasn't adding up here.

"No, she usually takes Mia with her, like she did this time."

I looked to Shamus who was looking intently at his computer screen.

"Has she ever taken you or Sherman with her?"

Caleb went into deep thought, "No, she's only ever taken Mia. My dad never had time and she never wanted me to go. She always just took my sister."

My gut was screaming at me. What woman didn't take both of her children along when she went away on vacation? I could see it happening once in a while, but according to Caleb, this was a regular occurrence.

"How often does she go away?"

Before Caleb could answer, Shamus began to speak.

"Three hundred and twelve times, always on Virgin Airlines. The first time she took Mia with her there was an issue with her birth certificate matching her passport."

Caleb and I quickly turned to Shamus.

"The note here says that the flight attendant questioned the validity of the documents and so the state of Mississippi had to verify the authenticity of the record."

I looked to Caleb who was staring slack-jawed at Shamus.

"I told you, there isn't a firewall that Shamus can't get past."

Caleb turned his attention to me, the look of shock written clear as day.

"She was born premature and my father was concerned about letting her travel, or at least that's the story I've always heard," Caleb said as Shamus continued to click away. Before Caleb could go any further, Shamus interrupted again.

"How can a baby be premature when the birth weight is over ten pounds?" Shamus was still clicking on his keyboard. He was clearly thinking out loud.

This time Caleb moved around to the computer screen, peering over Shamus's shoulder.

I watched as Caleb's eyes looked over the screen wildly.

"You see, right there, ten pounds three ounces," Shamus looked to Caleb.

I watched Caleb's face closely as it roamed the screen over and over. "This can't be right. She was a preemie, my mom always said so. I've kidded Mia all of her life that she was always in a hurry to do things."

I was still pondering who I knew in Montepulciano.

"Could it be that your parents had to get married?" I questioned Caleb. "Maybe the 'premature' thing was a ruse to cover up an unwed pregnancy."

"Malloy, I got the same speech from my mother as you did yours, that she was a virgin when she went to her marital bed. They knew each other for ten days before he returned and took her to the courthouse."

So clearly it wasn't a case of "oops, we're pregnant" here.

"It doesn't make any sense, Caleb, why would she lie about the baby being premature?"

Then it hit me like a Mack truck.

"Mia isn't Sherman's."

Caleb's head quickly snapped up. He said nothing and his eyes became emotionless as he pondered my statement.

I continued to watch as his face reflected memories flowing through his mind. "Shamus, check the dates of Eileen's trips to Italy against the dates the money went missing," I instructed.

Shamus began to quickly type and his brow furrowed.

"Her name is Mia," Caleb whispered.

I looked back to Caleb, he too, was thinking out loud.

"Her birth name is Mia. Not Shannon or Megan, or Claire, something that would reflect her Irish heritage. My dad might not be Ireland born, but his grandparents were."

This time Shamus looked away from his computer screen, his eyes meeting mine.

"Caleb, what the hell are you talking about?" I asked as Caleb's face never changed as he continued to stare blankly at the wall.

"That doesn't prove anything. Your wife's name is Paige, which is English." Apparently, Shamus wasn't following what Caleb was thinking.

"Paige's name is actually *Padraige*," I added before Caleb could respond.

The room grew deathly silent as all three of us looked at each other.

"Mom has insisted that all of our children are given proper Irish names. She said it would be a disgrace to the family if we didn't choose Irish names to honor the family heritage," Caleb thought aloud.

My eyes became huge as the memory of Anthony's last words returned to me. *"If you kill me, you'll never know..."* I finished his declaration in my head. *'The truth.'*

"Boss," Shamus's voice brought me back to the present. "Your on to something. Every time Eileen go to Italy, a large amount of money was transferred to a new account. I'm almost through the last firewall and we'll know who..."

Shamus's eyes became huge as he stared at the screen, *"Cac Naofa."* (holy shit)

I sprang from my chair and crossed the space between us. Nothing could have prepared me for the name that was written on the computer screen.

"Caleb, where is your mother today?"

Caleb looked at me as he began to retrieve his cell from his pocket. "She heard about Christi and insisted on visiting her today."

Dialing Christi as quickly as I could, I began to run out of the office. Her phone rang and rang before it went to voicemail. I then tried my ma's phone, but got the same. Next, I tried the house phone, but it only rang and rang, as well.

Finally, after reaching the last step, I threw open the door and ran to my car, Caleb and Shamus hot on my heels.

"Shamus, get all the men to my parent's house. Tell them not to stop for anything, just get the fuck over there."

How could I have been so stupid? My eagerness to make Christi safe had clouded my judgment once again. I began to pray that I wasn't too late. I should have taken his words with an ounce of warning. Anthony had not been man enough to pull off something like this alone. He would have had to have had help, like in everything else he did. Velenci didn't need Chicago. He had New York and Miami, not to mention Italy, so why was he doing this?

My speedometer read ninety as I rounded the ramp to get onto the highway. Traffic was heavy as I began to wind around vehicles and then drove on the shoulder when I noticed traffic had stopped.

Hitting the speed dial on my phone, I had to get someone over to the house. I could just feel it in my bones that something was very wrong.

"Patrick," my father's voice filled my car.

"Da!" I shouted into the microphone above my head.

"What's wrong, Patrick?" He asked his voice full of concern.

"Where are you right now?"

"I'm having lunch with Sherman, why?"

I pounded my fist into my steering wheel, as I again changed lanes onto the shoulder.

"Excuse yourself, I need your help and I need it now, but you can't let Sherman know something's up. I don't know if he can be trusted right now."

I glanced over to Caleb, who was holding on for dear life as I increased my speed.

"Well, I think that's a nice thank-you gift."

God, I loved my da. He was quick on his feet when he needed to be.

"I don't have all the facts yet, but I think Anthony was acting for someone and I think it was Velenci."

Traffic seemed to clear suddenly, and I pushed my foot further to the floor, my speed now at one hundred thirty.

"Your Mother is always telling me the latest gossip she's heard and I think you may be right."

"Da, I have all my men headed there now, I can't get Ma or Christi to pick up the phone."

"I'll drop by Matthew's house and see if he has any we can borrow."

I watched as Shamus picked up his cell and began dialing what I knew to be Matthew's number. Seconds later, it was confirmed when I heard him speaking in Gaelic, telling Matthew what we already knew and what we were doing.

"Da, if this is true you know what I'll have to do."

"Patrick, I thought that horse was dead. Quit beating it."

"I'm nearly there, Da, hurry and get here."

I didn't wait for a response, I knew my da would make up an excuse and Sherman would be none the wiser.

I began to pound on the gate remote as soon as it came into sight. I didn't care if it wasn't open enough for my car, I would crash it. The gate was open, but not quite enough as I heard my side mirrors being ripped off. Slamming on the brakes, I could hear my tires protesting the sudden demand. Shamus was a little faster, he didn't wait for the car to stop or bother trying the door knob. His body seemed to go through the door like a cartoon character. The house was too quiet as I entered, shouting for Christi. When I received no response, I began taking the stairs two at a time.

I was nearly to the top when I heard the distinct sound of a gunshot.

CHAPTER TWENTY-SEVEN

"So, what flavor will it be this morning?"

Since I had been home from the hospital, Nora had served me ice cream with nearly every meal. She was trying everything to help me gain my weight back.

"Surprise me," I chuckled.

Nora had placed a tray of hot tea on the side table when she first came in the room. I had begged her to show me how to make a proper cup of tea. She told me to get back to my previous weight and she would show me her secret.

"I do have a confession."

I looked to Nora as she poured the tea, "Okay?"

"Makenna phoned me this morning. She's having an issue with some paperwork a client has given her and since it's entirely in Gaelic, she's asked for my help."

I sighed slightly. "Don't worry about it, Nora. She's still a friend of yours."

"No, she's not, but the client she's working for is..." Before she could say anything more, the doorbell sounded. "Speak of the devil."

Nora gently patted my knee, turned, and left the room. Grasping the handle of the cup, I slowly brought it to my lips. I closed my eyes as I allowed the warm, sweet goodness to flow down my throat. Lord, she could make a good cup of tea.

I could faintly hear the front door opening and I had to snicker as I thought of Makenna walking through the massive foyer. She had to have been desperate and swallowed a lot of crow to pluck up the courage to face Nora again. Grateful, I wouldn't have to deal with her for my wedding.

Maggie was due to join us later. She hadn't been feeling very well lately. Nora came right out and asked if she could be pregnant. Maggie denied the possibility. She swore up and down that she would be going to her wedding bed as a virgin, but the way she and Angus were around each other had me skeptical. She was going to the doctor today at the insistence of Angus.

I had just poured my second cup of tea when I heard the doorbell again. It must have been later than I thought as I was certain that was Maggie. Taking in the warmth of the tea, I continued to relax into the chair.

"Christi?" Nora's voice sounded from the hall and I looked to the doorway as she entered the room, with a look of disgust on her face, "I'm sorry to do this to you, Lass," her voice was low yet emotionless. "Eileen is here to see you. She heard what happened and she *says* she wants to make certain you're all right."

I smiled at Nora, "It's all right. She's technically family and we do have to treat her as such."

Nora again placed her warm hand on my knee, "You have the heart of a lion and the touch of a lamb."

"Oh, Nora, hasn't there been enough fighting and hating? I just want some happiness." Nora return my smile as she turned back to the hallway.

I could smell her before she ever made it into the room, the overwhelming cloud of Eileen's signature Chanel perfume preceding her into the room. I had never been a fan of that particular scent, but to each their own I believed.

"Christi, I just could not believe it when I heard the terrible news."

She moved across the room and began to pour herself a cup of tea, all the while continuing to tell me how she's been in an area of Italy and that she couldn't get good cell coverage.

I looked to Nora who was standing in the doorway, arms crossed against her chest and eyes rolling. "Yes, well, as you can clearly see, our Christi is doing just fine."

Did I mention how much I loved Nora?

"Oh," Eileen stopped stirring the tea in her cup. "Dare I ask, is the wedding postponed?"

I couldn't help but laugh. The woman standing before me was not the Eileen I had been used to seeing. This one was acting as if we had been best friends for years.

"No, we're actually just finishing up the plans today."

The look on her face was of surprise, maybe a little shock.

"Yes, and speaking of planning, I have to leave you two alone for a few minutes," Nora's voice sounded reluctant, as if she would rather have a root canal than to help Makenna who was still waiting downstairs.

"Oh, Nora, don't worry about us, I'll be more than happy to keep Christi company," Eileen smiled brightly.

The look on Nora's face was of apology, but it wasn't her fault. I smiled and gave her a loving wink.

"I'll make this as quick as possible," Nora began, only to be quickly interrupted by Eileen.

"Take your time, Christi and I will be right here when you're finished."

Nora shot me a look that said she was sorry and she would hurry as she left the room.

My tea was lukewarm and Eileen was quick to offer to warm it up for me. I closed my eyes and let my head rest against the back of the chaise. I still wasn't a hundred percent and it frustrated me that I tired so easily. I had nearly fallen asleep when I heard Eileen stirring my fresh cup of tea before handing it to me with a smile.

"So tell me, Christi, what are your colors?"

I took a quick sip of my tea, the last thing I wanted to do was share my plans for my wedding with her.

"I'm going with the Malloy family colors."

There, truthful answer, yet completely avoided. She wouldn't question as to what that would mean. I knew she hadn't done her homework enough to know such an important detail about her daughter-in-law's family.

"That's very admirable of you." Eileen turned to gaze out the window as she continued to sip her tea. "You know, Christi, I was a lot like you when I was your age," she rested her cup on her saucer as she continued to look into the garden. Lost in her thoughts, she began to smile just a hint.

The tea was doing its usual job of relaxing me, perhaps a little too much.

"I was once in love with a man who I thought the sun rose and set in."

My body was so placid at this point, I felt so warm and relaxed from my toes to my eyebrows.

"How long have you and Sherman been together?" I asked. My words were becoming slurred and my arms suddenly felt heavy.

Eileen quickly turned toward me again, a look of pure hatred crossing her face. "Who said I was talking about Sherman?" Her voice was sharp and laced with sarcasm. I tried to respond, but my voice wouldn't come. "How are you feeling now, Christi?" she smirked. She moved directly in front of me, kneeling to place her face even with mine. "I've watched you Christi." She ran her index finger along my new bracelet, "I heard Sophia took your original, such as stupid girl that one." I couldn't feel my legs at this point; Eileen must have drugged my tea. "Hardly her fault. Her mother was a whore, so she came by it naturally."

I looked at her questioningly.

"Well, well, I take it by that look you know about the Porchelli family. So do I, and all too well." She rose to her feet and then took a seat in the chair across from me. "Well, let me tell you a few things you may not know about them." She crossed her legs and picked up her cup of tea, delicately bringing it up to her lips. Her memories played across her face, making her look deceptively pleasant and happy.

"It was the summer of my eighteenth birthday and my parents took me to Italy to celebrate. My sister and I had been shopping and stopped by this little café to have lunch. She and I had been talking and we were ready to head back to our hotel when we asked for our check. The waiter told us that the gentlemen across the way had taken care of it.

"Velenci Porchelli, as I later learned, was the most handsome man I had ever seen. He kissed mine and my sister's hands and said all the right words at the right time. He made me feel special, needed, and for the first time...sexy."

Her free hand went loosely around her neck and she smiled at me almost shyly, before looking out the window again. "He was so gentle with me and after only three days, he told me he was in love with me. I returned the sentiment. He was going to be my forever."

Suddenly she looked my way again, the memory gone from her mind, her face vacant of emotion.

"I returned home and wrote to him every day. He would send me gifts almost daily. He swore he would come to Ireland to visit me and ask my father for permission to court me properly. Two months later, I found out I was pregnant. I was so excited and I couldn't wait to tell him."

The look on her face changed again as she continued to sip her tea, her eyes never meeting mine. "That's when he told me he was already married."

She slowly set her tea on the table as she, again, rose from her chair. "He told me we would have to wait to be together. That if his wife found out, she would take all of his money and he would have nothing. I believed him and he paid my way and sent me to America."

I could just make out the sound of my cell phone vibrating on the table across the room. I prayed it was Patrick, knowing if I didn't answer he would send one of his men or even come himself to check on me.

"I was pregnant, alone, and needed help in a strange country. I only brokenly spoke the language and I had no support here. I was in the states less than twenty-four hours when I met Sherman Montgomery. He was a nice enough man, young and easy to fool, and so eager to please. I knew what I had to do. So I seduced him and he fell for it hook, line, and sinker."

My phone began to vibrate again. *Dear God, please let it be Patrick.*

"He came back a few days later and professed his love for me and we married immediately. When the appropriate amount of time had elapsed, I told him we were pregnant. He was thrilled, and then went and spoke with his family. Turns out he'd been on the fence as to whether or not he wanted to run his family's business. I had gone from one crime family to another, it was perfect."

The house phone began to ring. It continued several more times and I began to worry about Nora, why wasn't she picking it up?

"Velenci kept telling me he loved me and that soon we would be together." The house phone began to ring again. "I named the baby Mia after his Mother. Sherman never questioned me. Never once did he question anything I ever did, the fool. We only ended up pregnant with Caleb after a night of heavy drinking on my part, out of loneliness and missing Velenci. Sherman always thought me a bit frigid, but he wasn't who I wanted touching me. He was always so...ignorant."

Her arms wrapped tightly around herself.

"Caleb was a year old when Velenci's wife paid me a visit. She told me she knew all about me and my daughter. It was then I found out that I was one of many women Velenci had made promises of love to. His wife informed me that she had divorced Velenci and was with a man who treated her with dignity and respect."

She turned now to face me. "She was smart like you, Christi. She made the man pursue her, prove himself worthy of her. He's a butcher in New Jersey. She has a huge house and she wants for nothing. You have the most powerful man in this city at your beck and call."

She slowly began to walk toward the door, stopping once she reached the table where her purse sat. "I did everything for that man and he treated me like nothing, he tossed me aside. After I heard that he was no longer married, I went to him, with our daughter. I just knew he would take me as his wife, but instead he told me he wanted nothing more than for me to just be one of his goomahs."

She then turned back toward me and I could see the shiny gun she had in her hand.

"It was then I began to plan." Her hand caressed the gun like a mother caressed a baby's face. "I began to take money from Sherman's accounts and sending it to bank accounts I set up under Velenci's name so if they were ever discovered, he would be blamed. Of course, I had a part to play, too. Who would believe shallow, greedy, stupid, redneck-marrying Eileen capable of detailed planning and years of patience, being belittled and ridiculed as a social spectacle? No one, and that's the beauty of all this."

"My Mia has been denied all these years, but she's also been patient. She knows her part in all of this as well. My precious girl is brilliant, just like her Mother. She's going to run the Porchelli family now. It was always my plan to get Sophia and Anthony out of the way. Their stupidity just made it easier.

"It was Mia's idea to have Velenci attend the wedding you know. She told Caleb that she and Sophia were old friends, practically like family. Again, Sherman never questioned anything. Nice job, by the way. It was a beautiful wedding, and once I make sure my son marries properly, I'll deliver the baby quilt to its rightful mother to use with my grandchildren."

My phone began to vibrate again.

"Yes, you were just too pretty at the wedding for that sick bastard Anthony to resist and I encouraged him to pursue you. I even told him you and Patrick were fighting and that you had mentioned you found his eyes erotic. I honestly think he believed you would find him desirable, the poor nutcase."

"I knew how Patrick would react with you gone. I knew he would do all the dirty work for me, including getting rid of those bastard children of Velenci's before he took care of himself. Men are such basic, simple creatures. But Anthony took too long. I told him to move quicker, but he insisted he wanted to break you down first, make you want him completely. So, I took my opportunity and flew to Italy while he enjoyed his game, and this time, I called all the shots," she said blowing on her pistol as if she had just fired it.

I wasn't certain I wanted her to tell me what she meant by that.

"So you see, in the end I'll have everything I want. Mia is the head of the Porchelli family now, and once I do some damage control, Caleb will take over here as soon as a few loose ends are tied up. I'll finally take my place as the Mother to two of the most powerful people in this country and Europe."

She was serious. This had all been her plan.

"Nora made it far too easy today and Makenna was all too eager to help me. Well, it did take a little promise of a large sum of money on my part, but not to worry as I plan to kill her as well."

I could feel my breathing becoming erratic as she stepped closer to me. God, please let Patrick get here quick.

"The only thing I haven't decided yet is, do I kill you first or do I let you watch everyone else die."

I could feel the tears rolling down my face, yet I was powerless to do anything about it.

"Only one thing wrong with your little plan there, Eileen." Nora stood in the doorway once again. Her hair was a mess and her shirt was twisted. Eileen's face was one of shock and I wanted to scream for Nora to run, but again nothing would come out. "Your partner in crime downstairs can't throw a right hook to save her ass."

I had always known Nora to be a graceful woman, she moved with a particular air about her. Not this time, though. She was a mother bear protecting her cub.

Eileen didn't know how to react as Nora tackled her to the floor, smashing the lamp that had sat on the table that was now on its side. The motion caused the door to slam shut. The bodies of the two women had blurred into one as they fought for the gun in Eileen's clenched hand.

"Christi!" The sound of Patrick's voice echoed from downstairs as Eileen and Nora continued to thrash around on the floor. I could hear the thunderous sound of feet, hitting the wooden steps and I questioned if all of Patrick's men were on their way up the stairs.

The sound of a gunshot drowned out the sounds coming from the stairs and the thrashing of the women abruptly stopped.

Seconds later, Patrick and Shamus burst through the door, splinters flying as the frame gave way.

Eileen and Nora lay motionless, Nora currently pinned under Eileen. I couldn't control the tears that ran down my face. This family wouldn't survive without Nora.

I held my breath as Patrick crossed the room towards the two women, his gun pointed at the back of Eileen's head. I watched as Nora's hands began to move, struggling to get Eileen off of her.

Patrick moved quickly as he rolled Eileen's body to the side. Nora lay on the floor, her shirt stained with bright red blood, her breathing heavy and her eyes closed. All eyes were on Nora as she blinked and slowly sat up, Patrick was quick to help her as he began to check her over. Eileen's lifeless eyes were still open as she stared blankly at the ceiling.

Nora's nose wrinkled as she looked at the dead woman's body beside her, "You'd think someone would have told that awful woman that perfume has an expiration date."

CHAPTER TWENTY-EIGHT

Once the dust settled, Patrick took Thomas out into the hallway. Moments later, an ambulance arrived to take me back the hospital. My biggest fear was that the drug she had given me would have an adverse effect. Tonto came in while Patrick and Thomas were talking, and took my teacup in hand and sniffed it.

"Troll killer," he spoke with assurance.

"Not to worry, Ms. O'Rourke, I've used that drug a number of times and although it seems potent, it wears off quickly."

Patrick and Thomas entered the room again; Patrick was at my side before I could even blink.

"I saw the tapes, Love."

Tapes?

Thomas was quick to answer my questioning look. "Nora wants this to be a nursery, she had audio and video placed in the room for when the grandchildren are over."

If I could have laughed, I would have. Nora was always a step ahead of everyone.

My father was the next to enter the room, and as much as I loved and needed Patrick, I would always want my dad to comfort me. He looked to his right, the covered body of Eileen stopping him in his tracks.

His eyes then turned back to me, "Christi, you responsible for this?" When I lay there motionless and didn't answer, he rushed past Patrick to get to me.

"Sir, she was drugged by Eileen with troll killer, it's an herbal concoction. We use it sometimes to get answers we need. It wears off pretty quickly, but I can give her an antidote," Tonto informed.

Patrick took my hand in his, "Are we sure it's troll killer?"

Tonto nodded and then passes the teacup to Patrick. With a quick sniff, Patrick agreed. "Give her the antidote."

Tonto left the room and I heard a loud clatter of voices coming up the stairs moments later. Brandon entered first, followed by Muscles. Nora came in behind Muscles, her small frame nearly blocked by Muscles larger one. Her clothes were changed and her hair perfect. She crossed the room, shooing away Matthew and Thomas.

"Let me see my lass." Nora took my arm and began cleaning a spot on my skin in a circular motion, the smell of alcohol flooding my nose. "This will sting just a little, Lass."

Seconds later, I felt a slight sting which was followed by an overall warm feeling filling my body, much like the feeling I got from the original drug.

"I still want her to be checked out," Patrick's sharp voice resonated.

"Of course, Patrick," Nora replied condescendingly.

The medication must have been working, as I could finally move my fingers.

"Someone want to tell me exactly what happened here?" My father's concerned voice questioned from across the room.

Nora took in a deep breath and then turned to face him. "It's all my fault, Matthew."

Nora sounded so sad and broken. It wasn't her fault, and as soon as I could talk, I was going to inform her of that very thing.

"Makenna called early this morning in an absolute panic. She was recently given the Fitzpatrick christening. Mrs. Fitzpatrick wanted all of the programs in Gaelic. You know as well as I do that Makenna may be of Irish blood, but she never took the time to embrace it."

This wasn't a surprise to me. Most of the Irish families that lived in the neighborhood embraced their heritage. You either got with the program or you were left behind.

"Mrs. Fitzpatrick does so much for the women's shelter over on Main that I couldn't say no." She lowered her head and began to rub her hands up and down her pant covered thighs.

"Makenna walked in, thanking me profusely, not knowing I wasn't doing this for her benefit," her head shaking as she spoke. "I told her to have a seat in the sunroom and that I would make us a pot of tea." Nora rose from her chair and began looking out the window into the garden, just as Eileen had done not long ago.

"Had she stayed in the sunroom, her plan might have worked." I was finally able to move my head, so I tried to clear my throat, but it was still silent.

"She came into the kitchen, the look of confidence on her overly tanned face," Nora sneered. "She raised the knife she'd smuggled in, like I had reason to be afraid of a knife," Nora let out a huff; clearly she wasn't afraid of the blade of a knife.

"You're very brave, Nora," my father spoke.

Nora turned to face us once again, "Bravery has nothing to do with it."

Patrick and Thomas began to chuckle. Matthew looked between the three, frustrated he wasn't in on the joke.

"She had the balls to try and throw a punch when I knocked that pathetic pocket knife out of her hand." I would have given anything to have seen that.

"She forgot the one rule in engaging an enemy." The men began to chuckle harder. "Never bring a knife to a gunfight."

Nora was clearly unscathed from her run in with Makenna. It was as if Makenna had forgotten to flush the toilet rather than pulled a knife on her.

"Why would her plan have worked if she would've stayed in the sunroom?" My father finally asked the question I wanted to know the answer to as well.

"Because her favorite gun is in the kitchen. The sunroom only has a shotgun and Nora isn't as good with a shotgun," Thomas answered and a smile came across Nora's face as she leaned into his side, nodding in agreement.

"It's a very nice nine millimeter with a silencer on it. Eileen never knew what was happening down here. Now, had I used the shotgun, she could've heard what happened, and killed my girl," Nora said seriously.

And just like that, Nora became my hero.

The next day, I was once again sitting in the Malloy house. This time I was allowed, to get up long enough to set the table. Nora had insisted on having a big family dinner. I watched in awe as she scurried around the kitchen, as if doing the most graceful ballet dance. No matter how long I lived, I would never look that good in the kitchen.

Once everyone was seated and grace was said, the only noise you could hear was the clanking of forks against plates and an occasional moan of someone enjoying their food. While everyone else had plates of salad, I was forced to eat yet another bowl of ice cream.

Maggie had arrived late yesterday after the guys had cleaned up the two bodies. Had I not been here and seen all the blood everywhere, I would never have guessed there had been a gunfight. Even the front door had been re-hung and was absolutely perfect. Nora had insisted that Maggie and Angus be here for the family dinner as well.

"Christi, I have only the programs left to put together and I thought we could do some this evening as long as you're not too tired," Maggie offered.

"No, I'm more than willing to do a few. But first, Missy, I want to know what's been going on with you."

The smile on Maggie's face dropped and her head lowered. It was instant waterworks. Angus quickly took her hand and drew her into his side.

"Oh, my, Maggie. Whatever is the matter?" Nora asked concerned.

I watched as Maggie's body began to convulse with sobs. Poor Angus just continued to rub her back.

"It's my fault she's so upset, Mrs. Malloy," Angus's voice was sad, regretful, and I wanted to go over and hug it all away.

Maggie took in a deep breath and wiped her eyes with her dinner napkin. "Since I was a wee little one, I've had my wedding planned out," her voice was so small, not the usual strong person she was.

"I made a promise that I'd save myself for my husband and give him all of me." No one moved or tried to say anything as Maggie continued. "I love Angus with everything I have, but I'll never be able to show him that love and give him all of me now."

I quickly turned to Patrick; I wanted to know why he wouldn't let Angus marry Maggie.

"Angus isn't in the country legally," Patrick's husky voice filled the table, clarifying the situation for everyone. "He's not able to apply for a legal marriage license here."

It was as if the angels from heaven above shouted it themselves as three female voices cried out at the exact same time.

"Da, you have to fix this!" Amex slammed her tiny hand down on the table.

"Who do you know, Thomas?" Allyson's voice was not far behind.

"Dad, call someone and do something!" I wasn't about to be left out, either. Shannon also nodded vehemently in agreement.

Nora shook her head as she began to chuckle. We girls were all talking over one another, demanding that our fathers do something.

Poor Maggie sat gob-smacked in her chair.

Finally, Thomas raised both hands in surrender, "Fine, yes, I'll make a call."

"Right now, Da!" Amex shouted.

I turned to see Patrick's face growing red, his eyes boring into mine. "What?" I questioned him.

"What am I, Christi, chopped liver?"

I was confused at his question and his anger.

"Calm down, Son. These ladies know who can do certain things and who they need to call on," Thomas said in defense.

"Oh, so only you can forge some documents?" Patrick's voice was tight and clipped, his anger now spilling over in his words.

"No, I could forge them just as easily as you could, or I can call Governor Stamford to play some golf and then have him sign an executive order so everything's aboveboard."

I watched as Patrick hung his head and began to chuckle. "Touché, Da, touché."

Muscles was sitting back in his chair shaking his head, his look was of disbelief.

"What has your crow, Muscles?" Thomas questioned.

"Just an observation."

"Continue."

"It's just that with one word from these little daddy's girls, they have the two of you snapping to attention."

My dad let out a deep bellied laugh. Thomas followed.

"What, what's so funny?" Muscles questioned.

"Son, when you're blessed to have a little girl, you'll learn there's nothing you won't do to make her smile."

"Pfft."

"Muscles, when my three were little, I was their mannequin when they wanted to play dress-up. I was their guest at more tea parties than I can count. I cleaned up scraped knees and broke up fights over favorite shirts. I've had the pleasure to be the first boy they ever danced with and to have warm, wet, strawberry-scented kisses every night before bed. I held my daughters as they cried over first crushes and even one particularly persistent young man who had my daughter followed," my dad turned to Patrick and winked.

"I was blessed with Abby and again I sat at that small table with my knees to my ears and I sipped the tea she made me, no matter what it tasted like. I let her put lipstick on me and paint my nails. My own girls have long since grown up, but I can assure you that when Patrick and Christi bless us with a little girl, you'll once again find myself *and* Thomas with barrettes in our hair, feather boas around our necks, and frilly hats on our heads."

Not a dry eye was left at that table after my dad's speech.

"Sorry to disappoint you, Sir, but Christi and I will only be having boys," Patrick was trying very hard to be serious.

"Oh, well, I'm certain I can speak for Thomas when I say this to you, Patrick. You can only pray to be blessed with a little girl."

I noticed Sherman had grown very quiet and I was certain he was thinking of Mia. My heart broke for him.

"Sherman, do you need any help with the funeral?" Nora's voice was warm and gentle.

Sherman's head quickly turned in her direction. "We're just having a small service, since it'll only be Caleb, Paige, and me."

Nora reached over and took Sherman's hand in hers. "We'll all be there, Sherman. She was still your wife and I know that at one point in time, you loved her. She gave you a wonderful son and we'll all benefit from his devotion to this family," Nora patted Sherman's hand as his other discretely wiped his eyes.

When the truth about Eileen was finally told, Sherman could only shake his head in disbelief. He knew all along that Eileen had never loved him, but he had loved her. He admitted that they only shared two moments of intimacy their whole time together. She had lied to him, saying she didn't care for sex and he had been gentleman enough not to push. Meanwhile, she had been enjoying regular visits to Velenci.

After the shootings, my father had contacted a friend of his who had moved to Italy several years ago. He had become a constable in a town not far from where Velenci lived. He alerted him that there might be an issue. When the police arrived at Velenci's estate, they found a very happy Mia shouting out orders to men who wouldn't listen to her. They also found a naked Velenci with a knife through his chest in an upstairs bedroom. He had been dead for some time. Mia was taken into custody and was awaiting trial for murder.

Caleb had been concerned that Patrick would think he'd been involved in Eileen's plans. Patrick had made it quite clear that he knew Caleb better than that. The tapes had also proved Caleb and Sherman had no knowledge of what Eileen had been plotting.

"I'll never fall for a pretty smile and an accent again," Sherman's words brought me back to the present. "With present company excluded, women are nothing but headaches."

I felt so bad for him, he was such a good man and he deserved someone to love him, we all deserved that.

"Mr. Montgomery, you sound just like my poor Ma," Maggie's voice was now back to its jubilant tone. "When my Da left, he took a huge part of her heart with him., he did"

Maggie continued to tell us of how her parents married extremely young and quickly had two girls, herself and her sister, Caitlyn. Her Da left literally in the middle of the night. Her Ma was left with huge debts and two small girls to raise on her own. He'd said he had found the love of his life in a neighboring village, too bad the love of his life had a husband already. One that shot him to death when he came to profess his love.

"She's been alone all these years and she swears she'll never fall for a man again."

I remembered seeing a picture of Maggie's mom and sister one day while visiting her shop. She was a beautiful woman who looked like a slightly older version of Maggie.

"How long has it been since you've seen your Ma, Maggie?" Amex questioned.

Maggie closed one eye and tilted her head to the ceiling, "Almost four years, I'd s'peck."

"Oh, my," Nora spoke.

"Oh, not to worry, Lass, I've been so busy since Mrs. Montgomery's nuptials that I've paid for my Ma and my sister to come over and help me. They'll arrive this weekend," Maggie's face became even brighter as she spoke to Nora.

"Maggie, what's your Ma's name?" Nora questioned.

"Ma's is Sharon, and my little sister is Caitlyn Gael. They'll be here on Sunday. Just in time to help with Ms. Christi's wedding."

I couldn't help but to smile at her joy. I knew that since Paige's wedding, her business had really picked up and I knew she was booking events into the next year. I was happy for her. She made people feel special and tried to make their day perfect.

Now, about Sherman...

Three days later, we all stood under a huge tree behind Nora and Thomas's house. Sherman and Caleb stood side by side as the soft breeze ruffled their jackets. I had questioned Patrick about how they would explain the death of Eileen to her family back in Ireland. He said that in families such as ours, you knew that if you did something as sinister as what Eileen had done, the family would shun her. It would be as if she had never existed. Mia could ask for all the help in the world, but none would be given. In our family, trust was everything.

"I found your letters you got from him. I read all the promises he made you, the dreams he said he had about you," Sherman's voice rang strong and clear.

"I tried to love you, I was always faithful to you, and even though you spit in my face, I stayed true to my vows to you. I took back all of the money you stole and I'm helping my son build our company, the one you tried to destroy. Goodbye, Eileen." I watched as Sherman opened the urn and dumped the container onto the ground.

Caleb said nothing as he continued to stare at the ashes at his feet. I watched as a ray of sunshine danced off his hair, the red strands glistening in their path. "When my children ask me what their grandmother was like when she was alive, I'm going to lie and tell them that you loved everyone and had a good heart. No child should ever have bad memories of the woman who gave them life. That's all you did, but I'm going to work on forgiving you."

Nora was beside Caleb so fast that she was almost a blur. She wrapped her arms around him tightly and kissed his cheek. She whispered in his ear so quietly that no one else could hear. Softly, she cradled him, as if he were a small boy as he shook with silent sobs in her arms. They stood like that for several minutes, no one making a single sound.

Caleb slowly looked into her eyes as he and Nora shared a smile. "I'd be honored to call you Ma," Caleb's voice broke the silence.

"Come on then, Lad, we have so much to make up for," Nora's warm motherly voice chuckled.

It was days like these that I was so glad I'd worn waterproof mascara.

CHAPTER TWENTY-NINE

I'd heard that what didn't kill us made us stronger. If that was true, then Christi was one of the strongest people I knew.

I had taken too many chances with her safety as of late, not seeing what was directly in front of me. That changed today.

Last night after dinner, I spoke with Matthew. I asked him if he was happy with the department he currently worked for. He questioned me, pushing me directly to the point. I told him I wanted Christi better protected, by someone who wouldn't be swayed by sex or money. I needed someone who would protect her as if she was the most precious thing in the world.

He thought about for several minutes. When I said I would double his salary, he continued to ponder. Then I offered to triple it.

Matthew finally agreed to matching his current salary and placing additional money away for his retirement. He formally resigned from the Chicago PD last night.

Christi's warm body lay still and peaceful beside mine. I could feel her every breath and muscle twitch. I had never prayed as hard as I did, while we waited for the toxicology results to come back from the lab. Tonto had been correct, it was troll killer.

No one could really pinpoint the origins of troll killer. I could remember my father using it on a particularly uncooperative man when I was much younger. He refused to tell my father who had stolen a shipment that had gone missing so my father gave him the drug and then placed him in a bathtub, and then turned on the water. It was quite effective.

The beauty of the drug was that it rendered the extremities useless, yet the mind remained clear and breathing was unaffected. Speech was hindered, yet awareness remained sharp. Everything that was happening was still discernible, but the recipient was powerless to do anything about it. It was essentially undetectable in the bloodstream and that was again proven with Christi's blood tests.

The sun was just beginning to break across the horizon, beautiful shades of pink and gold lighting the sky. Today would be a good day. Today was also the last day I would be a single man.

Muscles had pulled me to the side last night and asked if I wanted him to book a quick flight to Vegas so that I could have a bachelor party. I only looked at him and he knew the answer to that. I didn't need or want to have a party involving half-naked women parading around. I was far too happy to toss my single days away to mourn them ending.

Christi's quiet stirrings brought me back to the bed we currently lay in. She had extra blankets covering her. Ever since her kidnapping, she had been obsessed with being warm. She said that being so cold had been the hardest part. I would sweat every night for the rest of my life to keep her as warm as she wanted to be.

With one final stir, Christi softly and sleepy called out my name, "Patrick?"

Placing my hand on her arm, tracing the soft,warm skin that lay beneath the covers, I buried my nose into her brown, silky locks as I inhaled, taking in the most pleasant aroma I had ever experienced, pure Christi.

"Good morning, Beautiful."

CHAPTER THIRTY

Staying at Nora's had its advantages. First, she was as neurotic about having things in their place as I was. Second, she could cook like there was no tomorrow. Breakfast this morning consisted of the crispiest and most amazing waffles, I had ever had with this phenomenal berry compote, and a cup of coffee that Juan Valdez himself would have been proud of.

I had a counseling session first thing this morning. Dr. Green was well aware that the wedding was tomorrow, and that Patrick had a very long honeymoon planned, thus the reason for the appointment today.

Patrick had informed me that my father would be my new bodyguard and honestly, it felt like the whole world was lifted off my shoulders. My daddy was the one man I trusted completely, besides Patrick.

Dr. Green and I discussed a few fears I was currently having. One having so much attention shoved my way. The second, being intimate with my new husband. She was honest when she told me that only time would tell.

Arriving back at Nora's just before lunchtime, I was immediately assaulted with the smell of pasta sauce cooking. Maggie was large and in charge, with her phone in one hand and a clipboard in the other. She looked up when she noticed me walking into the room.

"Yes, that's right, Saint Josephine's church. And if the runner isn't delivered by three, you'll be hearing from me."

Her smile was bright and I knew by the look on her face she was having the time of her life.

"Christi, you're looking sprite today, Lass."

With a quick kiss to my cheek, her phone began to ring and she quickly answered. "I fail to see how that's my problem. You were contacted months ago so I suggest you go find more."

I didn't want to know what the issue was. I didn't care if the food was cold and the beer stale, I was getting married.

"Christi, my love," Nora came from the kitchen, hair perfect and not a single stain on her apron. "Patrick is on his way to drop your things off at your father's, and then he's picking up the family from the airport."

Nora had invited every single family member from Belfast. Patrick had chartered a commercial plane and pilot. I thought it was a bit ostentatious, until Nora told me it was actually less expensive than purchasing sixty round-trip tickets.

Maggie pulled a few strings and had gotten the entire Plaza hotel reserved, all fifteen hundred rooms. Nora had no problem filling all of them.

With the size of the wedding, Maggie suggested we hire a number of vendors that provided the same services. She said that with the sheer numbers we were having, there would be no room for error. Charlotte had a decent relationship with another caterer in the next town over and they had worked it out between them who would supply what.

Maggie had informed me that the most difficult part was finding enough bells for each of the guests to have one. With Paige's wedding, she had chosen not to perform this particular tradition. I, however, wanted to have the bells at my wedding. Tradition had it that each of the wedding guests would be given a bell, and this bell was rung several times during the ceremony. Once the wedding was over, the bride and groom chose a single bell from the guests to take home. Later, when the couple would have an argument, they would ring that bell to ward off the evil spirit that caused the fight.

This became an issue when you needed nearly a thousand of them, all made from fine china with an Irish Claddagh on the side. Maggie assured me she had it covered.

So for the first time in months, I had nothing to do except slip into a hot bubble bath and relax, so that was exactly what I did.

Several hours later, I made my way down the large staircase. Once I reached the bottom of the steps, my father and Brandon stood waiting to escort me to the limo that would take us to our wedding rehearsal.

I was next to last to climb into the back followed by my dad. As I sat down, I was greeted by cheers and catcalls. Everyone had a drink in their hands and the music was blaring. Brandon and my father sat at each door while I sat between them. Abigail was a bundle of energy as she excitedly sipped her glass of what looked like sprite with grenadine. She was just like all the other girls who had a drink in their hand.

I took a good look around, examining each face of the people I loved. Maggie took her role very seriously as she began to pour everyone a new glass of champagne. It was then I noticed that she put the champagne bottle down and opened up a new can of sprite. She first filled up Abigail's glass and smiled as Abigail thanked her in her sweet little voice. Then she moved to my sister and Paige. She poured each of them a Sprite instead of champagne...holy fuck! Was there something I should know about?

Maggie glanced in my direction. She realized that I had noticed what she had just done. She quickly and quietly shook her head no. I could only smile at the thought of both of them being pregnant. It would be amazing.

As the limo continued down the street, my dad reached over and took my hand in his. "So I'd guess you're pretty glad now that you didn't tell him to take a hike, huh?"

I chucked and leaned into his side. "I'm so glad I listened to my heart and not my head on this one."

Saint Josephine's church came into view. The limo smoothly pulled into the drive and I watched as Tonto, Patrick, Thomas, and Sherman stood at the curb.

Patrick told me this morning that Sherman had come to him and asked to join his security team. Sherman had already discarded Eileen's belongings and had moved in with Caleb and Paige. He told Patrick that he just wanted to do something different for a while, prove to the family he could be trusted.

Sherman was a handsome man and the essence of a southern gentleman as he assisted all the ladies out of the limo. Once Maggie was out, she leaned over and kissed his cheek. The blush that spread across his face caused a round of laughter.

Patrick wrapped his hand in mine and helped me up the stairs. Once inside the church, Maggie was in full coordinator mode.

I was floored as I looked at the decorations that were already in place. Beautiful, yellow bows were attached to the pew ends waiting for the flowers to be attached tomorrow. The flower arches were already in place, again just waiting on the fresh flowers to be placed in them.

Maggie came jogging up to me, instructing me where to stand. It was then I noticed the two beautiful women that flanked her.

"Who are these lovely ladies, Maggie?" Thomas questioned.

Thomas was Patrick's best man. Since he didn't have any brothers, and he didn't want to pick one of his friends over another, this decision only made sense.

"Aye, Mr. Malloy, this is my mum, Sharon, and my little sister, Caitlyn."

The two beautiful women stepped aside and made their way over to the precession line. Honestly, it was hard to tell who was the daughter and who was the Mother.

"*Athas orm bualadh leat, a dhuine usasail, Is e mo ainm na Sionainne agus is e seo mo inion alainn, Caitlyn.*" (Pleasure to meet you, Sir, my name is Sharon and this is my daughter, Caitlyn.)

I was about to open my mouth and introduce myself when a husky voice behind me sounded.

"Oh, my..."

I turned and came face to face with a slack-jawed Sherman, his eyes locked with Sharon's. I turned back to Sharon to find a huge smile across her face. Sherman gently passed by me and took Sharon's hand in his, he leaned over and slowly kissed her knuckles.

"Please, allow me to introduce myself. I'm Sherman Montgomery and may I say, it's a true pleasure to make your acquaintance."

The area where we were standing was so quiet that you could have heard a pin drop as Sherman and Sharon continued to stare at each other.

"How do you do that?" Patrick whispered in my ear, I turned to him and gave him a questioning look. "You bring people together, even those who've given up on finding love again."

I could only smile at him as he placed a sweet kiss against my temple.

Maggie had us run through the entire ceremony three times before she was happy. Since I still tired easily, Patrick had insisted that a bench be placed at the altar so I could sit during the ceremony. Maggie wasn't happy with what was available at the church so she had someone make one.

When Maggie was finally satisfied, we loaded up into one of the chartered buses she had arranged for, and headed off to the reception hall that Patrick owned.

Nothing could have prepared me for the absolute glory of the room. Each place setting was set with a very classically-styled Wedgwood china service, elegant crystal and silver, and beautiful centerpieces adorned each table. But what really brought it all together was the canopy of lights that hung from the ceiling. It was as if we were sitting under the stars.

Maggie ushered us to the head table where Patrick pulled out my chair, kissing my forehead as he joined me in his own.

Two of Patrick's cousins from Ireland had been given the task of handing out the gifts to the wedding party. Maggie, bless her heart, had taken care of acquiring all of them, since I was a little busy being held captive by a fucking madman.

Each of my bridesmaids received a beautiful diamond drop pendant, while Patrick gave his guys each a Rolex watch.

Again, the room had different pictures of Patrick and I growing up and several from when we had first started dating. The most amazing one was of Patrick down on one knee with that shamrock in his hand. I made a mental note to have Maggie keep that one and have it framed. I wanted it in our home.

I was brought out of my daydreams by the clanking of a knife against a glass. I looked over and saw that Patrick was standing.

"If I could have everyone's attention," Patrick's manly voice quieted the room and all eyes were soon on him. "I just wanted to thank everyone for making the long journey here. It means the world to Christi and me." He turned to look at me as he reached for his beer. "A wise man once told me that the woman you want to marry isn't the one you can live with, it's the one you could never live without."

He then looked to Thomas and raised his glass to him.

"From the very second I laid eyes on this beautiful creature, she owned me. I couldn't get her out of my head." His eyes now focused on me, "Christi, you made me take a long hard look at myself and question the man I was. You made me realize that having everything was nothing if I didn't have the other half of my soul. That's exactly what you are, my soul mate. You help me be the man I was destined to be. I swear to always be there for you the way you are for me, I love you."

The room erupted in applause as Patrick took my hand, lifted me out of my chair, and placed a gentle kiss to my lips.

"Now, in the Malloy family, it's tradition for the groom to give a gift to the bride as a sign of his ability to care for her. So with that in mind..."

Patrick motioned for Abigail to bring over an envelope. I knelt down, took it from her, and kissed her cheek, making her giggle.

Nothing could have prepared me for what was in that envelope.

Patrick had already purchased us a home so as I looked at the picture of a grand log cabin, I was speechless.

"It's for when we just want to get away, somewhere to take the children and make some memories."

I threw my arms around his neck and hugged him tightly. "Thank you."

Thomas was gracious enough to tell the room what Patrick had given me.

Finally, we broke apart and I took his hand in mine. "I have a little something for you as well, Patrick."

Nora had asked me if I wanted her help with his gift. I told her absolutely, since I had no clue what to get the man who had everything. I took his hand and led him out of the building. There in the valet circle, was a black Bentley.

The look on Patrick's face was that of a kid on Christmas who had just gotten the one special toy he had asked Santa for. He picked me up and swung me around in several circles.

"Your Ma said you wanted this one."

"I did, I'd planned on getting one after we got back from the honeymoon, but this is so much better."

I watched as he ran his hand up and down the sleek hood of the car. It was merely seconds before the majority of the men at the party were standing around the car, hands in pockets, staring at it in awe.

"Christi, it's getting late. We need to get you to your father's house so go say goodnight to groom. That is, if you can get him away from that car long enough," Maggie grinned. She was on her game till the end.

Nora had suggested making Matthew's house bridal central and her house for the groom. The distance was enough that the chances of us seeing each other were quite slim.

I made my way over to kiss my soon-to-be husband goodnight when I noticed a love-struck Sherman give Sharon a kiss that would have made Hollywood stand up and cheer.

"Mmm," Patrick's silky voice sounded in my ear.

"It's time for me to go," I spoke softly.

"I know, I'm just not ready to see you leave yet," his lips brushed the shell of my ear.

"Oh, I think you'll have a little something to hold your attention," I giggled and gestured toward his new car.

"Oh, Babe, that car has nothing on you. It can't love me back."

"I do love you, Mr. Malloy, so much," I looked him directly in the eye as I spoke.

"I love you, too, Mrs. Malloy."

"I'll see you tomorrow?"

"Yep, I'll be the one in the tux at the end of the aisle trying not to run to meet you halfway. I'll be waiting for you, my love."

I smiled as I said, "Yes, and you'll get to guess whether or not I'm wearing any panties under my dress." With those words, I removed myself from my stunned fiancé's arms and ran to the waiting limo, giggling the whole way.

Tomorrow would be the first day of the rest of my life. I couldn't wait to start it.

CHAPTER THIRTY-ONE

The church could not have been more beautifully decorated. I would have to remind myself to have Books give Maggie a huge tip.

As the organ softly played I began to remember the sight of my Christi when she was just a girl. How I tried to get the very essence of her out of my life. How now I couldn't get enough of her.

I turned to my left to see Father Murphy standing reverently, bible in his hand ready to bless this holy union.

I could hear faint whispers from the sea of guest that were currently seated in the wooden pews. The constant smiles that graced each face as they mirrored my glances.

I could feel the bead of sweat as it rolled down my back. Why isn't this thing starting already?

Christi was extremely punctual and I began to worry that she may have had a problem with her dress. Looking at the clock that hung on the back wall, I noticed it was now twenty minutes past the time we were to have begun. The murmurs from the crowed and the lack of smiles, confirmed that I wasn't the only one who was worried.

The thump of the door that kept the bride from the church caused me to look up to find a distressed looking Matthew making his way down the aisle toward me. The look on his face was one of sadness and I could feel my heart rising to my throat.

"Patrick," His hushed voice sounded in my ear.

"I'm sorry, but she changed her mind."

With those words, he placed her ring into my hand alongside her shamrock pendant.

Sweat was running down my face and body as I shot straight up in bed. I looked around the pitch black room. I was still at my parent's house. It had all been a dream.

When my breathing finally returned back to normal, I tossed back the covers and made my way down stairs, pausing at the bar long enough to pour myself a tall glass of scotch.

I wanted to call Christi. Make certain she was all right and that she still loved me. It was foolish I know, it was only a dream for Christ's sake. The tinkling of the piano keys echoed in the room as I began to softly play random keys. That was my mood right now, random and uncertain. Would my dream become a reality? Would I do something to cause her to leave me? Would she someday wake up and find that she can do so much better than me?

"This is a good sign you know"

The sound of my da's voice, startled me.

"Fuck, Da, you scared the shit out of me."

He could only chuckle as he made his way into the room, sitting down on the leather couch that rested not far from the piano.

"Sorry, I figured I would find you in here."

I turned my head in a questioning glance. He lifted his glass as his eyes never left mine.

"I heard you shout."

Oh...

"Bad dream, I take it?"

I didn't reply immediately. Honestly I was a little embarrassed, my dad having to make sure I was all right after a bad dream. What was I three?

"She changed her mind." I spoke softly, terrified that God was listening and mistook it for a prayer.

My father let out a deep sigh as he placed his empty glass on the bar.

"The night before I married your Ma, I was so sick that my father had to take me to the emergency room and have fluids put back into me. They had to give me medicine to make the vomiting stop."

I turned my attention back to him.

"I was terrified that she would come to her senses and see what a douche I really was."

Hearing my father call himself a douche made me chuckle to myself.

"I will tell you what your grandfather told me."

He had my full attention now. Thomas' father was a bad ass. He would shoot you between the eyes just because he could. He died in his sleep a few days after my grandmother passed. My da said he died of a broken heart. I didn't believe him at the time, but now I got it.

"You can set back and worry everyday about how you're going to do something incredibly stupid to cause her to leave. Or you can wake up every morning and have a plan on how you will make her smile."

Does the tub in my new house have jets? If not, I am so asking Patrick to change that.

Maggie had arranged for me to spend the morning at a local spa. I had just finished this amazing salt wrap that was designed to get rid of dead skin and leave your skin silky soft. I was currently resting in a jetted tub getting the salt and skin taken off from me...it felt like heaven.

Last night was some of the best sleep I have had in a long time. I dreamed of Patrick having a tea party with three little girls. His hair was full of colorful barrettes and his lips were painted bright pink, the lines of his lips not taken into consideration as the lipstick was touching his nose. He was laughing and talking to the little girls in the most adorable British accent. Would I have three girls?

With recent events, Patrick had insisted that I have five of his men surrounding me at all times before the wedding.

When the limo finally reached the church, a huge group of black suited, Ray ban wearing, beef cake men surrounded the limo, effectively blocking anyone from getting to me. My wedding dress was waiting for me inside the dressing area of the church. I didn't want to one, risk getting anything on the dress, and two, I didn't want to look like a raving lunatic trying to move around with the full skirt.

"Time for tradition," Charlotte announced.

She was the honorary 'mom' for me today. She would be on my left while my father was on the right. She would kiss Patrick and pass him the traditional mother of the bride gift, a lock of the bride's hair that is carefully placed in the pocket watch of one of the bride's grandfathers.

Charlotte carefully placed the lace handkerchief inside the bow that secured my bouquet. Legend has it that the handkerchief will be used to dry the tears of the first born child, and then it will be used in the making of the baptismal bonnet.

My hair had been pulled back and several braids were placed as a sign of strength and fertility. It was held back with a beautiful silver clip, with green stones. Green was the traditional Irish wedding color and It was important for this to be as authentic as possible.

As I slid on my peep toes shoes, Charlotte inserted the coin Patrick had given me.

Next came the horseshoe that I would carry as a sign of good luck. Many brides wore it as a necklace, but I chose to carry it instead.

With one final deep breath, I gathered my skirt and nodded my head as a sign I was ready.

"Auntie Christi?"

Abigail's small voice caught my attention and I glanced down at her.

"Yes, Baby?"

"Are we marrying Patrick today?"

I had to smile at her, it wasn't if I was marrying him she felt the whole family was going to marry him. I guess in a sense we were.

"Yes, we are. Are you ready?"

Her face suddenly looked upset.

"But I don't want to marry Patrick. I want to marry my daddy."

I looked to my sister who had her hand firmly covering her mouth, a small sob escaping as she quickly turned to gather her flowers.

"Abby, I think that if you want to marry your daddy, Patrick will understand."

The smile that covered her little cherub face was enough to brighten the room. And she began to jump up and down excitedly, the yellow ribbon of her dress following her every move.

My father stood at the end of the hall, dressed in a crisp black tuxedo. He, like Patrick, would not have the same tuxedo as the groom's men.

With Charlotte on my left and my dad on my right, I focused my eyes on my sister who stood directly in front of me.

The beautiful one shoulder dress that we had chosen would truly be one of those you could wear after my wedding. I had ordered one for myself as a matter of fact.

Once Shannon was on her way down the aisle and the doors again securely closed, I could hear the rustling of the runner as it was being laid down the aisle. Nora had insisted that it be made of real lace and not the waxed paper version that so many brides did these days.

The doors opened, and with a final breath and a quick close of my eyes, I took my first step at becoming Mrs. Patrick Malloy.

As I placed the ring on Patrick's left hand, I spoke the words I'd memorized since I was a little girl. As I looked into his deep green eyes, I tried to picture what my life with him would be like. Will he remember this day as a day he will never forget, or will he wish it was just a bad decision he made in his youth? I would spend the rest of my days reminding him how wonderful this day was.

"Ní féidir leat a bhfuil liom go mbaineann mé liom féin.
Ach fad is mian linn an dá é, mé a thabhairt duit go bhfuil mianach a thabhairt.
Ní féidir leat gceannas orm, mar tá mé ag duine saor in aisce.
Ach beidh mé ag freastal ort sna bealaí de dhíth ort,
Agus beidh an honeycomb blas bhinne ag teacht ó mo lámh.
Geallaim duit go mbeidh mise an t-ainm a bheith caoin mé os ard ar an oíche,
Agus na súile isteach a aoibh gháire mé ar maidin.
Geallaim duit an bite chéad mo feola agus an deoch chéad ó mo chupán.
Geallaim duit mo bheo agus mo bháis, gach cothrom faoi do chúram.
Beidh mé a bheith ina sciath do do ais agus tú mianach.
Ní dhéanfaidh mé clúmhilleadh tú, ná mé tú.
Beidh mé honor tú thar aon rud eile, agus nuair a quarrel beidh muid é sin a dhéanamh i
Phríobháideach agus insint Ní hannamh ár casaoidí.
Tá sé seo vow mo bainise a thabhairt duit
Is é seo an pósadh ar comhionann."
("You cannot possess me, for I belong to myself.
But while we both wish it, I give you that which is mine to give.
You cannot command me, for I am a free person.
But I shall serve you in those ways you require,
And the honeycomb will taste sweeter coming from my hand.
I pledge to you that yours will be the name I cry aloud in the night,
And the eyes into which I smile in the morning.
I pledge to you the first bite of my meat and the first drink from my cup.
I pledge to you my living and my dying, each equally in your care.
I shall be a shield for your back and you for mine.
I shall not slander you, nor you me.
I shall honor you above all others, and when we quarrel we shall do so in private and tell no strangers our grievances.
This is my wedding vow to you
This is the marriage of equals.")

"It is my great honor to present to you, Mr. and Mrs. Patrick Malloy."

The master of ceremonies' voice vibrated the floor I currently stood on. Patrick lips firmly attached to mine and I could feel the smile he was wearing against my lips.

"I love you." His word carried a promise, one I knew he would keep.

Patrick, never one to do anything the normal way, quickly picked me up bridal style as he walked into the massive ballroom.

We had to use the same room that Paige and Caleb had used due to the number of guests. The same companies set up monitors for all to see. Though the threat was gone, the security was even tighter. This was the first time I had seen the room completed.

Just like Paige and Caleb, we cut our cake first. The multi-tiered cake had our initials setting majestically on top. Patrick carefully placed the tiny bite of cake to my lips and then quickly kissing me. Maggie handed me a glass of champagne and I quickly took a drink.

"Go easy on that stuff. We have plans for later and I want you to remember every detail."

His words alone caused my body to shiver and left me completely speechless.

That night, I danced until my feet nearly fell off and I laughed until I cried.

I hugged, flirted, and had the time of my life.

When I look back on this night, I doubt that I will remember how the food tasted or what brand of wine sat on the table.

I won't remember what music was played or who left together.

I won't remember what time Abigail finally fell asleep in her daddy's arms.

What I will remember, was the look on Patrick's face as he glided me across the dance floor.

I'll remember how my father let a single tear fall as we danced to *I loved her first* by Heartland

How Tonto and Caitlyn were caught making out in the back of the limo.

And how Abigail announced to the whole room that she was glad Patrick was married so he wouldn't cry when she married her daddy.

But most of all I will remember that today I married the man of my dreams…

Epilogue

I had dreaded this day for as long as I could remember. Our son, Declan, was getting ready to board a plane for Ireland.

Patrick was with him now, just as Thomas had been for him. I could still remember the night Patrick had decided to go, the night of Shannon's bachelorette party. Oh, how many of those I had attended since then. Thank, God there hadn't been anymore serial rapists in attendance.

Patrick and I were blessed with three children, not the twelve he'd desired, or so he'd said. It was after Katie was born, that I learned that he had really wanted a little girl, too, not the twelve boys he had so boldly spoken of. Nora was overjoyed when we announced that we would be naming two of, however many sons we had, after her two brothers that had been murdered all those years ago.

Declan was our oldest and first in line to run the family business. He was so much like his father that I felt a little sorry for his girlfriend, Katie. Katie, on the other hand, was a little on the nervous side and a bit high-strung. She overanalyzed everything and cried at least once a day. Declan assured me he would work on helping her toughen up her skin. She would need it to survive in our world.

Yes, that was right, his sister and his girlfriend had the same name. It wasn't planned that way. Patrick and I had chosen to keep our baby's name a secret, and so had Maggie and Angus. Maggie and I had delivered our girls within minutes of each other. Thomas had made good on his word and Angus received his official citizenship a few short months later. Shamus stood beside him as they raised their right hands and took the oath.

Our second son we named Connor. He was my mini-me. He wanted nothing to do with the running of the family business and chose to be a 'positive' part of the family as Nora had labeled it. Connor was in his second year of medical school. Patrick and I couldn't have been more proud.

"Christi!" Katie's voice was quivering as she raced into the room in tears, effectively putting an end to my walk down memory lane. "Christi, why does he suddenly have to go to Ireland? I mean how important can his business be if I can't go with him?"

See what I mean?

"Katie, what have both your Mother and I told you about your behavior?"

Her head fell and she plopped herself into the chair she was closest to. "You said that if I plan to be a part of this family, that I need to grow a backbone and not cry all the time."

Her voice was so tiny and I continued to question if Declan had made the right choice in asking her father for her hand in marriage. Declan had always had the maturity of a thirty-year-old man. From the day he was born, not that he'd had a choice in the matter.

"So, why are you sitting here crying your eyes out?"

I watched as she raised her head, straightened her shoulders, and then wiped her eyes with her tiny fingers, "Because I just don't get why he has to do this."

I remembered questioning Patrick as to why he had to go. I had simply accepted that he had business, but Katie wasn't me.

"Katie, there are going to be things that happen in life that you have to just accept and go on."

"I get that, Christi, but he won't even talk about it. He tells me it's something he has to handle and that I can't go," she pouted.

Her attitude was that of a three-year-old and it bothered me the most.

"Well, Katie, you don't follow him to the bathroom do you?"

Her nose wrinkled up in disgust. "No!"

I laughed, as I had changed far too many of his diapers not to find that thought amusing.

"Well, then think of this as an extended bathroom break."

She began to giggle at my statement. At least she had quit crying, for now.

"So, Christi, you know what's happening while he's in Ireland, can't you tell me anything? Are they buying more buildings?…Is he going for fun?…Does he have… a…a girl there?"

All of my children had a very clear view of how Patrick and I felt on the issue of cheating. Katie knew that as well. So it puzzled me as to why she would even think that.

"Katie," my voice was clipped.

"Sorry, Christi, I know he'd never do that, not after…"

"Exactly." The tone of my voice quickly ended that conversation.

I knew I had to give her something, a glimmer of hope, and yet not ruin the proposal that Declan would have for her upon his return. I thought for several moments until the right words came to mind.

"I can assure you that what he's about to do in Ireland will be to your advantage as well as his. Don't worry, Sweet girl, it's just a whole lot of shamrocks with a touch of secrets."

Declan did both his father and grandfather proud when he walked back through our front door six days later. His clothes were just as tattered and torn as Patrick's had been. Katie again worried me as she turned her nose up in disgust as Declan made his way toward her.

"Are you thinking of the day this all happened for us?" Patrick wrapped his strong arms around me, chasing away the chill that had crept into the room.

"Has it really been twenty-five years?" My voice a little thicker than it was back then, the hair a little grayer.

"Um hmm. It has." He responded as he kissed the top of my head.

I watched as Declan slowly bent to one knee, saying the same words that men have spoken to their intendeds for years.

"I wish your mother could have seen this." I spoke softly, missing Nora terribly, especially during times like this.

"Yes, I miss her, too. But the past twenty-five years have been good years, haven't they?" Patrick seemed to have a different memory of those years than I did. Granted the majority of them were wonderful, but I questioned if he forgot the first few that our marriage nearly didn't survive.

"I seem to recall things a little differently." He said against my temple. I turned my head slightly, my cheek now against his broad shoulders, my eyes locked with his.

"Oh, really?" I challenged, his green eyes now dusted with age, the laugh and worry lines trophies he wore with pride.

"Yes, *really*, Mrs. Malloy." He tossed back at me, his teasing and highly playful tone shining thought his voice.

"And pray tell, Mr. Malloy, how do you remember the last twenty-five years?"

Patrick snuggled in closer to me as the crowd that had been invited to share in this moment, were clapping with congratulations for the happy couple. Katie of course was crying.

"Well, my beautiful wife, I remember…"

Want to know what Patrick remembered? Find out for yourself in

CLADDAGH AND CHAOS
The sequel to Shamrocks and Secrets. Coming soon.

ABOUT THE AUTHOR

Cayce Poponea is from southern Georgia. From an early age, she discovered the amazing world that resides in the pages of books. She shared that love for reading with her two children and both were able to read at very early ages. With encouragement from her friends and family, she took the plunge and decided to share her own thoughts in the form of her books. A true romantic at heart, Cayce brings her ideas and desires about love and relationships to life in each one of her novels.